The
Lost
Letter

The
Lost
Letter

Jillian Cantor

RIVERHEAD BOOKS
New York
2017

RIVERHEAD BOOKS
An imprint of Penguin Random House LLC
375 Hudson Street
New York, New York 10014

Copyright © 2017 by Jillian Cantor
Penguin supports copyright. Copyright fuels creativity,
encourages diverse voices, promotes free speech, and creates a vibrant
culture. Thank you for buying an authorized edition of this book and
for complying with copyright laws by not reproducing, scanning,
or distributing any part of it in any form without permission.
You are supporting writers and allowing Penguin to
continue to publish books for every reader.

Library of Congress Cataloging-in-Publication Data

Names: Cantor, Jillian, author.
Title: The lost letter : a novel / Jillian Cantor.
Description: New York : Riverhead Books, 2017.
Identifiers: LCCN 2016039408 | ISBN 9780399185670 | ISBN 9780399185694 (ebook)
Classification: LCC PS3603.A587 P76 2017 | DDC 813/. 6—dc23
LC record available at https://lccn.loc.gov/2016039408
p.   cm.

International Edition ISBN: 9780735219397

Printed in the United States of America
1 3 5 7 9 10 8 6 4 2

BOOK DESIGN BY LUCIA BERNARD

For Grandma Bea and Grandpa Milt: I remember.

(The edelweiss) is an alpine plant . . . that is said to grow on the line of perpetual snow,—in fact under the snow. . . . Only the boldest alpine goatherds and hunters venture to pick the hardy little plant from its native soil. The possession of one is a proof of unusual daring.

—Berthold Auerbach, in *Edelweiss: A Story*

❋

The
Lost
Letter

Austria, 1939

S HE CLUTCHED THE LETTERS *tightly in her hands, careful not to damage the stamps. It was snowing and her toes were freezing, wet through the worn soles of her boots, but she kept walking through the woods toward town, shielding the letters underneath her coat to keep them dry. Only a few steps more, she kept telling herself. It was a lie, but she kept on walking.*

Only a few steps more. Just a few more.

All she had to do was make it into town, drop the letters at the post on Wien Allee. All she had to do was mail the letters, and everything was going to be all right.

That was a lie, too, of course. But she kept on walking through the snow.

At the edge of the woods, she reached the clearing, and through the swirl of snowflakes, the pink-blue onset of dawn, she could see the remaining red-roofed buildings in town, up ahead.

Wien Allee. She was almost there.

The sudden cold butt of the gun against her temple surprised her. She didn't even let out a cry before the man grabbed her arm, and the letters fell from her hands, onto the unblemished snow.

Los Angeles, 1989

T HE FIRST TIME I show up at the stamp dealer's office, I consider not even getting out of the car. It's an unusually cold
morning in LA, I don't have a sweater with me, and I'm
fairly sure all I'm doing here is wasting my time.

But my hatchback is filled to capacity with the former contents
of my father's hobby room: pages and pages of books filled with
stamps under plastic, large clear boxes filled with thrift shop finds,
mostly yellowed letters, unsent or unopened but adorned with a
stamp from some other era. If I don't unload it all here, I'll have to
find somewhere to put it back at my house. And besides that, I feel
like I owe it to my father to at least try to do something with his
collection. At that thought, I get out of my car and open the trunk.

When I was a kid, I used to accompany my father to thrift shops
and yard sales and estate sales on the weekend, sifting through
other people's trash, looking for an old letter, or maybe a deceased
collector's newly unwanted collection. I would ask him what he was
looking for then, and he would turn to me and smile, and say, *a gem.*
That's what stamps are to him, gems. Or were, anyway. Diamonds,
rubies, emeralds. He saw himself as a jeweler who could determine

flaws and beauty in what looks average to all the rest of us. Once, after we took a family trip to DC and saw the Hope Diamond at the Smithsonian, he turned to me and said: *That's what I'm looking for, Kate.* Though I doubted my father would ever find it in the thrift stores of Southern California.

According to my father, the Hope Diamond of stamps will be one that is a mistake. One that will be rare because it was issued too early or too late, because it was printed wrong. And I guess that's what all these boxes stacked up in the back of my car really signify: his search for some kind of accidental greatness amidst thousands of little paper squares.

All I see when I look at stamps are paper and ink. Stamps are a means to an end, a utility. They get my mail from one place to another, pay my bills, take my letters to my best friend, Karen, who moved to Connecticut last summer. And most recently they've sat staring at me, three little flowers in a row, pasted on the manila envelope from Daniel that I've left unopened on my kitchen counter. The end of everything. I hate the finality of it and that's why I haven't actually opened the envelope yet.

I'm certain that my father, who never much liked Daniel, would've been altogether annoyed by the choice of flowers for such a correspondence. But my father doesn't know. And even if he did, now I'm pretty sure he wouldn't remember.

❀

The stamp dealer's office is a nondescript one-room tucked into a strip mall, just near where the 405 meets the 101, on the edge of Sherman Oaks. Not a place I'd expect to find or unearth any kind of gem. But I'm already here; I have an appointment. I take the first armload of boxes out of my car and walk inside.

The dealer, Benjamin Grossman, sits behind his desk, which is covered in a disorganized mess of papers and has a small black-and-white TV perched on the corner. He's watching the noon news, and the newscaster is talking about the protests yesterday in East Berlin.

He looks away from the TV when I walk in, but he doesn't turn it off. He's younger than I'd been expecting after talking to him over the phone. Stamp collecting always felt to me like an old man's hobby, and I'd expected an elderly dealer. But Benjamin looks like he's my age, mid-thirties, possibly early forties. He wears wire-rimmed glasses, and has a full head of curly light brown hair. "Mrs. Nelson?" he asks.

I'm still unsure what I'm supposed to do with my married surname. "You can just call me Katie," I tell him.

"Okay, Katie," he says, absentmindedly. He couldn't care less what he calls me. He reaches up and fiddles with the antenna on his television, adjusting the picture to his liking, and I get the feeling I'm intruding, interrupting something by showing up here, even with an appointment.

"Um . . . what should I do with these?" I shift the boxes. They're heavy.

"Oh, sorry. Here. Just put them on my desk." Benjamin lets the antenna be and sits back down. I glance at the mess surrounding him. "Anywhere you'd like," he says, and I put the boxes down on top of some papers. He leans forward and riffles through carefully for a moment, and I wonder how he became a stamp dealer, what one even majors in in college to get on such a career path. History?

I majored in English and work for a lifestyle magazine, where I review movies. It's not a very well-paying job, but until recently it was, at least, a fun one.

"I'll go through this," I realize Benjamin is saying. "And then I'll give you a call, let you know what I find." I've already told Benjamin over the phone about my father, his failing memory, his inability to keep up his collection, and his continued insistence that there are gems in here. He used to tell me all the time that when he got older the collection could be all mine. And he reiterated that when I moved him into the Willows a few months back. But I honestly don't know what I'm supposed to *do* with it. And that's really why I've brought it all here.

I walk back out to my car to grab another pile of boxes, and when I walk back in, Benjamin looks away from the news again, raises his eyebrows. "There's more?" I nod. "Sorry. I'll help you carry it in." He gets up and follows me back out to the parking lot. "I didn't mean to be rude."

"It's fine," I say, not in the mood for small talk.

But Benjamin keeps talking. "I just didn't realize how much your father had when we spoke over the phone." He peers into my trunk.

"He's seventy-one," I say, and it comes out sharper than I meant it. "It's just . . . it's been a lifelong obsession for him." Though even as I say it out loud, seventy-one doesn't sound as old as it should. Many people at the Willows are older than him, and I'm constantly angered by how unfair it is; the disappearance of his memory feels like a punch, something that takes my breath away, again and again.

"It usually is," Benjamin says kindly, as if he understands, as if he, too, shares this obsession with stamps. As if I am the weirdo who doesn't get it. Maybe I am.

After the last box is unloaded, Benjamin Grossman simply says, "Give me a week. Maybe two. I'll let you know what you have here."

But I hesitate for a moment before leaving, wondering how my father would feel about this, me leaving his most treasured possessions with this man I found in the yellow pages under "Stamp Dealers." I'd called and left messages for all three dealers listed. And Benjamin Grossman had been the first one to call me back. "Do I need a receipt or something?"

Benjamin shakes his head, pulls a business card from underneath a pile on his desk, and presses it into my hand. "I'll call you when I'm done," he says. Then he adds, "Don't worry. I'll take good care of them." As if the stamps are flowers, something that need to be nurtured, tenderly.

"I'm not worried," I say. I've let something go that wasn't really even mine to begin with. But as I get into my car, pull out of the parking lot and back onto the 405, I can't shake this unexpected feeling of emptiness.

Austria, 1938

A T FIRST, Kristoff didn't understand the power of the burin. He didn't know that the one small simple-looking engraving tool could eventually save them. Or get them killed. All he knew, in the beginning, was that the burin was impossible to use precisely, and that he was not naturally suited for metal, the way he'd always been for canvas.

He didn't like the way it felt in his hand either. Oddly heavy, hard to maneuver. He felt it should create lines with the agility of a brush, or even charcoal, and yet his hand kept getting stuck, and he became repeatedly frustrated at his inability to achieve the perfect lines and grooves in the metal the way Frederick showed him. He worried that Frederick would fire him as his apprentice, and then he would have to find not only another job, but also another place to live. As Frederick's apprentice, Kristoff had been receiving room and board with the Faber family in their beautiful home on the outskirts of Grotsburg, as well as five schilling a week. But most important, the opportunity to learn the trade that Frederick Faber was known for throughout Austria: engraving. His greatest creation was the country's most popular—and, Kristoff would argue, artistically perfect—postage stamp, the 12 Groschen Edelweiss. The stamp was a stunning replica of the pure white flower, and Frederick had both designed and engraved it himself in 1932.

Kristoff remembered placing that stamp on a letter he'd written to his mother once, but had never sent. He could not mail a letter to someone who didn't exist, or whose existence and location he could never determine in spite of his best efforts. But even as a young boy of thirteen, Kristoff had admired the artistry of that stamp, the perfect bows of the petals. He'd always wanted to make a living as an artist. So when he'd heard the rumor last fall from another street artist in Vienna, that Frederick Faber, *the* Frederick Faber, was searching for a new apprentice, Kristoff had packed up his art supplies and spent most of his small savings to hire a ride to take him the two hundred kilometers out to Grotsburg. And when he'd arrived, he'd convinced Frederick to give him the job after he showed Frederick some of his charcoal sketches of Vienna.

"You have a good eye," Frederick had said, staring at what Kristoff thought was his most noteworthy sketch: Stephansdom, elaborate in all its detail of the two wide turrets in the front. Frederick had raised a thick gray eyebrow. "But what do you know of metal, my boy?"

"I'm a quick learner," Kristoff had promised, and that had seemed enough to convince Frederick to take him on. Though, so far, this had turned out not to be true, at least where engraving was concerned.

Though he didn't master the burin right away, Kristoff did learn two things in his first few weeks working for Frederick. One, Frederick was older than Kristoff had initially thought, and sometimes his hands began to shake when he tried to teach Kristoff how to use the engraving tools. Frederick had told Kristoff he needed an apprentice because there was business enough for two master engravers to work on his stamp assignments for Austria, but now Kristoff suspected the real reason was that Frederick might not be able to continue on with his trade much longer. And Frederick didn't have any sons.

That was the second thing Kristoff learned. Frederick had two daughters: Elena, who was seventeen, a year younger than Kristoff, and who reminded Kristoff of the edelweiss with her snowy skin, waves of long light brown hair, and bright green eyes. And Miriam, who was thirteen. If Elena was a flower, then Miriam was the buzzing bee who wouldn't leave the flower alone. Or, as Mrs. Faber called her with an exasperated roll of her green eyes, a *flibbertigibbet*. But Kristoff still found her amusing, even when her family did not.

Kristoff quickly became accustomed to life in Grotsburg, where the world was green and very quiet, and instead of buildings and throngs of people, he woke up each morning to a view of the forest and rolling hills. But even more, Kristoff reveled in the warmth of the Fabers' dining room, of the fragrant smell of Mrs. Faber's stews, of the bread they broke on Friday nights in the glow of their candles. The challah was a savory bread, and Kristoff had never tasted anything like it growing up in the orphanage in Vienna, where the nuns had led him to believe there was only one religion anyway. Not that he was necessarily a believer. Kristoff was much more drawn to the Fabers, the light and wholeness of their family, than he had ever been to God or the institutional church.

"Miriam, sit still," Mrs. Faber chastised, one night a few weeks after Kristoff had begun his apprenticeship. Almost a month in,

Kristoff was still failing miserably at the metalwork. Though earlier that day he had impressed Frederick with his sketch of the hillside, and even hours later, he was still basking in Frederick's compliment that it was "not half bad."

"I'm sitting still, Mother," Miriam said in a singsong voice, bouncing slightly in her chair and casting a sideways smile at Kristoff.

Kristoff hid his own smile in his spoonful of soup. He glanced at Elena, but she refused to look at him. He had yet to determine whether she was shy or rude, whether she acted so standoffish around everyone, or whether it was just around him.

"Elena, dear. Go fetch another log or two for the fire. It's chilly in here," Mrs. Faber said. It was the deepest, coldest part of winter, and the Fabers' three-story wooden house was drafty. Kristoff's room in the attic had a small woodstove, but he had to huddle under two blankets to stay warm at night. Still, it far surpassed the orphanage, his bed in a row of ten others in a large cold room, and only a thin blanket to cover him. And Mrs. Faber's cooking was much better than the nuns'.

Elena put her soup spoon down and stood. Kristoff tried to meet her eyes again, but she wouldn't look up.

"I can help." Kristoff stood, before he lost his nerve, and Elena turned toward him. At least he'd caught her attention.

Her beautiful face sunk into a frown. "It's not—" she began.

Mrs. Faber spoke over her: "Thank you, Kristoff. I'm sure Elena would appreciate that."

He smiled at Mrs. Faber and followed Elena. They went wordlessly through the kitchen, out the back door, toward the woodpile, which rested across the Fabers' sprawling yard in front of Frederick's workshop. The earth was frozen, and the ground crunched beneath their feet; the night air was biting and neither Kristoff nor Elena had grabbed a coat. Elena shivered, and her hair fell into her eyes as she reached down to grab the wood. Kristoff resisted the urge to pull her hair back, and instead reached down and took the log from her hands.

"Really," she said sharply, pulling it back and holding it toward her chest. "I'm just fine. I've been doing this on my own long before you came here. I don't need your help."

"But I want to help," he said. "And it's no trouble." Elena glared, and he was suddenly certain that she was not shy—she just didn't like him. And this realization bothered him. He had the urge to fix it.

But before he could say more, Elena turned and began to walk back toward the house. Kristoff picked up another log from the pile and ran after her. He caught her just before they reached the back door, and he reached for her shoulder. "Have I done something?" he asked her, slightly out of breath from running in the cold. His words came out jagged and smoky against the chilly air.

"Something?" she echoed back.

"To upset you?"

"Why should you think that?" Her breath made frosty rings in the air, and she shivered again.

"Never mind," he said. "We should get back inside. You're freezing."

"Look," she said. "It's just that we're not friends, okay? We're not going to be friends. I don't expect you to be here long. They never are."

"They?" he asked, considering, for the first time, Frederick's last apprentice, or maybe his last few? Were they all terrible with the burin, like him, and promptly fired?

But Elena didn't answer. She carried the wood inside and placed it into the fire. Kristoff did the same, and then he excused himself to go to bed. Up in the attic, wrapped in two blankets, he took out his sketch pad and a nib of charcoal. He found himself sketching Elena's angry green eyes and wondering how long this place would stay his home.

❁

The next day, inside Frederick's workshop, Kristoff had trouble concentrating. His work with the burin was even worse, his practice lines even sloppier. And when they were cleaning up before dinner Frederick turned to look at Kristoff and frowned. "Are you going to fire me?" Kristoff asked.

"Fire you?" Frederick was nearly bald, but his eyebrows were still bushy, thick, and gray, and they framed eyes as vividly green as Elena's.

"I'm not doing well with the metal," Kristoff said, unable to keep the note of desperation he felt from creeping into his voice. "Maybe I'm not meant for this. Maybe you should fire me." As much as Kristoff did not want to be fired, he also knew the longer he was here, the more accustomed he became to the warmth of the Fabers' house and Frederick's workshop and Frederick himself, the harder it would be to leave. Should Frederick want to fire him, it would be better for him to do it now.

"Do you want me to fire you?" Frederick asked, looking confused.

"No, of course not," Kristoff said. "I just thought . . . Elena said . . ." He felt his cheeks turning red.

"Ahhh, Elena." Frederick sighed. "Don't mind my Elena. She's just mad about my last apprentice."

"That you fired him?" Kristoff asked.

Frederick shook his head. "No, no, my boy. I've never fired anyone."

"So what happened to him?" Kristoff asked.

Frederick frowned again but didn't answer his question. "You want to be here?" he finally said. Kristoff nodded. "Then I want you to be here. I want you to learn. If you still want to learn?"

"I do," Kristoff said.

"Good." Frederick put his hand gently on Kristoff's shoulder. "There are two necessary skills to becoming a stamp engraver, Kristoff. First is the ability to draw something worthy of going on a postage stamp for our beautiful Austria. You have that skill down." Kristoff felt his cheeks grow warm with the unexpected compliment. "The other part is learning how to replicate that all to scale, in reverse, in the metal with the engraving tools. And you will learn. It just takes time. And patience. I didn't have complete control of the burin either when I was your age." Kristoff smiled, grateful for Frederick's kindness. "Here, try one more time before dinner." He handed Kristoff back the burin, his hands shaking a little, the tool vibrating in his palm. Kristoff pretended he didn't notice.

❀

Mrs. Faber had a routine for weekly dinners. Thursday nights she made beef stew, and this became Kristoff's favorite night of the week. They'd rarely had beef in their stew in the orphanage because it was too expensive, and so now the taste of Mrs. Faber's delicious meat each Thursday night reminded Kristoff that he was no longer an orphan, no longer entirely alone.

After dinner, Miriam and Elena would finish their schoolwork, and Frederick would smoke a pipe in the armchair by the fire in the living room and read a book. Kristoff wasn't sure what to do with himself at first and he would excuse himself to go up to his room.

But one Thursday about two months into his apprenticeship, after the girls had finished clearing the table, Miriam bounced up to him and asked him to play Monopoly with her. Frederick had brought the game back from a trip to London two years earlier, and Miriam loved it. Elena didn't seem so enthusiastic, but Kristoff had seen her sitting on the floor by the fire, playing with Miriam before. This was his first invitation to play along.

"Come on." Miriam tugged on his shirtsleeve. "Don't be a bore and run up to the attic like you always do. Play with us tonight. It's so much fun. You'll love it."

He glanced at Elena, who quickly looked away. "I don't want to intrude," he said quietly, willing Elena to turn back and look at him, to tell him that he wasn't intruding at all. The truth was, he wasn't exactly sure how to play Monopoly and he knew that was most likely why Miriam wanted him to play, so she could win. Not that he minded. He was happy she'd invited him at all. His belly was full from the stew, his skin warm from the fire. He wasn't ready to retreat to the cold attic alone.

"You aren't intruding," Elena said. "I have a book I want to finish, anyway. I'll go upstairs. You play with Miri tonight."

"What are you reading?" Kristoff asked.

She finally looked back at him, her eyebrows raised, and maybe she couldn't believe that a person like him, a person who had left school at fourteen to become a street artist, might be interested in books. But he was. Ever since he was a little boy, he'd read everything he could get his hands on in the orphanage, and his favorite nun, Sister Marguerite, would often give him books when she'd finished reading them. Books on art, history, and war, and sometimes even novels.

"She's reading something boring," Miriam said, tugging again on his sleeve, trying to pull him toward her game.

"Dr. Freud is not boring," Elena said. "Maybe when you get older, Miri, you'll understand him." Miriam rolled her eyes in response.

Kristoff had nothing to add, as Freud's books were not something he'd ever seen, and he only loosely knew of the man. Some kind of doctor practicing in Vienna, with all kinds of crazy thoughts. But maybe Elena didn't think they were crazy the way the nuns had?

"Elena," Mrs. Faber chimed in, then leaned over to blow out the candles that had been burning on the dining table during dinner. "Why don't you leave Dr. Freud be, and play the game with your sister and Kristoff." She tugged affectionately on one of Miriam's braids. "Someone needs to make sure this one doesn't cheat. And three people can play together."

"I don't cheat, Mother." Miriam crossed her arms. "I can't help it if I always get London's best properties."

Mrs. Faber laughed, pulled Miriam close, and kissed the top of her head. "Right," she said. "You never steal Elena's money when she's not looking."

"Never," Miriam gasped, and Elena broke into a grin.

"All right. Come on," Elena said. "The game takes forever. We might as well get started."

He followed the girls to their normal spot on the floor in front of the fire and he tentatively sat down. Frederick lowered his pipe and his book, and he looked at Kristoff as if he was about to say something, but then he changed his mind, smiled warmly instead, and announced he was going up to bed.

❋

Later that night, Kristoff couldn't sleep. He lay in bed for a long while, wide-awake. The sound of Miriam's laughter as she'd counted up her money, and Elena's chuckle as she'd lost to her younger sister (yet again)—intentionally, Kristoff thought—all felt so near to him. As if they were his, as if he belonged to them now.

The engraving tools felt so impossible still. The metal so different from canvas. Frederick continued to insist that Kristoff would learn. But what if he didn't? What if he never did? Frederick couldn't stay patient forever. But Kristoff couldn't imagine losing him. Or Mrs. Faber's beef stew. Or Miriam's laughter and chatter, and Elena's beautiful smile, even if it was rarely directed at him. He couldn't fail at engraving and be forced to leave the Fabers behind. He just couldn't.

Though it was very cold now, and the middle of the night, he got out of bed and tiptoed down the two flights of stairs. He would practice at night. While Frederick slept. He needed the extra time in the workshop, alone, without Frederick's watchful eye making him nervous.

The dining room was quiet and still at this hour, and the fire had burned down to tiny orange embers. Kristoff put on his boots and his coat, and he opened the back door slowly, so as not to make noise. He ran across the snow-dusted grass to Frederick's workshop.

When he opened the door to the workshop, his eye immediately drew to the unexpected light of a candle flickering inside on the worktable.

"Who's there?" he called out.

He felt the crush of metal against his skull, and he cried out in pain as he sunk to his knees.

Los Angeles, 1989

SUNDAY MORNINGS WHEN I was a kid, my mother would sleep in late, and my father would wake me early, sometimes before the sun even came up. We lived in the Fairfax District, in walking distance to twelve different synagogues, a farmer's market, and CBS Television City. Most of the week we were ensconced in our own little section of LA. My father taught at Fairfax High (I eventually went there, once the rebuilt/earthquake-safe campus opened my junior year); my mother worked at a law firm across the street from Canter's Deli. But on Sundays, my father and I would get into his red Mustang convertible and ride, with the top down, to parts unknown. Or unknown to me, as a kid, anyway. Every week it was a thrift shop in the valley, a yard sale in West Hollywood, an estate sale in Beverly Hills, all in the name of my father's never-ending quest for stamps.

Each week, we'd return home just before lunch—I'd be full from the donuts my father would buy me to eat on the way (a treat neither one of us divulged to my mother)—and my father never came home empty-handed. Sometimes, he'd have someone else's old collection (or a piece of it); other times, letters—sent and saved or unsent and lost. Every once in a while, when our endless riffling through yard sales turned up nothing, we stopped at the post office on the way back, and he bought a sheet of the newest stamp that had come out that month.

So you're not actually going to use those to send letters? my mother asked when we came home with new stamps, her voice rising skeptically, the way I imagined it did at work. She was a paralegal for a firm that handled real estate law. I sometimes pictured her in the courtroom, even though I knew that the lawyers she worked with mostly did paperwork.

My father just smiled at her, and took his stamps up to his hobby room to file them away with the rest of his collection.

This memory returns to me today, this Sunday morning, as I drive toward Santa Monica to visit my father at the Willows. Not in a red convertible, of course, but in my old blue Toyota hatchback, which is on its last legs, pushing a hundred thousand miles. I remember so suddenly, so vividly, exactly what stamp he bought at the post office once—a five-cent Humane Treatment of Animals stamp, featuring a cute black-and-white dog, just like I always wanted for a pet as a kid, and never got.

And what lingers in my mind as I arrive at the Willows is this: I am no one's child anymore. I can never return to those Sunday mornings with my father. We haven't done one of those trips in years. Not since before I left for college, since before my mother died. But still. Now there's no going back.

❀

The good thing about the Willows is that it's only a half hour from me, in a beautiful section of Santa Monica. The bad thing is also that it's in a beautiful section of Santa Monica, which, in LA terms, translates to outrageously expensive. My father will run through his savings, his teaching pension, and his life insurance collection from my mother's death long before he's ready to leave the Willows, I'm sure. But the Willows is also the best memory care facility in LA, and every time I've been to visit my father so far, it seems he has been mistaking it for a grand hotel. He asks me if I can help him locate his plane ticket, when he's going home. He can't seem to find his itinerary, he says. And rather than reminding him, gently, of the truth, I promise him I'll look. That I'll find his documents, somewhere.

"Morning, Mrs. Nelson." The nurse at the front desk greets me as I walk inside.

"Hi, Sally." I wave, and walk up to the desk and sign in. Sally's in her twenties and clearly green enough that dealing with memory care patients on a daily basis hasn't worn her down yet. She's petite and wears a giant sparkling engagement ring on her left hand, and though she's a licensed nurse, she's dressed in jeans and a sweater. The Willows doesn't feel anything like a hospital or a nursing home. And one of the requirements for my father living here is that his health, his physical health anyway, is good.

"You're here early today," Sally comments.

I nod, but don't offer a reason. What would Sally think if I told her that I haven't been sleeping? That since Daniel left, I wake up at five a.m., even on Sundays, even if I don't fall asleep until two. That my house, my bedroom, my bed, all feel strange and dark and empty. But I would never admit that out loud, especially not to someone who barely knows me.

I've come to visit every Sunday since I moved my father in

here three months ago, and to the staff, I'm still Mrs. Nelson. Okay, so I'm technically still Mrs. Nelson everywhere, given that I haven't actually signed the papers yet. But in my head I dropped the *Mrs.* (and the *Nelson*) months ago. My father doesn't know about Daniel leaving me, and why upset him or confuse him? Sometimes I feel a little guilty that his disease has turned me into such a liar.

"So how's he doing today?" I ask Sally. I like to prepare myself before going back to his room.

"Not bad," she says. "Ted's having a good day so far. Lucid at breakfast. He went to art class this morning, and that put him in a good mood. Told me he was going to knitting with some of our ladies after lunch." She laughs, and I smile in return. The Willows *is* like a cruise ship. Packed with classes and activities, to stimulate the mind and pass the time. No wonder my father always thinks he's on vacation.

Sally tells me I can go back, and I walk down the long hallway toward his room. The hall is decorated with patterned wall-to-wall carpet like a hotel, and large glass chandeliers hang from the ceiling, making the pathway brightly lit. Too brightly lit, for someone who drank a little too much chardonnay last night, as I am apt to do these days, and I pull my sunglasses down. *He'll know me today. He'll be totally fine*, I chant to myself in my head as I walk, as if by thinking it, wanting it enough, I can make it true.

When I reach his room, I stop, stand in the doorway and watch him for a moment, before he notices that I'm here. He sits in a blue velvety armchair by the wide picture window, reading a book, his reading glasses arched at the bridge of his nose. He looks the way he always did, the way he always has: he's very tall and thin, but also strong. He's a little thinner now, maybe, and also mostly bald. But still my father.

He looks up and sees me, and he breaks into a smile. "Kate the Great!" I smile back when I hear his childhood nickname for me. He knows me. Sometimes he thinks I'm my mother or even a nurse. But today, Sally was right. It's a good day.

"What're you reading?" I ask as I walk into his room. He holds up the book so I can see the cover. "*The Philatelist's Guide to the Universe*. Oh, Dad. That sounds so boring." But I'm happy he remembers who he is this morning. What he loves. My father was never a reader of novels like me and my mother. He taught high school history for years, and he read nonfiction, thick books about wars and generals and history and, of course, stamps. This particular book is worn, and he must've looked through it many times before, whether he remembers that now or not. Though, maybe he does. It's mostly his short-term memory that's affected by his disease so far. The past is often still vivid to him, sometimes so vivid that he believes he's reliving it in the moment. That he believes my mother is still here.

"Speaking of stamps," I say, and I pull up a chair to sit near him. "I'm having your collection appraised."

He opens his mouth and slams the book shut. "Why would you do that?"

That wasn't the reaction I'd been hoping for, and I immediately try to mollify him. "Well, you always said you were looking for the Hope Diamond of stamps, and I wanted to see if you'd found something valuable." I try to keep my voice light, but I notice the way his face seems suddenly paler, his brown eyes a little darker, and I wish I hadn't brought this up at all.

He turns and looks out the window, as if the pale blue sky and the arch of the barren brown mountain beyond hold some kind of answers I can't see. "Every stamp is valuable."

"I know, but that's not what I mean."

"Where'd you take it?" he asks.

"A stamp dealer. Benjamin Grossman," I tell him.

"A Jew at least," he says, and his voice softens, as if he's coming around to the idea of getting his collection appraised. It hadn't occurred to me that Grossman is a Jewish name. The only thing more important than stamps to my father is his Judaism. But to me—as a grown woman who married a non-Jewish man—I've left almost all of my religion behind. I'd never tell my father, but one of my favorite times of the year throughout my seven years married to Daniel was decorating our Christmas tree. Maybe because it was such a novelty or maybe because it was something I purely associated with my marriage. The thought of Christmas, practically right around the corner, saddens me now. What reason does an almost-divorced Jewish girl have to get a Christmas tree?

"You won't sell anything," my father says, emphatically, interrupting my thoughts, and I bring my mind back to the stamps.

"If you don't want me to, I won't." I lean in and put my hand on his. "I didn't mean to upset you. I didn't know what else to do with your collection when you told me I could have it. But I can go get it back. And I'll just . . . keep it." I wonder what Benjamin Grossman will think of me when I do, or how much I'll owe him, for simply wasting his time.

But my father doesn't respond. He turns back to stare out the window. "The stamps were everything," he murmurs, and maybe he's pushing himself to remember the specifics of his collection.

Once, it wouldn't have surprised me if he had committed every single stamp in it to memory. But now, who knows what's still in his mind and what's lost.

"I know. Your collection is huge. It filled up my entire car."

"But you never understood it, Rissa. Never even wanted to."

Rissa. I sigh. In an instant I've turned into my mother in his mind. I've wasted his few good, lucid moments this morning talking about stamps, and I want to take them back and talk about something real with him instead. To tell him about what happened with me and Daniel, about how I haven't been able to bring myself to open the envelope with the divorce papers yet. About how a part of me is still hoping Daniel will change his mind, that we could figure out a way back to each other if we really, really tried. About how thinking that makes me feel weak, and I hate that. I want to ask for his advice, the way I always have. "Dad." I touch his shoulder gently.

"You never understood it," he repeats. "You never even wanted to."

"Don't worry, your collection is safe. I'll go get it back, and I'll take good care of it. I promise." I'm echoing the words Benjamin Grossman said to me when I left everything at his office. Though my promise feels empty. I'm not sure what I would do to take good care of it.

His book falls from his lap to the floor, but he doesn't seem to notice. He watches the outside world carefully, as if he can envision my mother there, beyond the hills, beyond the Pacific Ocean. I look, too, as if she might really be there, visible, a ghost, until the brightness hurts my eyes and I finally look away.

I pick his book up off the floor, and it's filled with stamps, pages and pages of stamps categorized by year, country, engraver. Was all of this committed to his memory once, too? But these days does it appear just as new, as foreign, to him as it does to me?

I hand him back the book and kiss the top of his head. He turns to me, and something brings him back. I can see it in his eyes. He sees *me* again. "Kate," he says, sounding surprised. "You came today."

"Yeah." I put my hand on his arm. "I come every Sunday." I pause and wait to see whether this information registers, but his stare is blank and I'm not sure. It's so hard to watch him come and go, when I really need him to be here. "I have to go to work." I give him a hug. "But I'll be back soon. Next week, okay?"

"Kate," he calls after me as I walk away, and I turn. "My tickets. I can't seem to find my passport."

"I know." I force myself to smile. "I'm still looking."

❋

Every time I leave the Willows I feel like I'm sinking. Like I've dived into the cold waters of the Pacific without a wet suit. I am numb, cold. Tired. I really do have to work. I'm supposed to go to a movie premiere, but I still have a little time, so I head home first to collect myself. I don't live in Fairfax any longer, but near UCLA, in Westwood, where there are still a fair number of synagogues—I just haven't been in any of them.

When I get back home, I consider calling Daniel, asking him to assign someone else to the premiere. Sitting in a dark theater and concentrating on a movie, a Chevy Chase National Lampoon movie about Christmas no less, feels nearly impossible after this morning. But these days, I try not to ask Daniel for anything. I've tried to avoid him at work, communicating mostly through notes in our inboxes and outboxes on our desks, and I certainly don't want to call him now and ask for a personal favor.

I make myself a pot of coffee and try to regain my composure. But then I sit in the kitchen to have a cup at the very same table where Daniel and I ate dinners and breakfasts for so many years. Daniel offered me this house in the divorce settlement as a gesture of kindness. He said he didn't want to force me to sell so we could split the equity, force me to move out of my home when everything else in my life was in upheaval, too. And so he'd graciously just . . . given it to me. *Graciously*. That was the word my lawyer had used, anyway. But there are so many memories of us together, everywhere in this house.

When he had first said the terrible words to me last spring, we were eating dinner at this table. I'd made lasagna and a salad, and I'd taken the day off work. Earlier that morning I'd visited the Willows for the first time and had made the decision to put my father on the waitlist for a room there. In a way, it had felt like a relief. I'd come home and thrown myself into chopping, cooking, baking. I'd also made a cake—chocolate chip with buttercream icing, Daniel's favorite.

"But I made dessert," I said that night, in response to his unexpected announcement that he was done, that he no longer wanted to be married, that he'd be moving out. I'd thought, at first, that he was joking. That I'd offer him the cake and he'd laugh and take the words back.

"We're just not working anymore," Daniel had said, calmly. "This is the first time we've had dinner together in months." Was it? I tried to recall the last dinner we'd shared at this table, and I couldn't. My father really shouldn't have been living alone at that point, and I'd been spending all my free time with him.

There were probably a thousand things I could've or should've said, starting with the fact that things were going to get better once I moved my father into the Willows. I could've gotten angry, yelled at him that taking care of a parent was no reason to leave someone, or that it wasn't okay for him to just decide all this without even discussing it with me first. Or that no matter how many dinners or nights we'd spent apart I couldn't imagine my life without him. But I was so shocked by his announcement that instead, I just kept talking about the stupid cake. "Cake," I'd emphasized. "I made you a cake." I never baked a cake, unless it was his birthday. The cake was my apology, in a way. I knew we'd grown apart. I'd just believed, right up until that moment, that it would be okay. That we could still fix things, that this was just a rough few months in a marriage that would last forever.

"Katie," he said, evenly. "Our marriage is over."

And then it hit me: He was giving up on us? I cut him a slice of cake. I shoved the plate toward him, harder than I should've, and the cake bounced off the plate. Daniel stared at me, then at the cake, half on the table, as if suddenly he wasn't sure what he was supposed to do with it.

"It's your favorite cake," I finally said, and though it'd felt like a gesture of kindness when I was making it, I sounded bitter, angry, when I said this to him.

Daniel looked down, picked up his fork, and took a bite of the cake.

After dinner he packed a bag, and left to go sleep at a hotel.

❋

A few hours later, after I get home from the premiere, I sit in bed, chewing on my pen, trying to find the words for my review. But the page in front of me is totally blank, and my mind is still lost in my morning visit to my father. I have the urge to pick up the phone and call him now, the way I often used to back in college when something occurred to me, late at night, or when I just wanted to talk, hear his voice. After my mother died of cancer my freshman year, I knew he would be awake, no matter how late it was. He was always a night owl; so am I. *Daniel left me*, I might tell him. *I can't even bring myself to open the divorce papers because I still can't accept that we're done.* Once, years ago, when Daniel and I were first married, we got into a stupid fight and Daniel left me then, just for the night. I'd called my father in tears, sometime after midnight. And I still remember what he said: *Kate, when you really love someone you don't run.* Any goodwill he'd had for Daniel dissipated after that, and I'd felt a little bad that I'd called him at all. But now I'm grateful for the memory of it, his words. That's probably what he'd say to me, if I did call him tonight. But anyway, I can't call him. The Willows doesn't accept phone calls after eight p.m.

I remember the promise I made to him earlier that I'd get his stamps back, and I decide to call Benjamin Grossman now and leave him a message instead. But after two rings, Benjamin, not his machine, picks up.

"Oh," I say. "I didn't expect you to answer, to be in your office so late on a Sunday night. I figured I'd leave you a message."

"Who is this?" he asks.

"Right, sorry. It's Katie. Katie Nelson. I brought you my father's collection last week." He doesn't say anything, so I jump in, with the reason I called. "I need to come back and pick his collection up. I changed my mind. I don't think I want it appraised after all."

He's quiet for another minute, and I have no idea whether he's surprised or annoyed, or just uncaring and maybe doing something else in the background. I picture him sitting at that messy desk, adjusting the antenna on his TV. "I found something unusual in his collection," he says.

"Unusual?"

"There's a stamp on a letter," he says. "A World War Two–era Austrian stamp. And I've never seen anything like it before."

"It's valuable?" *Every stamp is valuable*, my father had said to me this morning. But what if he really did find a gem? My father would be thrilled. I know he would be. Not to mention we could use the money for his care, for the Willows.

"It's unusual," Benjamin counters.

"But unusual means valuable to a stamp collector, right?"

"Philatelist," Benjamin corrects me, the technical word for stamp collector rolling easily off his tongue, though I've never really liked that word. It strikes me as oddly sexual, a little embarrassing.

"But unusual is good, isn't it?" I ask.

"Maybe," Benjamin says. "Can you meet me? I want to show you what I mean. In person."

"Now?" I glance at the clock, at my half-drunk glass of wine. It's almost ten, but I'm wide-awake. I haven't drunk enough wine yet to begin to feel myself ready to slide into sleep.

Benjamin exhales on the other end of the line. "Sorry," he says.

"I'm an insomniac. I do my best work at night. Sometimes I forget that other people sleep."

"I don't sleep either," I admit.

We're both quiet for a moment, and then Benjamin says, "I know a diner, Frankie's, off the 405 just a little south of my office. It's open twenty-four hours. If you want to meet over there?"

"I'll be there in thirty minutes," I say.

Austria, 1938

KRISTOFF OPENED HIS EYES and saw Elena's round face hovering close above his own. She looked worried, and as he tried to sit up, he felt a sharp aching in his head. He reached up and felt a painful lump on his forehead. "What happened?" he asked.

"You're alive." Elena exhaled and stepped back. She held a thick piece of metal in one hand, a candle in the other, and her hands were shaking.

Then he remembered the clunk against his skull. "You hit me? Why would you do that?"

Elena put the metal down and reached out her free hand to help him up. Her hand was tiny in his, cold and soft, and he let her lead him to the corner armchair in the workshop, where Frederick often sat and smoked his pipe, just before lunch.

Once he was settled in the chair and Elena seemed satisfied that he wasn't going to die, she put the candle on the worktable and folded her arms in front of her chest. "It's the middle of the night," she admonished him. "Why are you sneaking around in my father's workshop?"

"Why are you here?" he countered. His head throbbed, and he put his hand to his forehead in an attempt to quell the ache.

"I live here," she said, as if that gave her the right. Frederick would most likely be angry to know that either one of them was in his workshop in the middle of the night, much less both of them. "Were you trying to steal from my father? I knew you couldn't be trusted," she added. It seemed a strange thing to say, when only hours earlier she'd teased him as they played a board game together, and he'd thought they were finally becoming friends.

"No," he protested, and tried to sit up, but Elena had hit him hard, and the workshop spun all around him in dizzying waves. The metal engraving plates, the tools, they all seemed misplaced, upside down. "I don't want to steal anything," he said as the world tilted around him. "I just wanted to practice. I . . . I need more practice. With the engraving tools."

Elena opened her mouth slightly, and she leaned forward, her shoulders slumping. She kneeled on the floor in front of him and reached up and touched his forehead lightly. Her fingers were cool, her touch gentle against his throbbing head. "I thought you were an intruder. It's dark. That's why I hit you."

"An honest mistake," he said, wondering how long it would take for the aching in his head to subside. He might suspect it wasn't a mistake at all, given Elena's clear dislike for him, except her face turned in such a way that she genuinely seemed to feel bad. "You still haven't told me what you're doing in here," he said.

"I'm practicing, too," she said quietly, her eyes moving to the worktable. Her hair fell across her face, and he couldn't read her expression. He had the urge to lean down and move her hair behind her shoulders so he could see her eyes, but he didn't.

He raised his eyebrows, and felt a new flash of pain across his forehead. "Why?" he asked. "Why would you be practicing?"

"None of your concern." She stood and moved toward the door.

"Elena," he called after her.

"It's late," she said. "I should get some sleep. We both should."

He heard the door click shut behind her, and he sat for a little while longer until the dizziness finally subsided.

❊

The next morning at the breakfast table, Mrs. Faber noticed Kristoff's head right away. He'd overslept, and Frederick was already out in his workshop. Kristoff hoped he wouldn't be angry, but after Elena left and his headache had subsided a bit, he had practiced, and he hoped today the progress would show. That Frederick would be happy with him, in spite of his tardiness.

"Oh, dear boy," Mrs. Faber said, handing him a cup of her strong black coffee. "Whatever happened to you?"

The bump had already turned purple and ugly, and protruded from his forehead, the size of a small apricot. He glanced at Elena, who stared very hard at her toast. "I fell out of bed," he finally said. "Hit my forehead on the side table."

"That looks nasty. Oh, I feel terrible. I'll have Miriam move that table for you after school today," Mrs. Faber said.

"It's fine," he said. "I'm just clumsy sometimes. It wasn't anyone's fault."

Elena finally looked up at him, and it seemed she couldn't help herself. She gave him a small, maybe grateful, smile. He shrugged in response, to say, *I'll keep your secret. For now.* If he was being honest, he didn't care so much why she was in Frederick's workshop in the middle of the night, why she was practicing with his tools. He cared about falling into her good graces. About seeing her smile again. At him.

❀

"You're late," Frederick barked at him as Kristoff walked into the workshop. It looked different in the daylight, all the engraving tools more menacing again.

"Sorry," Kristoff apologized, and went straight for the burin. Last night he had gotten it to make a small, straight line, just the exact size that he wanted it to be. Even with his head throbbing. But as he picked it up again, he felt nervous, uncertain.

"Kristoff," Frederick said. "I know you came back in to work last night."

"You do?" Kristoff touched the swollen lump on his forehead, and he wondered how Frederick knew.

Frederick held up an engraving plate, and Kristoff saw it bore a strong resemblance to his drawing of the hillside, the one Frederick had told him was *not half bad*. But he wasn't nearly skilled enough with the engraving tools yet to do anything like this, in the metal. He was still learning to make simple lines behave the way he wanted underneath the pressure of the burin, never mind trying to replicate an entire drawing. In order to make an engraving plate for a stamp, a drawing had to be engraved on the metal plate, backwards and to scale. Each line and detail of the original drawing had to be replicated with perfection, in reverse order, before the plate could be taken to the printer in Vienna. "I couldn't . . . I didn't . . ." But Elena had. She must've. Elena had said she was practicing. And, looking at the plate in Frederick's hands, Kristoff realized that she was actually good. Far better than him, anyway. Why wouldn't she tell her father that she was interested in engraving, in fact very skilled at it? Sure, engraving wasn't a trade for a woman, but Frederick seemed the kind of man who wouldn't pay any attention to what other people would think. So why all the secrecy? But he remembered the smile Elena had shot him at breakfast, and he wasn't about to give her away now.

"I was practicing last night," Kristoff finally said. "I'm sorry. I just wanted to get better. I needed the practice." None of that was a lie, he reasoned.

"Okay," Frederick said. "But you need to start from the beginning, my boy. You are getting ahead of yourself with this." He pointed again to the hillside engraving. "It's too messy. There are many mistakes. If you want perfection you'll learn slowly. In the daylight hours. With my help." Kristoff nodded, relieved that Frederick wasn't going to ask him to repeat what he had supposedly done, what Elena had done. Frederick placed his shaking hand on Kristoff's shoulder, and he handed Kristoff the burin.

Kristoff took the tool from Frederick. "I understand," he said.

❋

Kristoff thought about Elena all day. His hands ached as he practiced painstaking lines with Frederick's tools, the time passing slowly. He pondered Elena's motives, what she was doing, why she was teaching herself Frederick's trade, and in secret. But also her small, cold hands. The way her skin felt soft against his own. The way his aching head had felt when her finger had traced his skin, just below his hairline.

At last the sun began to fade behind the hillside, and Frederick told him it was time to stop work for the day. "It's the Sabbath," Frederick reminded him, and Kristoff nodded, having already learned the importance of this Friday-night ritual in his short time living with the Fabers. "I understand it's not your religion," Frederick said. "But it's mine. And this is my workshop. I can't have you in here until after sundown tomorrow night. Promise me."

"I promise," Kristoff said, and he meant it.

❈

Elena wouldn't look at him throughout the Sabbath dinner and seemed to concentrate very hard on the prayers, the candles, the breaking of the bread. Kristoff tried to concentrate, too. Because he felt still very much an outsider in this world. He listened carefully to the words of the prayer (*Baruch atah, Adonai, Eloheinu* . . .) as he had done each week, trying to commit them all to memory, so that one week, soon, he could say them easily along with the Fabers.

As they began to eat and Mrs. Faber chastised Miriam for tapping her spoon against the side of the soup bowl, making it into song, Elena stood to get more wood for the fire, and Kristoff jumped up to help her. This time she didn't protest.

Once the back door closed behind them and they'd sunken into the sharp chill of the night air, Elena turned and put her fingers gently to his forehead. "Does it hurt a lot?" she asked.

"Not so much," he lied. She went to move her hand, but he moved his hand up to catch hers. "Your father found your engraving plate. The one you made of my drawing." Her eyes widened, and he said, "He thought it was mine. I let him believe that it was."

"Thank you," she said. "I . . . thank you." She pulled her hand away and started walking toward the woodpile.

"Why are you lying to him? Teaching yourself in the middle of the night?"

"I'm not lying," she said. "I don't have to tell my father everything."

"But tell me, then."

She grabbed a piece of wood from the pile, and he did the same. "Look," she said. "I'm sorry about your head. I am. But we're not friends, and like I've told you before, we're never going to be friends."

She began walking back toward the house. "I disagree," he called after her. "I think we are going to be friends."

But she just opened the door and walked inside the house without another word to him.

❀

Later, he lay in bed with his sketch pad and drew Elena again. This time her hair was a flower, like the edelweiss on Frederick's famous stamp. His side table had been moved as Mrs. Faber had promised this morning, but rather than moving it back he laid his materials out on top of the sheets. His bed was his workspace, but he didn't mind. He felt vaguely comfortable, a feeling that was strangely unfamiliar to him.

Someone rapped softly on his door. *Elena?* And he tried to hide the drawing, so obviously her, before he told her to come in.

But when the door opened, Miriam, not Elena, stepped inside his room. "Kristoff," she said, her small brown eyes open wide. Her brown hair was tied back in a messy braid, and she wore a long white nightgown that was too large for her—it dragged on the ground as she walked—and Kristoff guessed it had been Elena's once. "I'm so glad you're still awake. I need your help."

"What do you need?" he asked. They didn't play Monopoly or other games on the Sabbath. So he expected her to ask him to gather more firewood or to say that the mouse was back in her room again. This was all the talk when he'd first come here—the mouse that Miriam swore she heard scratching in the walls of her bedroom at night, and Mrs. Faber's insistence that the mouse only existed in Miriam's too-vivid imagination.

"Elena's gone," she said. "And I can't tell Mother or Father because it's the Sabbath and they'll get really angry. We're not supposed to go anywhere on the Sabbath."

"What do you mean, gone?" Kristoff pictured Elena inside Frederick's workshop teaching herself the engraving tools by candlelight. "Maybe she's just—" He stopped himself because he wasn't sure what Miriam knew of her sister's secrets.

"She's not in the house, and she's not in Father's workshop either. I checked."

"Maybe she just went out with a friend." Kristoff didn't know Elena's friends. Had she snuck out to meet a boy? The thought angered him, not that he had any right. But he didn't want Elena to have a suitor, especially not someone she would risk upsetting her parents for, running out on the Sabbath.

Miriam hesitated for a moment, and then she said, "She does go to meetings sometimes."

"What kind of meetings?"

"People who worry about the Germans. Elena says it'll be very bad for Austria if we agree to an annexation with Hitler."

The breadth of little Miriam's political knowledge, and Elena's, surprised him, especially living all the way out here in Grotsburg, where the entire rest of the world, the city, felt out of reach to him. In Vienna, in the rush of the city, people had often spoken of political change in Europe, and in Austria. Some people thought it would be better for Austria to remain independent; some people thought it wouldn't. Kristoff didn't like Hitler, and he wasn't in favor of him moving into Austria either. "Where are these meetings, Miri?"

Miriam shrugged. "I don't know. I just know she goes. And she doesn't tell Mother and Father because she doesn't want them to worry about her. But she's never left on the Sabbath before." Miriam paused for a moment and twirled her braid in her fingers. "Sometimes she stays out all night. But tomorrow is Saturday. Father won't be working, and he gets up so early. He'll notice she's not here. I don't know what she was thinking. Everybody says that *I'm* the flighty one."

It occurred to him why Miriam had come to his room. "You want me to go out and look for her, don't you?"

"Would you?" she asked.

He hesitated. "She won't listen to me, even if I find her. She doesn't like me very much, you know."

"But you like her." Miriam reached across the bed for his sketch pad.

"Don't." He grabbed it back from her.

"I already saw it this afternoon." She smirked a little. "When Mother asked me to move your table away from your bed."

"You shouldn't have been going through my things." He could feel warmth creeping across his cheeks at the thought of Miriam in here, looking through his drawings. The idea that she had seen all of his most personal thoughts, his sketches, his feelings about Elena right there on paper, in charcoal, made him feel worse than if she had walked in here and caught him undressing.

"I wasn't trying to," she said. "But it was right there. Sitting on the table. I had to move it to move the table." She was lying, the same way she fibbed about not cheating at Monopoly, but it wasn't worth arguing with her. What was done was done. "You're a pretty good artist, aren't you?" she said, her voice turning more serious. "I wish I could learn to draw as well as you."

"I'm okay," he said. Then he added, "Look, I know you want my help. But I wouldn't even know where to search. I'm sure Elena will be fine." He rubbed his still aching forehead. "She can take care of herself."

"There's a cabin in the woods, about halfway to town, just off the path." Miriam put her hands on her hips. "You could at least check there. I know she's gone there before and it's not that far."

❋

Outside it was surprisingly light, the round moon piercing the black sky and leading Kristoff into the woods behind Frederick's workshop. The town of Grotsburg was about a fifteen-minute walk, on the other side of these woods and at the bottom of a hilly clearing. Grotsburg was very small, much smaller than Vienna, a little village of red roofs, much like the Fabers'. But it had everything the Fabers needed: the market, the school the girls attended, and the post office. Kristoff found the bucolic walk to and from civilization refreshing after the constant bustle of Vienna for so many years. But he had only ever walked through these woods before in daylight.

At night the woods felt thicker, the path to town longer and a little steeper. He knew the cabin Miriam spoke of, but as he approached it, he didn't want to go in. After last night in Frederick's workshop, he didn't relish the idea of sneaking up on Elena again, surprising her.

"Kristoff?" Elena's voice coming through the woods toward him startled him, and he jumped.

He held up his hands and stopped walking. "Don't hit me," he said.

He heard the sound of laughter, a boy's laughter. No, a man's. And that's when he made out two shapes in front of him. Elena was holding on to someone's arm. Someone taller than him. A man who looked rather frightening to Kristoff in the half light of the moon.

"Who's this?" the man asked.

"Oh, no one," Elena answered, and Kristoff felt her words like a slap, or the crack of metal against his skull. "Just my father's new apprentice."

The man laughed. "Another one to go join the Hitlerjugend?" He took a step closer to Kristoff. "If you plan to go, why don't you go right now? Don't waste any more of Frederick's time."

"Josef, stop. He's all right." *All right?* Kristoff felt pleased that Elena didn't completely despise him. "What are you doing out here?" she asked him.

"Miriam was worried. She thought your father would notice you were gone during the Sabbath and get upset."

"I know. I'm on my way back. It just couldn't be helped tonight." She turned to Josef. "I'll walk the rest of the way with Kristoff."

"Are you sure?" Though Kristoff couldn't really make out Josef's expression in the dark, he guessed that Josef was eyeing him skeptically, or with annoyance.

"Yes," Elena said. "It's not far. We'll be fine."

Josef grabbed on to her arm, and Kristoff felt his senses heighten; he had the feeling that she was in danger. But Josef whispered something in her ear, Elena gave him a quick hug, and Kristoff realized she'd wanted to be pulled toward Josef.

"Come on." Elena tapped his shoulder a moment later, and she began to walk through the woods, back toward the house.

"What were you doing out here in the woods?" Kristoff asked her, trying to keep up with her quick pace. "And why did Josef ask if I was going to join the Hitlerjugend?"

"Are you?" Elena asked.

"Why would I ever do that?" He felt hurt Elena would think he would intentionally join a group so hateful of the Fabers' religion.

"I don't know," Elena spat back. "Why wouldn't you?" Then she added softly, "My father's last apprentice did."

So that explained what had happened to Frederick's last apprentice. He hadn't been fired at all but had left the Fabers to go join the Hitler Youth movement. No wonder why Elena had mistrusted Kristoff. It wasn't fair maybe, but suddenly it felt a little more understandable. "You know I have never had a family," he said. "Before I moved here, to learn from your father, I spent most of my life in an orphanage in Vienna. I never had a mother or a father. Or a sister," he added. "I never had anyone."

"I'm sorry," Elena said. "I didn't know that."

"You don't need to be sorry. But what I'm trying to say is, I like it here. I like your family a lot. I would never do anything to hurt them. Or you," he said.

Elena stopped walking and turned to face him. "You're different than I was expecting when you first came to live with us," she said.

He remembered what Miriam had told him about where Elena had been tonight. "I don't want Austria to become a German state either."

Elena sighed. "The German troops are already marching into Vienna. By tomorrow at this time, we'll all be Germans."

❀

In the morning the entire Faber family broke the rules of the Sabbath and turned on the radio. Even Miriam sat completely still as they waited and listened. The reception was crackly all the way out here, but they understood enough: Hitler's troops had marched into Austria and had announced the annexation of the Austrian state, just as Elena predicted the night before.

"Well, they'll still have to vote," Mrs. Faber said, shaking her head and moving to turn the radio off.

"Mother, don't," Elena said. "I want to hear what they're saying."

"They can't just take over Austria without a vote." Mrs. Faber's voice rose, unnaturally, and she wrung her hands on her apron.

Frederick reached across her and ignored Elena's protests and turned the radio off. "They can take Austria," he said quietly. "But we can't let them take the Sabbath, too."

Los Angeles, 1989

ENJAMIN IS ALREADY waiting in a booth by the window at Frankie's when I get there. From my parking spot, I can see his sand-colored curls near the glass. They look unruly, and I wonder if today has been as long for him as it has been for me.

I walk inside, slip into the booth across from him, and glance at the cup of coffee in my spot. "I ordered you a cup when I got one for myself," he says. "I didn't know if you drink coffee or not?"

"I do. Not normally this late at night." I pick up the cup and sip. "It's good," I say. "I'm a bit of a coffee snob." I'm not sure why I'm talking so much, but I feel a little flustered, out of my element, and I can't stop myself. "This is really good coffee," I repeat.

Benjamin ignores my nervous chatter and opens the manila folder in front of him, revealing one of the plastic sleeves from my father's many, many stamp-filled books. He slides it across the table to me.

Inside the plastic there's a sealed, addressed envelope, what appears to be a letter. The envelope is yellowed and crumbling with age, and it has an upside-down stamp in the right-hand corner.

"This stamp is upside down," I say. Benjamin nods. "That's what's unusual about it?"

"No. That's just a message."

"A message?"

"People used to do it all the time. Stamp placement meant something. There was a whole language of stamps."

"A language of stamps?" I had no idea.

"Upside down meant *I love you*," Benjamin adds.

"So is this a love letter?" I turn the envelope over carefully in my hands, the journalist in me caring less about the stamp and more about what the letter inside this envelope might say.

"You're missing the point," Benjamin says, running his hand through his hair. He reaches across the table and points to the stamp. "This stamp is not something I've ever seen before."

I turn the envelope upside down to inspect the stamp more closely. It's a black-and-white steeple, printed on an orange background with an eight in each corner, partially covered by the words *Deutsches Reich*. "I don't know what I'm looking for."

"The top of the steeple," Benjamin says, his voice edgy. He seems impatient with what he probably sees as my incompetence, my total lack of understanding.

I hold it up, closer to my eyes, and now I see at the very top of the steeple there's an outline of what appears to be a minuscule flower. It's barely visible. "The flower?" I ask.

He nods. "After Hitler took over Austria, they did a series of stamps to commemorate Austrian buildings, landmarks. This stamp is St. Stephen's Cathedral, in Vienna. But it's not supposed to have a flower in the steeple."

"So what does that mean?" I ask him. "Someone made a mistake when they made this particular stamp?" Is this my father's Hope Diamond? A tiny, barely visible flower on an Austrian steeple? Upside down on a love letter?

Benjamin takes a sip of his coffee. "I doubt it was a mistake. The way everything was done back then, it was all painstaking work, transferring an illustration to metal. Stamp engravers were highly skilled. You wouldn't just, ooops, slip and throw in a flower." He chuckles, and I feel silly for having made the suggestion.

"So then how did the flower get there?" I ask.

"Exactly," Benjamin says. But he shrugs. He doesn't have the answer.

I look at the envelope again. The address is typed: *Frl. Faber*, it reads. And below, an unintelligible address that I assume to be Austrian, based on what Benjamin said about the stamp's origins. "I wonder what's inside the envelope," I murmur.

"You can't open it." Benjamin pulls it back from me, holding it protectively. "You could diminish the value of the stamp."

"So it is valuable?"

"Maybe," he admits. "Or maybe not. Ninety-nine percent of irregularities I see turn out to be nothing. The stamps aren't even real, sometimes."

"Promising." I sink back in my booth, suddenly tired. It's close to midnight now, and I've driven out to this random diner to see a nearly invisible flower that is most likely not valuable, or real.

Benjamin looks at me for a moment as if he's about to say something more about the stamp, but he seems to change his mind, and takes another sip of coffee. "You don't happen to know where your father got this, do you?" he asks casually.

"It's hard to say at this point. He was always finding letters in thrift shops, at rummage sales. God, he dragged me to yard sales every weekend when I was a kid." The memory sounds insulting, and I instantly want to take my words back. Because what I remember, what I really remember, is the feel of my father's large hand against mine, the warm California sunshine against our faces when we got into the convertible so early on a Sunday morning, the smell of the bakery from the donuts we'd pick up on the way. *The stamps were everything*, my father said to me earlier, when he thought I was my mother.

Benjamin finishes off his coffee. "Can I ask—why do you want the collection back?"

"My father got upset earlier when I told him I brought it to you."

"How does he remember his collection? I thought you said his memory is gone."

I look down at the table and trace the edge of the plastic top with my thumb. The plastic is cracked and peeling. "Memory loss is a widening sieve." I'm repeating what one of his doctors told me once, but his voice was stoic; mine sounds bitter. "Small things fall through small spaces, slowly at first, then more and more. The spaces widen. With my father, it's mostly his short-term memory that's gone now. I go to visit him every Sunday, so next week when I go back, he probably won't remember that I told him today about bringing the collection to you. But he'll still remember the collection, for sure."

"That must be hard," Benjamin says. "I mean, for you."

"It is," I say, and I realize it's the first time I'm ever really admitting that out loud. The first time someone else is recognizing that what's happening to my father is harder for me, in a way, than for him. Daniel never once acknowledged that. He saw my father's memory loss only inasmuch as it affected our marriage, the way it took my attention away from him. And I feel a surge of warmth for Benjamin, this strange man whom I don't even know. "I'm sorry about this," I say. "I'll pay you for your time."

Benjamin hesitates for a moment. "Are you sure you want to take the collection back and just forget this whole thing?"

"I mean, it would be one thing if you thought this stamp was valuable, but it sounds like it's probably not. So what's the point, anyway?"

"I didn't say that," Benjamin says. "I said it *could* be valuable."

"What, a one percent chance?"

Benjamin smiles a little, maybe pleased I listened to him so carefully, and I get the feeling he's not used to that. "It could be higher," he says. "I'd have to put some feelers out, figure out what was going on with this." His finger lightly traces the flower through the plastic. Then he pushes it back across the table toward me. "But why don't you take this for now? Maybe you could show it to your father next time you see him, see what he says. Maybe he'll still remember where he got it, or know what the flower means." He pauses. "And then you can decide whether you want me to appraise the whole collection or whether you want it all back."

Benjamin's words feel like an unexpected kindness, a space in which to take a breath, reconsider. He doesn't sound angry that I've wasted his time, and I feel the need to thank him, though I can't put my finger on exactly what I'm thanking him for. Still, I do. "Come on," he says in response. He stands up, pulls a five out of his pocket, and leaves it on the table. "Let me walk you to your car. It's late."

❀

The next morning on my way to work, I find myself taking an unintentional detour, and I end up in the parking lot of the public library instead of the parking lot of *LA Lifestyles Magazine*. I go inside and use the pay phone in the lobby to call in sick to work, which is something that I haven't allowed myself to do since Daniel told me he was leaving me. Even when I had that horrible head cold last May that would've justified using a sick day, I went to work. I didn't want him to think that I was avoiding him. I wanted to show him that *I* was a consummate professional. I know I really need a new job. I'm not planning on spending the rest of my life working for my soon-to-be ex-husband. I just haven't found anything yet, though, truth be told, I haven't been looking all that hard either.

I'd stayed up most of the night last night after my meeting with Benjamin at the diner, my heart racing from drinking too much coffee, too late. And from everything Benjamin had said. I don't care about filing my review on time, or what Daniel will think of my absence today. I want to know more about this stamp, where it came from, why it might be important.

I hang up the pay phone and walk inside the library, feeling wonderfully unfettered at the thought of not having to go to work today. I'm not sure what I'm looking for here exactly, but maybe something like the book my father was reading yesterday, and I walk up to the desk and ask if they have a copy. They don't, but the librarian finds me another, similar-looking guide, a catalog of every stamp created in the first half of the twentieth century, divided by year, country, and engraver. "I had no idea there were so many stamp collecting books," I say to her as I flip through the pages.

She glances at me sideways. "We actually have an entire section devoted to philately." I follow her toward the back of the stacks. She turns right, and motions to several tall rows of books. "Lot of collectors in LA," she says. "Let me know if you need help finding anything else."

I thank her and begin to walk down the aisles. I'm still not sure what I'm looking for. But I feel a certain sense of allegiance to my father, to this curious stamp Benjamin noticed. With my father's memory failing him, I can't give up on his lifelong passion, just like that. It needs to mean something. Maybe if it means something, I can hold on to him just a little longer. And my father won't completely disappear along with his memories.

❋

A few hours later, at home, I look through the books I gathered at the library and pour myself another cup of coffee. I squint through the tiny pictures in the large guide the librarian had found for me, scanning through the stamps of Europe shortly before the war, so many of them of Hitler's horrible profile. Only the amount of postage or the color seems different. I flip back the pages, as if I can flip back time, go to a world before Hitler existed. I've flipped too far, the early 1930s, but I decide to start there and work my way forward.

I flip past many busts and buildings I don't recognize, until one stamp in 1932 catches my eye. It's a flower. The entire square filled with its enormous petals. But something about it looks remarkably similar to the tiny flower in the steeple that Benjamin found.

Edelweiss, it reads underneath the stamp. Engraver: *Frederick Faber* (1885–1938).

Austria, 1938

GROTSBURG WAS APPROXIMATELY two hundred kilometers southwest of Vienna, and while Vienna was as flat as the sheets of metal Kristoff had now come to find familiar, Grotsburg was a town of snowy hills, which led into snowcapped mountains on its western edge. Grotsburg was not easily reached by train, and only by car should one definitively want to go there by choice. It wasn't on the way to Salzburg or Graz; it was entirely out of the way.

So even as they heard reports of Nazi soldiers moving into Vienna, Kristoff naively believed everything would stay exactly the same in Grotsburg. What should the Germans want anyway with such a small village all the way out in the countryside?

Even in the middle of April, just as the snow had begun to melt, when there was an official plebiscite, 99.7 percent in favor of the annexation (Mrs. Faber had been right, they did have to vote, though it seemed Hitler had bought the vote, or had scared everyone into agreeing with him)—Kristoff saw no change in their lives in Grotsburg.

Perhaps the only change at first was this: Frederick worked Kristoff extra hard throughout the spring, longer hours, some days straight through dinner until darkness overcame the workshop, and then they practiced only by candle. Mrs. Faber would leave food for them warming in the stove, and Frederick and Kristoff would eat together late, in semidarkness, after the girls had gone to sleep. But Kristoff didn't complain. Not even when his fingers ached and became calloused in new ways. The calluses meant to him that at last he was becoming *something*. He was becoming an engraver.

By the summer, Kristoff's hands understood the burin more. Kristoff could finally make a simple sketch on paper, and then translate that drawing onto a metal plate, in reverse, with some semblance of precision.

Frederick picked up the plate and smiled. "You are getting there, my boy." He clapped his hand on Kristoff's shoulder and smiled at him, with what Kristoff believed was pride. "I knew you could do it."

Kristoff wanted to say something, but he couldn't find the right words. He'd never had someone believe in him before, the way Frederick had, and the feeling of Frederick's warm hand on his tired shoulder nearly brought him to tears.

❁

As summer turned into fall, and the leaves began to turn golden on the hillside, Kristoff became more confident in his engraving skills. And by the time the leaves fell and a chill nipped the November air, Frederick shared something with him.

"What's this?" Kristoff asked as Frederick handed him a stack of letters. He noticed the stamps. Hitler busts. Deutsches Reich stamps.

"They've been sending me letters for months," Frederick admitted. "The new government. The Germans." He said the word *Germans* like it was a rotten apple and he wanted to spit it out. He motioned for Kristoff to open one of the letters, so he did.

Kristoff read the words, disbelieving. They were asking Frederick to report to Vienna immediately and to hand over all of his engraving tools and drawings to the new government.

"They can't do that," Kristoff said, his voice shaking in fury for the demands they were placing on Frederick. Frederick was an artist. Frederick had already given Austria so much, and now that Austria was annexed by Germany they wanted to take everything away from him?

"They can," Frederick said sadly. "They've already torn up Vienna. Half the universities have had to close for losing Jewish professors. Hospitals, too. Losing so many doctors."

"But Grotsburg isn't Vienna," Kristoff protested weakly. And that's when he understood that Grotsburg did have something that the Germans wanted: *Frederick*.

"Everything is growing more serious," Frederick said. "Tensions are rising. I read in the newspaper that a Jewish boy shot a secretary at the German Embassy in Paris." Frederick sighed. "As if they need another reason to hate us."

Kristoff had read the newspaper as well. It had been sitting on the table in the dining room as he'd drunk his coffee this morning. A headline decreed that all Jews were "murderers," and Kristoff had put the paper back down on the table, the headline facedown, not having the stomach to read on. "What are you going to do?" he asked Frederick now.

"I'm going to go do what they're asking. I'll go to Vienna." He paused. "But then I'll tell them about you," Frederick said.

"Me?" Kristoff didn't understand.

"I've been engraving stamps for my Austria my entire adult life." Frederick spoke slowly, evenly, attempting to keep control of his emotions. "They will still need someone to engrave stamps for them. Someone who is skilled and who is not a Jew. They will need you."

"But I'm not ready," Kristoff protested, altogether unsure that he could create an engraving plate from scratch without Frederick's guidance. Or that he wanted to.

"You are ready enough," Frederick said. "You are as ready as you have to be." Frederick sat down in his armchair. He looked around the workshop as if trying to memorize it, and then he put his head in his hands. "We will be leaving. For Vienna."

"All of you?" Kristoff didn't want Frederick to go, but he wouldn't admit out loud that even more he didn't want to let go of Mrs. Faber's cooking, Miriam's laughter, and most of all, Elena. She had kept her distance from him all these months, but at times he would say something to her at dinner, and she would smile, and it would make his entire evening. Over the summer, he'd stayed in Frederick's workshop practicing some nights after Frederick went to bed and Elena had come in and worked with the metal alongside him sometimes. Elena couldn't draw as well as him, but she had a better eye for copying lines in the metal. So Kristoff sketched flowers for her, the edelweiss that bloomed along the hillside all summer long, and then gave the sketches to her to use for engraving practice. They worked with the metal as if they both belonged there, as if they both knew what they were doing, as if they both could become master engravers. Someday.

He and Elena never spoke a word while they were in the workshop, and afterwards, it was like it never happened. But their arms occasionally bumped as they moved around, exchanging tools. Kristoff felt her closeness like a living warmth, the rays of sunlight that lit up the hillside in the summer, thawing all the snow and turning the world around them a verdant green.

"I'm going ahead this week, to find us a place to live," Frederick said, bringing Kristoff back to the chilly workshop. "The girls will join me soon, yes. Miriam can start at the Jewish school next quarter. And maybe Elena can take some courses at Universität in the spring." He paused. "I'm giving all of this to you." He motioned to the workshop and the house beyond.

"But you can't," Kristoff protested. He didn't want Frederick's things, but more he didn't want them all to leave him here. Alone. In a few short months it was as if Kristoff had never been an orphan, and he didn't want to become that lonely boy again.

"I want to give it to you while it's still mine to give." Frederick forced a smile. "Before they take it from me." Then he added, "Maybe someday I can return for it, but I want it to be taken care of in the meantime. You'll take care of it, won't you?"

Kristoff felt he had no choice but to agree. "Of course," he finally said.

※

Frederick set out for Vienna that afternoon, with a small brown suitcase and food Mrs. Faber made him: apricot jam on slices of challah, and a large jug of black tea. "I can buy food later in town, my love," Frederick said. But he accepted the food and the long hug Mrs. Faber gave him.

"I should go with you," Mrs. Faber said, with a weariness in her voice that made Kristoff think she had already said this before, more than once.

"You need to stay with the girls," Frederick said. "And besides, I'll only be gone a few days. A week at the most."

Frederick planned to walk to town before it got dark, and then spend the night at the temple. Tomorrow morning he would catch a ride to Vienna with Mr. Gutenheimmer, an old family friend who had a car, and who had business in Vienna. For many years he'd driven Frederick into Vienna with his finished engraving plates, when he was ready to deliver them to the printer. But Kristoff guessed Mr. Gutenheimmer had also been summoned into Vienna by the Germans. He was not only a lawyer, but also a Jew.

"I have to go," Frederick said, pulling back from Mrs. Faber. He kissed Miri and Elena on their heads, and he turned to Kristoff and held out his hand to shake. Kristoff felt he should say something, anything. But he didn't know what to say. He held on to Frederick's hand an extra few seconds longer than he should have, but then he let Frederick go. He had no choice.

※

That evening Mrs. Faber went to bed before supper, claiming her head ached. Elena spread apricot jam on the remaining challah for her and Miriam, and Kristoff stood by the back window, staring out at the yard and the workshop. He had promised Frederick that he would take care of things. But he tried to imagine working for the Germans, creating and engraving Deutsches Reich stamps for them, all the while thinking of how they made the Fabers leave their home, their life. That wasn't what he wanted; this wasn't why he'd come here. Maybe he should return to Vienna, too, and use the money he'd saved up while living here to rent a tiny flat. He could get a new job, something easier than struggling with the burin. (Most things would be easier.) And he could still see the Fabers, if they were nearby.

"Kristoff." Elena interrupted his thoughts. "Do you want some bread with jam?" Her voice sounded smaller, softer. He turned to look at her. Her face was paler than usual, her green eyes seeming brighter in contrast. Her long hair fell in a mess against her face. She noticed his gaze, and she pulled her hair behind her shoulders, self-consciously, in a way that surprised him. "Kristoff." Elena said his name more sharply. "Jam? Bread?"

"Yes," Kristoff answered her, though he didn't feel hungry. "If it isn't any trouble."

"No trouble." Elena cut another slice of bread and smeared it with jam.

The three of them ate at the dining room table in silence. Even Miriam sat completely still, chewing on her bread, not moving, not saying a word.

Frederick had left; the entire world was changing. Kristoff wanted to reach out and stop it, to hold everything else entirely still. He didn't want to be left here, in this house, this life, completely alone.

❀

That night, Kristoff couldn't sleep, and he walked downstairs and made his way out to Frederick's workshop the way he had done so many times before. Though Frederick had given it to him, Kristoff didn't know if he'd ever think of it as his. It was Frederick's. It always would be. In the middle of the night, he still felt like an intruder.

Inside the workshop it was so dark, quiet. Kristoff had been hoping Elena would be here. But she wasn't. He was all alone.

He lit a candle, and he ran his hands across all the tools, the metal plates. Frederick's stack of letters from Vienna still sat on top of the worktable. Kristoff picked one up, lit the edge on fire with the candle's flame, threw it in the woodstove, and watched it burn. As it turned to ash, he thought that maybe he shouldn't have. That maybe the Germans would decree him a criminal, too, simply for destroying their instructions. For being here, with the Fabers.

He was startled by a knock on the door. *Elena?* But no, why would she knock? It came again, and it was too loud, too hard, a pounding that couldn't come from Elena, or Miri. *German soldiers?* He hunted around for something to defend himself with, though he understood it was futile. Should soldiers be at the door wanting to take Frederick's things, Kristoff couldn't do anything to stop them.

"Elena," a man's voice called. It was familiar, but Kristoff couldn't place it, at first. The knock came again. "Elena, open up." *Josef?*

Kristoff knew Elena left at night sometimes still, to meet with

Josef, he assumed. He was a light sleeper, and Elena would climb in and out the side window, just beneath his room. Her footsteps would always wake him, and then he wouldn't be able to fall back asleep. He'd lie in bed awake for hours, unable to let go of the image of Elena, off in the woods with Josef.

"I see the candle," Josef said with another knock on the door. "I know you're in there. Open up."

Kristoff grabbed the candle and opened the door. In the candle's light he could see Josef more clearly than he had the last time, the only other time they'd met, that night in the woods last March. Josef had dark hair and dark eyes; a small beard framed his mouth, and he was a head taller than Kristoff. Kristoff stood up straighter.

"Elena?" Josef pushed past Kristoff to look inside the workshop, and then upon realizing Elena wasn't inside, he stepped back and frowned. "Where is she?" Josef asked.

Kristoff nodded his head across the yard to the main house. Why had Josef tried here first? Why would he not just knock on the door of the Fabers' house instead?

"Go get her." It was a command, not a question.

"It's late." Kristoff was reluctant to help Josef. He didn't think Frederick would approve of this, whatever this was. "She's asleep," he added, though he honestly wasn't sure whether she was or not.

"Wake her." Josef's voice was a growl, reminding Kristoff of an angry dog. "The Germans have made it to town. The temple is already burning."

"The temple?" Kristoff's voice shook as he repeated the words. "But Frederick was staying there tonight."

Josef nodded. He knew. That was why he was here. "Now go get Elena. You're wasting time standing here talking to me."

Los Angeles, 1989

THE NAME FABER STICKS in my head the next morning as I drive to work. *Frederick Faber*, the stamp engraver I'd found in the book. *Frl. Faber*, it had said on the letter, and I want to know who she was and if, and how, this fräulein was related to the engraver. *A love letter*, Benjamin had said, commenting on the upside-down placement of the stamp. And I'm still less interested in any possible value of this stamp and more in the story behind it.

I call Benjamin as soon as I reach my desk, but I get his machine. I remember what he said about not sleeping, doing his best work at night, and maybe it's too early in the morning for him. I leave him a message about the picture of the Edelweiss stamp in the book I'd found, the similarities, and the matching last name of the engraver and the recipient of the letter.

When I hang up, Daniel is standing right in front of my desk, and I hope he didn't hear the message I was leaving for Benjamin. It's not because I'm worried about doing something wrong by calling Benjamin when I'm supposed to be working, but just because I don't want him to know. I want something new, something that Daniel's completely not a part of. Something all mine. Daniel knows nothing of stamps or love letters.

Daniel is tall, lanky, classically handsome, with light blond hair and pale blue eyes. I like to think that leaving me has made him somehow less attractive, but then when I see him up close like this, I remember again that it hasn't.

"Feeling better?" he asks. He sits on the edge of my desk and tilts his head, genuinely concerned. He probably thinks he knows me well enough to feel sure that I wouldn't have missed work yesterday unless I was really sick.

"Yeah, I'm fine. Much better today." I force myself to smile but don't offer him any more. And besides, I kind of like the idea of him worrying about me. Although I shouldn't.

He leans in closer, lowers his voice a little. "Did you get the papers? My lawyer said they were sent."

I've misread his concern. It wasn't for me, my well-being, but about whether or not his divorce papers got lost in the mail. "Yes. I got them."

"Good." He glances at his watch. "I need your review in thirty minutes, okay?" His tone hasn't changed at all. He seems to care equal amounts about the divorce papers and my review.

"No problem," I tell him.

Truthfully I haven't started, but I can work fast under a deadline. And I just want him to leave my desk, go away, go back to his own office. I don't want to think about him, the divorce papers, or how my favorite part of working here used to be working with him, having him this close to me.

❁

I don't want to wait until Sunday to take the letter to the Willows to show my father, so I decide to drive over there after work, and I suffer through crushing rush-hour traffic. As I wait on the freeway, my mind wanders back to Daniel, sitting on my desk this morning, so close, so familiar, asking me about the divorce papers, as if they weren't a big deal.

I met Daniel at a reelection party for Mayor Bradley in 1981. I was there to cover the election for the *Tribune*, where I used to work the city beat, and Daniel was with his mom, Gertrude, as invited guests. (His mom was a big donor.) I was standing on the fringe, taking notes in my reporter's pad, when my pen ran out of ink. I searched my bag for another one, and then Daniel appeared, out of nowhere, pen in hand. "Looks like you could use this," he said. When I looked up, the first thing I noticed (after the pen) was how blue his eyes were, how tall he was, how his tux fit him perfectly. He owned it, I remember thinking. It wasn't a rental.

The formal party was out of my league, and I'd run out to Macy's the night before to buy a dress. (I'd chosen the cheapest one, having no need for such a fancy dress other than this night.) It was black velvet, with puffy shoulders, and too tight—a size too small, but that was what they'd had on sale. I felt outrageously uncomfortable, nothing at all like my normal self. And here this gorgeous man was standing in front of me, offering me a pen. This wasn't the kind of man who normally offered me anything.

I took the pen and thanked him, and he smiled. He had a perfect smile, straight white square teeth. "I don't know about you, but I'm bored." He leaned in and whispered conspiratorially, as if we were already friends. "Want to get out of here and get a drink?"

I did, but I was supposed to be working. That was, sadly, my most exciting assignment in months, a huge step up from dreary city council meetings I'd been covering. I told him that, and he laughed.

"Okay," he said. "Then how about you give me your number and I'll call you tomorrow and ask you again?" I wrote my number on a piece of paper, ripped it off my pad, and gave it to him. He touched my bare arm briefly, folded the paper, and put it into the inner jacket pocket of his tux. Then he disappeared back into the crowd.

My notes for the rest of the night were a jumbled mess, indecipherable to me the next morning at work. And when I got home later that night, I called my father, and I told him that I'd met this amazing man.

These days, my father can't even remember Daniel's name. One of the first signs of his insidious disease was when he began calling Daniel simply "your husband" when he asked after him. At first I thought it was because he didn't really like Daniel. Later, I realized it was because he genuinely couldn't remember Daniel's name. According to his doctor, it's fairly common for Alzheimer's patients to remember the names of their children, but not their children's spouses, or their children's children, because those memories were added later in life. Suddenly names are replaced by generic relation: husband, child, and so on.

Ex-husband, I think now, as I finally pull into the parking lot of the Willows. It's such a small distinction in the semantics but one my father wouldn't remember, even if I did tell him the truth.

❊

I don't recognize the nurse on duty at the front desk tonight, and when I tell her who I am, she reminds me, not so gently, that it's nearly seven, and I only have a few minutes with him before visiting hours are over. Then she asks if I've ever been to see him after dinner before. I shake my head. "He'll probably be worse than you're expecting," she says. But I hate her *probably*; she doesn't really know him. And I hate that he's here, surrounded by strangers like this, though I know it's necessary. "Sundowning," she adds.

I'm familiar with the term. When my father was first diagnosed, I read books, articles, anything I could find in the library about his disease. *Sundowning* refers to the fact that many patients with Alzheimer's and dementia get markedly worse at night, once the sun goes down. For a moment I'm tempted to leave, to just come back on Sunday, the way I always do, when it's morning, still light out, and my visit with my father is at its usual time, what I've come to expect of him. But I drove all the way out here and I'm excited to show him the letter, so I thank the nurse and walk toward his room.

I watch him from the hallway for a moment before I go in. He's already sitting in bed, and the TV's on, a special news report from West Germany, the commentators wondering, will it finally happen? Will the wall finally come down? I can't believe it will. Germany has been divided nearly my whole life. I still remember being at my grandparents' house sometime just after the wall first went up. I was eight or nine and Gram was crying, my mother trying to console her. The East, where my mother's parents had grown up, had become a Soviet-run communist state, its citizens locked in behind a literal iron curtain. Gram was certain she would never be able to return to the place she'd been born. And my mother had told her gently that she didn't need to, that she had a wonderful life here in the United States, with us.

My father seems to be listening carefully to the news report, considering the possibilities of a reunification of Germany, the way the newscasters are. He suddenly looks toward the doorway, notices me standing here, and he squints a little, so I'm not sure if he knows who I am or not. "Damn Germans," he says. My father was also born in Germany, like my grandparents, but he left when he was very young, a small boy, and he doesn't have any sense of connection the way Gram still does. He still bears just the slightest hint of an accent, barely noticeable, except in times like now, when he seems to be remembering a piece of the past, and his accent becomes somewhat more pronounced.

"East Germans, you mean?" I try to bring him back to here, to 1989. He frowns, but he doesn't say anything else. I tentatively step farther into his room, clutching the plastic tightly in my hand. "Dad." I hear my voice trembling a little. "Dad," I say again, a little louder, lending a forcefulness to my tone that I don't truly feel. "It's me, Katie. Kate the Great," I add, hoping to jog his memory back to the present with the familiar, his familiar term.

He looks at me, and he nods. I pull his armchair closer to the bed and I sit down. He's still watching the news, and I pick up the clicker from the nightstand. "Mind if I turn this off, so we can talk?"

He doesn't respond one way or another, so I turn it off. The screen goes black, his room is silent, darker than I'd realized. I switch on the lamp on his nightstand, and the yellow light illuminates his face, his sagging wrinkled cheeks, the pale liver spots on his mostly bald head, and the wisps of gray hair that I have to resist the urge to comb down for him. *Doesn't anyone do that here, remind him to comb his hair?* I feel an almost irrational anger. But it's nighttime, he's already lying in bed. Who cares what his hair looks like?

I look away from his hair, and back to the letter in my hand, the reason I came here tonight. "I brought you something," I say. "Something the stamp dealer, Benjamin, found in your collection. Something interesting."

"Benjamin?" He shakes his head. He can't place the name. He doesn't remember our conversation just a few mornings ago, his presumption about Benjamin's religion. Of course he doesn't. In the vast bleeding sieve of his mind, why would Benjamin Grossman's name remain, a name I mentioned to him only once?

"I took your stamps to be appraised, but then you asked me to get them back, and I promised I would. I am," I say gently, hoping to jog his memory with my even tone.

"You can't show them my stamps," he says. His voice sounds distant, and he doesn't look at me when he says it, so I'm still not sure he's really here, whether he really knows who I am.

"I know. I'm not going to sell anything. I'm getting them all back. I promise. It's just that Benjamin noticed an interesting one. I wanted to show it to you." My hands are shaking as I lift the letter and hold it out for him to see. I hate that I feel this way, that my hands, my body, betray me, show my fear, that I have fear sitting here, with my own father. I don't really know what I'm afraid of.

My father's eyes scan the letter, the stamp. He sighs a little, and I'm not sure if that means he recognizes, understands. Or if it means he doesn't.

"Benjamin said this particular stamp could be your gem," I tell him. That's not, of course, what Benjamin said at all. But I feel the need to be overly positive, upbeat.

My father shakes his head again. "You shouldn't have this," he says.

"You gave me your collection," I remind him. When he doesn't respond to that I gently put my hand on his arm. "Dad," I say.

"Your father's gone," he says sternly, as if I'm a small child and he's reprimanding me, in a way I can't ever remember him doing back then. But he's also right, my father *is* gone. The realization hits me all at once, and it's hard for me to breathe. "You need to go. You need to leave," my father shouts at me.

It's one thing when he thinks I'm my mother—his disease allows me a window of comprehension, understanding. I have my mother's gray-blue eyes, her dark brown curls, her apple-shaped face. At quick glance, I could be mistaken for her, as she was, once. But he has never yelled at me before, gotten angry like this.

That night nurse was right, I shouldn't have come. *Sundowning* is no longer just some clinical term I read about in a book I checked out of the library.

"I'll be back this weekend," I say softly, biting my lip to hold back tears, not wanting him to see me crying, even if he doesn't really see me at all. I gather my things, move the chair back, and walk toward the door.

"No," I hear my father say as I reach the doorway. "You can't ever come back."

❀

I run down the hallway, wanting to get out of the Willows as fast as I can, this awful beautifully maintained place where nothing makes sense. The nurse at the front desk looks up, notices me, and I half expect her to stop me and say with a smirk, *I told you so.* But instead she pulls a tissue out of a box and reaches across the desk, holding it out for me to take on my way by.

❀

My hands are shaking too much to drive home through traffic, so I drive just a few blocks west of the Willows to what used to be the Santa Monica Mall, but now, renovated, is the Third Street Promenade.

I park in the garage and walk down the promenade for a little while. The night air is chilly, it's close to eight, and I should probably grab dinner. I don't feel hungry, though. And I haven't yet remastered the art of eating in a restaurant alone. Once I calm down a little I'll drive home, pour myself a glass of chardonnay, and pop a frozen dinner in the microwave.

I spot a pay phone in front of the record store and I stop and fish around in my purse for some change. I put a quarter in, and dial Benjamin's number, which I realize I've memorized. I'm hoping to leave a message. *I'm done*, I'll say. *I don't care about the stamp. What it means or what it's worth. I'm coming to pick up the rest of the collection and then you won't hear from me again.* But Benjamin picks up on the second ring.

"Hello," he says, and I don't say anything for a minute. "Is anyone there?"

"Hi," I finally say. "It's me. Katie."

"You got my message?" he says glibly, assuming that I have.

"No. I'm not at home." I don't ask him about the contents of his message. I don't think I want to know. I picture myself hitting the erase button on my machine later tonight without listening to it.

"Where are you?" he asks.

But instead of answering him I say, "Look, this was a terrible idea. I'm just upsetting him."

"Who?" Benjamin asks.

"My father. I thought this would . . ." But I don't finish my sentence because what I thought was stupid. That these stamps, these silly inanimate squares of paper and faded ink would help me understand him, preserve him. Would keep me from losing him? *You can't ever come back*, he said to me. Come Sunday morning I guessed he wouldn't remember those words, our visit tonight. But I would. "I'm done with this stamp. Whatever it is."

"Then you didn't get my message," Benjamin says. This is just dawning on him. "I think maybe you were right. To connect the stamp to Faber. You have a good eye." He clears his throat as if the compliment has surprised him, caught him off guard, as if he is not used to anyone having a good eye, other than himself. "I noticed the Faber connection right away, too, when I saw the name on the letter," he quickly adds. "Except I knew this stamp couldn't have been issued until 1939 and Frederick Faber died in 1938. And this is a Deutsches Reich stamp, a Nazi stamp, and Faber was a Jew." Benjamin says it with such a certainty, an uncanny acceptance, but it takes a moment for his words to fully sink in, for me. Frederick

Faber couldn't have engraved the stamp even if he was alive then because a country run by Nazis would never have allowed a Jew to do such work.

"So he couldn't have been the engraver," I say. "So much for my 'good artistic eye.'"

"No, but I think it was connected to him. Somehow. I was at the library all day, searching through old microfilm. Faber had a family. A wife and two daughters. Two Fräulein Fabers."

"You speak German?" I know just a few phrases from Gram, but nowhere near enough to read articles in German.

"I found English articles. British newspapers. Faber was pretty well known in Austria before the occupation. In Europe even."

I try to imagine them, Frederick Faber's daughters. Did someone address this letter to one of them? Someone who'd admired their father's work? A love letter. Just after their father died? Were his daughters close with him? Did they love him the way I love my father? Did they miss him the way I already missed my father?

"So what happened to them?" I say. "His daughters?"

"I don't know," Benjamin says. "Jewish girls in Austria, after the occupation." He pauses for a moment and then speaks a little softer. "Probably nothing good."

Austria, 1938

KRISTOFF LEFT JOSEF OUT in the workshop and ran back to the main house. He stopped for a moment in the kitchen to catch his breath, and he stared at the half loaf of challah, still sitting out on the counter from supper. Only a few hours ago, when Frederick had most certainly still been safe. *He could still be safe*, Kristoff told himself. Maybe he made it out of the temple or maybe he hadn't arrived yet when the Germans set fire to it? Kristoff was sweating, though the air in the kitchen was cold; the fire in the dining room hearth had already dissipated into meek yellow and blue embers.

He tiptoed up the stairs, praying he wouldn't wake Miriam or Mrs. Faber, and have to explain to them, in the middle of the night, what Josef had told him. *Maybe Josef was mistaken*, he thought as he rapped softly on Elena's door.

Elena opened the door immediately. She couldn't have been sleeping. She looked at Kristoff and she frowned. "What?" she hissed. "It's the middle of the night." As if he didn't already know that.

He wanted to tell her to go to sleep, and while she slept and dreamed peaceful dreams, he would go into town, find Frederick safe and unharmed, and by morning all of this would be nothing more than a terrible mistake. She would never be the wiser. But he couldn't leave her and Miriam and Mrs. Faber here all alone. And it would be crazy to go into town, if the Germans had arrived, as Josef claimed. "Josef is here," he said instead, before he could lose his nerve.

"What?" Her tone changed. She was no longer annoyed with him for coming. "Now? Kristoff?" She grabbed on to his shirt-sleeve, holding tight to a sliver of fabric. "Is something wrong?"

He swallowed hard, unable to say the difficult words to her. "Get dressed and come out to the workshop," he said quietly. "We can talk out there."

❀

Back in the workshop, Josef sat in Frederick's armchair by the fire.

"What is it?" Elena demanded as soon as they walked inside. "What's happened?"

Kristoff shut the door behind them, and Josef spoke, his voice unwavering. He told Elena about the fire at the temple the same way he'd already told Kristoff.

"But Father got out," Elena said. "Right? He must've gotten out before the fire. I'm sure he did. Father's so resourceful."

"He's probably walking back here now," Kristoff said, and Elena shot him a grateful smile. Josef glared at him, stood, and went to Elena. He wrapped his arms around her, and Kristoff turned away and walked toward the fire. Josef had added wood when Kristoff had gone into the house, and the flames roared. Kristoff pretended to warm his hands, but really he stared at the fire just so he didn't have to stare at them as they embraced.

Josef whispered something to Elena, words Kristoff couldn't make out.

"Who cares about that. My father could be in danger still," Elena said.

"But, Elena." Josef's voice rose. "This only makes our work more important now. They're *burning* things."

"What work?" Kristoff turned back to look at them, and Elena had separated herself from Josef. She leaned against the worktable, her arms folded in front of her chest.

"I wasn't talking to you," Josef said. "In fact, I'm not sure why you're still here."

"Josef, don't," Elena said.

"What work?" Kristoff repeated, this time his question aimed squarely at Elena.

But Elena ignored him. She turned back toward Josef. "We have to go find my father. We're wasting time even talking about any of this now."

Josef nodded, briefly put his hand on Elena's shoulder. "All right," he said. "I'm going."

"I'll go with you," she said.

"No," Josef said. "You stay here in case your father makes it back before I find him. I'll be back as soon as I can." He turned to Kristoff, looked him solidly in the eye. "If anything happens to her while I'm gone," he said, "I'll kill you."

❀

"Don't mind Josef," Elena said, just after he left. "He's a little gruff. But he has a good heart."

"Right," Kristoff murmured. "That's why he threatened to kill me."

"He didn't mean it like that."

Kristoff felt certain Josef meant what he said. But Kristoff had no intention of letting anything happen to Elena. Or Miriam. Or Mrs. Faber. He'd promised Frederick, after all. But even if he hadn't, he would do anything to keep the Fabers safe.

"What work was Josef talking about?" Kristoff asked her. "What do you do together?" Elena had finished school last spring, and though there had been some talk about her enrolling in university in Vienna—Frederick wished for her to continue her academic studies, to broaden her reading even further—that had been put on hold after the annexation. Kristoff wasn't sure what she did all day, but he assumed she helped her mother with the household duties while Miriam was at school.

She hopped up and sat on top of the worktable. Her booted feet dangled down next to him, and Kristoff shifted a little, careful not to touch her. "We've been talking about ways to stop the Germans," she said. "And to help Jews get out of Austria. It's not safe here anymore. They've already taken everything as their own, and now they're setting it on fire, too." She sighed. "We have all the engraving tools here." She ran her hands across the worktable. "We've been talking about how we could use them to forge papers. Documents . . ."

"That's why you didn't want your father to know you were practicing in here?" Kristoff didn't think Frederick would approve of her learning to engrave only to do illegal things with the trade.

Elena nodded and jumped down from the table. "Father must be freezing. I should take a blanket, see if I can catch him in the woods. I wouldn't want him to have escaped the fire only to freeze to death." She pulled the old blanket from atop the armchair and gathered it in her arms.

"You can't go now," Kristoff said. She walked toward the door. "Josef said to wait. And, the Germans—"

"I don't care about the Germans," Elena said. "I know these woods better than they do. I'll be fine. And I can't just sit here and talk to you when my father is out there. I don't care what Josef said."

She opened the door, ran out into the freezing night before Kristoff could stop her. And he had no choice but to grab the lantern and run after her.

❋

Elena and Kristoff walked through the woods in silence, and it seemed even the owls and the deer could detect the danger in the town just beyond. Kristoff had never felt a night this quiet, this still. This cold. The only sound he heard as they walked was the crunch of their boots against dead leaves and twigs. But the faint smell of smoke invaded his nose. He tried to come up with a plan for what he would do if the German soldiers found them here, walking in the woods at night like this. Josef's threat didn't scare him. Losing Elena scared him, and he took her arm as they walked, a silly attempt to hold on to her, to keep her close, safe. Should the Germans find them, his arm holding on to hers would mean nothing. But fortunately, there were no soldiers in the woods; they were all in town.

At last they reached the end of the woods, and Elena pulled away from him and ran to the edge, just in front of him. The town spread out before them, down the hill, at the bottom of the clearing. They could see it all stretched out ahead of them, even in the darkness. The entire town glowed orange and red, towers of flame and smoke.

Elena put her hand to her mouth and gasped. "It's not just the temple. It's all burning," she said. Perhaps she hadn't truly believed Josef until she saw it with her own eyes. "They've destroyed everything."

Kristoff wanted to say something, but his eyes and his throat began to burn from the smoke. He instinctively reached for her hand, worried she might run toward the town, the fire . . . her father. But she stayed perfectly still.

He wanted to look away from the orange waves of flame that catapulted into the night sky. He wanted to look away but for a long while, he could not.

※

Kristoff didn't sleep that night. After he convinced Elena to walk back to the workshop, to wait there for Frederick and any news from Josef, he and Elena sat in the workshop together, in silence. They didn't touch the tools or practice with the plates the way they had before in the middle of the night.

Elena sat by the fire and watched the flames, saying nothing at all, and Kristoff wondered if in the flames she kept seeing the image of the town burning in her head, over and over again, the way he was.

Eventually, Kristoff picked up his sketch pad and drew her, almost by instinct, his fingers twitching for the charcoal. What he knew. What he loved. She was still here. Still perfect. The lines he made on the white paper made her safety feel real, made him feel calmer.

The fire in the workshop died down to embers, and the sun began to rise above the hill. Outside it had begun snowing; soft white flakes fell across the yard and they seemed out of place.

Elena stood at last. Her hair was unkempt, her dress rumpled and dirty, ripped at the bottom. She had circles under her eyes from lack of sleep. The temple was only a twenty-minute walk from here. If Frederick had made it out, certainly he would've gotten back here by now. "I have to tell Mother," Elena said.

"Do you want me to come with you?" Kristoff asked.

Her face remained expressionless as she jutted out her chin. Her stoicism was remarkable, beautiful in its own right. Kristoff wished he could get this across in his drawing of her, which, on second glance, seemed flat.

"Elena." He stood and reached for her hand the way he had the previous night, at the edge of the woods. He felt on the brink of tears, and he willed himself not to cry in front of her.

"No." She pulled away from him. "You stay here and wait for Josef. I'll go talk to her alone."

Los Angeles, 1989

THE PHONE RINGS and wakes me out of a surprisingly deep sleep. My bedroom is still dark, and my clock says it's just after six a.m. I get out of bed and fumble for the phone on the other side, on what used to be Daniel's nightstand, and I pick it up, filled with panic, dread. There are no good phone calls at this time of day.

"Honey, turn on the TV," Gram says as soon as I say hello.

I'm surprised to hear her voice. We usually talk once a week, on Saturday mornings, and I go to visit her a few times a year. Everything set up in advance. Gram doesn't like surprises. For that matter, neither do I. "Is everything okay?" I ask her.

"Just turn on the TV, Katie. The wall is coming down. Finally!"

I tell her to hold on as I go in the other room, and I yawn as I walk to the living room and switch on the television. Every channel is focused on the news. The Berlin Wall—people are dancing on top of it. East Germans and West Germans together, the newscaster reports.

"I've been watching it all night," she says when I pick up the phone in the living room. Gram grew up in East Germany, but she and my grandfather immigrated to the United States before the war, when she was pregnant with my mother. My mom always told me that it was their common German immigrant background that first drew her to my father on the tiny island of Coronado, where they met one night when my mom was working as a waitress at Mexican Village and my dad had come in for dinner. Though my father came over here from Germany as a small boy and my mother was actually born an American citizen, they had an immediate shared connection. My father—and Gram and Gramps—became citizens years before I came along. But even at age eighty-four, a part of Gram still thinks of Germany as her home. As her last remaining family member, I guess she felt compelled to share her joy with me this morning. "Isn't it wonderful?" she asks now.

"It is," I tell her. I'm happy that she's happy, and I know it's a good thing in a global sense that the wall is coming down. But it still feels very far removed from my own life.

"You know so many years I've wanted to go back," she's saying. "And I thought I'd be dead before I'd ever have the chance."

At eighty-four she isn't exactly spry, but she still lives on her own in her little cottage on the island, where my mother grew up. She stopped driving last year, and she pays someone to come help her out around the house. But her mind is perfectly intact. Though she's years older, she seems a lot better off than my father. She's well enough to travel, certainly, but the wall, the iron curtain, had made such a trip unthinkable for many years.

"I didn't wake Daniel, did I?" Gram asks, as if it just occurred to her.

I hesitate for a moment. "You know him. He sleeps through everything." I word it in a way where I tell myself I'm not lying. He *does* sleep through everything. She wouldn't have woken him, had he been here, sleeping next to me, the way Gram assumes he was. I kind of hate myself for not having already told her the truth. But I'm not going to tell her now, when she seems so happy. The problem is, what would I even say? I don't fully believe what's happened to us myself.

*

The office is all abuzz about the news out of Germany when I get there. Judging from the television coverage on every station, the entire world is buzzing this morning. Daniel has a black-and-white television sitting on top of the metal filing cabinet in his office, and he and a small group of my coworkers stand crowded around it, watching, listening. I'm glad to have already watched the news, processed, discussed, and been happy about it with Gram so I don't feel compelled to go into Daniel's office with the others, and I sit down at my desk instead.

I still have the plastic sleeve with the Faber letter in my bag. I've been carrying it around with me all week, unable to let it go. Unable to get Benjamin's answer about the Fräulein Fabers out of my head. What if they left Austria before the Nazis got to them? My own family made it out of Germany, after all. Granted, it was much earlier, well before this letter was stamped in 1939. But what if the Fabers also made it out? What if this letter would mean something to them, or their children, so many years later? Some connection to the father they lost, or the life they used to live?

Before I'd hung up with Benjamin the other day he said he still wanted to find out about the stamp, its origins, its value. He said he was going to a philatelic conference in the Bay Area this weekend and he was taking a Polaroid of the stamp with him, in hopes of getting some feedback. *Just give me another week*, he'd told me on the phone, *and if it's nothing, then we can give up*. I'd neither agreed nor disagreed but told him I'd give him a call next week to arrange a time to pick up the rest of the collection.

I grab my Rolodex from my bottom drawer and flip through it until I find my contact card for Jason Hirsch. Before I took this entertainment job at *LA Lifestyles*, before I married Daniel, I used to work the city beat with Jason at the *Tribune*. I'd hated the drudgery of it, reporting on city council meetings, mayoral races, and I'd been more than happy to leave that behind to review films. Jason left shortly after me and had become a rising star writing for the national publication *Voice*. He'd recently written a piece on Holocaust survivors living in LA, and maybe he'd be able to help me figure out how to find the Fabers.

"Katie! How've you been?" Jason asks when he picks up the phone. I haven't talked to him in months. I try to remember when we last saw each other. At a media party last winter, maybe. I was with Daniel; we were still together. But I haven't seen or talked to Jason since.

I'm tempted to say fine now, to lie to him the way I've been lying to everyone else. But we've known each other too long, and Jason is good at reading people. "I've been better," I say instead, almost surprised by my admission, the way the truth actually sounds. I tell him that Daniel and I are splitting up, that my father has had to move into a memory care home, and life feels strange at the moment.

"Shit," he says, unapologetically. "I'm sorry, Katie. I had no idea or I would've given you a call."

"Thanks." But I don't want to talk any more about myself, so I launch into the reason I really called. "I want to find somebody," I tell him. "A family, actually. Two Jewish girls, sisters who were probably living in Austria in 1939."

"Where's this coming from?" he asks. I tell him briefly about my father's collection and the letter with the unusual stamp addressed to Fräulein Faber. "Wow," Jason says. He's quiet for a minute, thinking. Then he says, "If you knew the city or the village they were living in in Austria, you could start with the archives there. That's what I'd do."

"But how would I access the archives? Do you think I'd have to go, in person?" The idea sounds preposterous as I say it out loud. Flying halfway across the world to Austria for a silly stamp and a letter that could still just be a piece of junk?

"Well, it depends. Maybe," Jason says. "I mean, were they in Vienna—in which case, maybe you could find the archives office there and give them a call? Or were they in some little village that doesn't exist anymore?" He pauses for a second, and I try to wrap my head around the gravity of that. Little villages that existed fifty years ago that are totally eradicated. "But say they got out." Jason is still talking. "Maybe they made it to the U.S., and in that case, maybe you could find an immigration record?"

"Wouldn't that be nice," I say, meaning that they got out of Nazi-occupied Austria, not the ease of finding them now. Though, of course, that would be nice, too.

"I know of a few organizations that have started up to help people search for family members, too. They're trying to create databases for people looking for loved ones. You could give them a call. Maybe they could help."

Jason sounds so confident that this is all doable, and I revel in his optimism. The idea of finding out what happened to these girls feels something close to exciting, the way I used to feel when I was younger, when I wrote a story I was really proud of and honed my reporter skills on a source.

"Hey, do you want to meet for a drink later?" Jason asks. "We could catch up and I'll go back and look through my notes, bring all the numbers I have for these organizations."

"Sure," I say, and it feels kind of nice to be making plans with an old friend, to have somewhere to go tonight after work.

❀

After I hang up with Jason, I decide to head back to the library to see if I can figure out where exactly the Fabers lived in Austria. The address on the letter could be a start to finding them—I just have to figure out what it's saying.

I peek my head into Daniel's office before I leave. The TV's still on, and Daniel, Janice, and Rob, who does our copyediting, are all standing there, transfixed. On the screen, a man is juggling on top of the Berlin Wall, and someone is holding up a boom box below him, blasting American music. Bruce Springsteen? I think it is. "Heading out to work on a story," I lie, but no one seems to notice.

❀

"You're back," the librarian says to me when I walk up to the main desk. "Becoming a philatelist after all, are we?"

I'm surprised she remembers me, but maybe not too many people, or not too many women my age, frequent this part of the library in search of philately books. Benjamin Grossman notwithstanding, I still think of stamp collecting as an old man's hobby.

I take the plastic sleeve from my bag and show her the letter, wishing my German and knowledge of prewar Austrian addressing conventions were good enough to decipher exactly what the address means. "I need to find this address, on the letter."

"So we're not interested in stamps anymore?" She frowns; I've confused her.

"No, I am, but I'm trying to find out about this specific stamp. This letter. I want to know where it was going, where this woman lived. I think this stamp is from around 1939, so maybe a map of Austria from that time?"

"Give me a few minutes." She walks over to the card catalog, searches for a bit, and then disappears. A little while later she returns with an armful of books, old dusty-looking monstrosities that it seems no one but me has asked after in a long time. "European geography, maps, and atlases pre–World War Two," she clarifies. "Maybe you'll be able to locate your address in one of these." I thank her and hand over my library card so I can check them out. "You know your letter was never sent, right?" she says. I nod, though I'm not sure whether I know that or not, or how she does. "No postmark," she adds.

"Of course," I say, feeling like an idiot. Benjamin must've noticed this, and he probably just assumed I did, too.

But as I walk out of the library, my arms piled high with the books, I think, maybe I can send it now. If I can just find out what happened to the Fabers.

＊

A few hours later, I wash my hair, shape my unruly curls with mousse, and put on a dress and even a little lipstick before going to meet Jason. It's not because I think this is a date, in any possible way, or that I want it to be. But more because I haven't left the house for anything other than work or seeing my father or this whole stamp thing in a few months. I remember that I can make myself look vaguely pretty, if I try. And it's kind of a nice feeling.

Jason is already there when I get to the Beverly Hilton, where we'd agreed to meet. And after I order a glass of wine and he orders a beer, I pull the letter out of my bag and show it to him. "It's a love letter," I say, explaining what Benjamin told me about the placement of the stamp and also about how the stamp is unusual, because of the tiny, nearly undetectable flower.

He glances at it. "I'll admit, I had an ulterior motive for inviting you out for a drink." He smiles at me. He has a nice smile, though his front two teeth are just slightly crooked.

"What's that?" I ask, my voice teetering a little. Maybe I shouldn't have put on lipstick.

"There's a story here." He's staring at the letter; he hasn't noticed my lipstick. He traces the stamp beneath the plastic with his forefinger before handing it back to me. "I don't think I told you, I got promoted. I'm in charge of features now."

"Wow, that's great." I raise my wineglass in a toast. "Congratulations." I hope I don't sound bitter. I'm not. I'm happy for Jason, but we both started in the same place at the *Tribune* years earlier, and now he seems light-years ahead of me.

"When you figure this story out," he says, "I want you to write a piece on it. For me." So that was his ulterior motive? He wants me to work for him?

I haven't considered this a story I could write. Nor had I considered asking Jason for a job, working for him. I feel a weird sense of déjà vu to when Daniel asked me to come work for him. We'd been dating for only a few months, but I was so tired of the day-to-day boredom of the city beat that entertainment stories sounded like the holy grail, and working with Daniel felt like a bonus. I didn't let myself worry about what would happen if things didn't work out. Anyway, I knew they would. And they had. Until recently. "You don't have to do that just because I told you about me and Daniel," I say to Jason now.

"I'm not," Jason says. "It would be fun to work with you again. And besides, I'm only hiring you once you figure this story out."

Jason isn't Daniel, I remind myself. And *Voice* would be a huge step up for me from *LA Lifestyles*. "Well, who knows if there actually is a story here," I say. "Or if I'll be able to find out what happened to this family, these girls."

"There is," Jason says. "And you will." He pulls a folder out of his briefcase and hands it to me. "Here's a list of all my contacts, people you could call to help you locate the Fabers, maybe." He lifts his beer bottle and clinks it to my wineglass. "Here's to new beginnings," he says. "And all good things in the future."

Or endings, I add silently in my head. *And all bad things in the past.*

Austria, 1938

THE NEWSPAPER WOULD CALL the events of the night they lost Frederick *die Kristallnacht*. Night of crystal. Night of broken glass. But to Kristoff it seemed that in Grotsburg, *Feuernacht* or *Tränennacht*, night of fire—or tears—would've been more appropriate.

The morning after that terrible night it began to snow heavily in Grotsburg. It snowed and snowed for days. Frozen tears, *gefrorene Tränen*, Miriam said without an iota of her usual joyfulness, as she watched the bitter flakes fall outside the kitchen window. It snowed so much that for a few days Kristoff couldn't even make it from the house to the workshop because the kitchen door wouldn't open from all the snowdrifts. He would feel certain, years later, that it was the snow that saved the Fabers' house and workshop from being destroyed during *die Kristallnacht*, too. The woods were too thick; the snow was too deep. The Germans gave up and turned toward Vienna, where they continued their destruction.

And yet it almost didn't matter that their visit to Grotsburg was short-lived at first: so much of the town was obliterated by the fire that the Germans had started in the synagogue. The buildings in town were all close together and made of wood. The fire had spread and burned until the falling snow finally put it out. And overnight, so many families were without homes, businesses, lives. Nearly everything that remained was charred, ruined. And now covered in snow.

The next time Kristoff walked into town, weeks later, he would think of it as a village of ashes and ghosts. One of the only buildings entirely intact was the post office, on Wien Allee, and Kristoff didn't think this was a coincidence. The Germans would still need mail, after all.

❉

Cooped up inside their house with Mrs. Faber's sobs, which shook her entire body every hour or so, Kristoff felt helpless for days. Lost. At least they had a large supply of canned food, which Mrs. Faber had stockpiled last summer in preparation for the snowy winter, so they weren't about to starve anytime soon.

When Frederick left, Kristoff never thought it would be forever, and he knew Mrs. Faber, Elena, and Miriam hadn't either. *What would Frederick want them to do now?* He paced back and forth in his attic bedroom. He paced and he paced, until he heard a knock at his door, and Elena barged into his room, without waiting for him to answer.

"You're wearing out the floor." She frowned at him, put her hands on her hips. She wore a brown baggy pair of pants and a raggedy-looking button-down shirt that Kristoff was pretty sure were Frederick's. Her hair was pulled back into a braid, and yet she still looked beautiful.

"I'm sorry," he said, but he didn't stop pacing.

"Kristoff!" She grabbed his sleeve. And finally he stopped. Not because she'd asked him, but because she was touching him. He could feel the warmth of her fingers through his shirt, to his skin.

"I'm trying to think," he said. "I can't sit still and think."

She let him go, walked over to the edge of his bed, and sat down. Before he could stop her, she picked up his sketch pad, and she began flipping through it. "All these of me? What makes me such an interesting subject?" He shrugged, and he felt his cheeks turning red. She continued to flip. "You've been drawing me . . . for months?" She laughed a little and closed his book. "You could've been practicing for stamps, and you've been wasting all this time on my ordinary face."

Kristoff sat down on the edge of the bed next to her. "There's nothing ordinary about it," he said, and before he could really think through what he was doing, he put his hand gently on her cheek, stroked it with his thumb. "Perfect lines," he said, and he didn't care whether Josef killed him or not. He did not want to take his hand from Elena's face.

She moved first, tilted her head down, and looked at the floor. "I can't," she said quietly.

"Because of Josef?" he asked awkwardly. He'd been wanting to ask Elena for months if she was in love with Josef.

Elena didn't answer right away. "The only thing I care about now is getting Austria back, the way it used to be. Getting the Germans out," she finally said. "I don't have time for anything, or anyone, else."

And then, for whatever reason, it occurred to Kristoff exactly what Frederick would want for his family. *He'd want them to leave*

Austria behind. All of them. Even Elena. Their country was no longer safe for them. Austria could no longer be the Fabers' home.

❀

The first person to make it out to the Fabers' house after the snow began to melt a week later was not a German soldier but Josef, and when he found Kristoff in the workshop, this time he asked Kristoff to walk with him through the woods. He didn't ask about Elena, and though Kristoff knew she was inside the house helping her mother scrounge up a supper, he didn't offer to get her.

"They need to go away," Kristoff said to Josef as sternly as he could muster as they walked through the woods. The snow was deep, up to Kristoff's knees, and his legs were cold and damp as he walked alongside Josef. "Mrs. Faber and the girls. They need to go somewhere safe. The Germans will come back when the snow melts. I'll be fine, but they might not be." As he said it, he wasn't sure he would be fine. Or what *fine* meant anymore.

"You're smarter than I thought," Josef said gruffly. And Kristoff supposed that was his version of a compliment, though it didn't exactly sound like one. "The town is almost all destroyed. You're right. There's nothing left for them here." Josef veered off the path toward town. "Many men are missing. Killed in the fires, or imprisoned. Arrested or murdered . . ." Josef's voice trailed off, and Kristoff realized they were headed toward the small shack—or tiny cabin, whatever the structure was—where he'd found Elena coming from that night last March when Austria was still Austria and their biggest worry had been that Frederick would find her gone on the Sabbath. That seemed so far away now, as if years, decades, had passed, not mere months. And Kristoff felt a numb sort of shock that this tiny little wooden thing in the middle of the woods still stood, when so much else around them was gone.

"What are we doing here?" Kristoff asked. Had Josef brought him out here to kill him, as he'd threatened once? Not that he truly believed Josef would do that. And besides, they had just seemed in agreement about the girls.

Instead of answering, Josef made his way toward the door. It didn't have a lock, nothing to keep the Germans out. "The Germans don't know this place exists. It's not on any map," Josef said as he fiddled with the handle, as if he could read Kristoff's mind. "You know they say an old woman lived here once, but that at night she took the form of a *Tatzelwurm*, scared everyone off."

"A *Tatzelwurm*?" Kristoff shook his head in disbelief, remembering how Soren, an older boy at the orphanage, used to intentionally try to scare Kristoff with stories of the mythical half-cat, half-serpent creature.

"Anyway," Josef said, finally getting the door to open. "It doesn't have an address. It's not officially a real place. Nothing that anyone would know was here unless they were coming through these woods and then went off the beaten path looking for it. And why would they? They've already destroyed half the town," he said bitterly.

"But what are you saying? About this place?" Kristoff was confused. "That the girls could hide here?" It seemed almost too easy, too close. If they were just here, a short walk from the engraving workshop, the Fabers' house, Kristoff could walk to see them anytime he wanted. He wouldn't have to let them go.

"No," Josef said quickly. "They wouldn't all be safe here."

"But you just said . . ."

Josef opened the door and walked inside. He motioned for Kristoff to follow. It was dark, and it smelled damp, musty in the cabin. But Kristoff followed Josef anyway.

"Not the girls," Josef said after a moment, and then he stepped aside so Kristoff could see what was inside the darkened room. Or rather, who.

Lying on the floor, covered by a torn blanket, was Frederick.

Los Angeles, 1989

ON SATURDAY MORNING I load up my hatchback with all the research books I've checked out of the library, and I make the two-hour drive down I-5 to Coronado to visit Gram.

I'm going partly because it's been a while, because she was so excited about the Berlin Wall coming down last week and I want to share this moment with her. We can go out for brunch, sip celebratory mimosas at the grand Hotel del Coronado just a few blocks from her house the way we did when I visited her just after Daniel and I got engaged.

But partly I'm also going for selfish reasons. Gram knows German, and most of the books of maps the librarian gave me, along with the address on the letter, are indecipherable to me. I'm hoping she can help me figure out where the Fabers were and maybe where they might have gone.

I leave my house really early, five-thirty a.m., to try to beat any weekend freeway traffic. I get to the large open bridge to the island before eight but I know Gram will be awake. I feel a little bad I don't get down here more often. The last time I was here was months ago—my father was still living by himself, in his house, and Daniel and I were still blissfully married. Well, maybe not blissfully, but I was somewhat blissful in my ignorance that he wasn't blissful.

I hate driving over the bridge—it has no sides, and I have to train my eyes to stay straight ahead, to not think about the bay lurching so precariously below me. I can see why Gram doesn't drive anymore, why she never leaves the island. Not that she needs to. Though it's only a short drive to downtown San Diego, the little village of Coronado has everything she needs within walking distance for her.

I park on the street in front of her small gray and white cottage, and when I get out of the car, I take a deep breath. Coronado Island really isn't far from LA but it seems worlds apart. I feel like I've been transported to a small Victorian town, with fresh sea air. No smog! And only the rumble of a military plane landing not too far in the distance, at the base on the end of the island where my grandfather once worked, many years ago.

I gather up my pile of books from the backseat and walk up the front path toward the white picket fence, but Gram already has the front door open and is coming out to greet me before I reach the door.

"Katie, sweetheart." She reaches around my full arms, to lean up and kiss my cheek. Then she looks behind me to the car. "Where's your other half?"

I turn around and look behind me, at my empty car, as if I'm really as surprised as she is that Daniel's not here, if only because I'm not sure how to answer her. But anyway, Daniel hasn't come down here with me for years. And she doesn't wait for me to answer before she notices the books in my arms and asks about those.

As I follow her inside her cottage, I tell her a little bit about the letter, about Jason's suggestion that I start with where the Fabers were from originally to figure out where they are now. About the maps the librarian gave me. "So much of this is in German," I tell her as I set the pile of books down on her antique dining room table, which she keeps protected with a thick plastic tablecloth. I run my fingers against the plastic and remember happier times at this table, Thanksgivings and Passover Seders of my childhood when both my parents were still here, physically and mentally. And my grandfather, of course, who died of a stroke just a few months after my mother passed away from cancer.

I push all those memories aside and pull the letter, still in the plastic sleeve, from my bag and hand it to Gram so she can see it. She puts her reading glasses, which she wears on a thin gold chain around her neck, up to her eyes, and she examines the letter, and the stamp, closely. "Marissa never understood it," she says as she carefully traces the stamp beneath the plastic with her arthritic finger. "Ted's obsession with these things."

My father had said almost the exact same thing, standing by the window in his room at the Willows, mistaking me for my mother. He wasn't wrong when he said it. Only about where he was, who he was with. "I know," I say to Gram. "And I guess I never really did either."

"So why this? Why now, sweetheart?"

I shrug. I'm not sure I know or understand the answer myself. "My father always told me he was looking for a gem in his collection. As a kid, I thought he meant something valuable, something that would make us rich." She laughs a little, and I smile sheepishly. As a little girl, I believed he would. That we would become the kind of millionaires who lived in a Malibu mansion, high up on the cliffs.

"But maybe that's not what he meant at all." I pause and take the plastic sleeve back from her. "Maybe he saw value in their stories." I have no idea if this is true or not, or if I'm just superimposing my own thoughts, Jason's insistence that there *is* a story here, in this particular oddity of a stamp, in the family behind it.

"It must be hard to see your father now," Gram says. "Him forgetting so much." The last time she saw my father, I drove down here with him. It was her birthday. Two years ago, I think. Pieces had already begun slipping away from him, and she, thirteen years older than him, had still been sharp as ever. He'd asked the same questions several times in the span of an hour, forgetting he already knew the answers. But she'd brushed it off then. He was tired. It was a warm day and he hadn't drunk enough water.

She pulls her reading glasses back down, letting them rest against her chest. And she rubs her watery eyes. "You'll drive me up to LA to visit him one of these days, won't you?" Her voice sounds wistful.

"Of course," I tell her, but I don't think I really will. He was so awful the last time I saw him, when he yelled at me, told me I could never come back. Why upset her like that? It seems better she remember him as he was the last time she saw him, here. When he was still mostly himself.

"Come on. Let's go get breakfast," she says. "And we'll look at your German maps there."

❀

Gram and I sit at the beachfront restaurant at the Del and sip our mimosas, staring off at the cool blue water. The morning fog has mostly burned off already, and the sun is shining, but the air is chilly, and Gram has wrapped her tiny body in a thick wool sweater. My jean jacket is much too thin for the cold breezes coming off the water, and after one mimosa I order a cup of coffee to warm me.

We don't talk much more, about my father. About the fall of the Berlin Wall. About the letter. But Gram pores over the maps in the library books, and every once in a while she murmurs something, a memory that has startled her, right there, in German, just like that.

"See this," she says, after a little while, her finger circling on the name of a city, or a village.

She pushes the book across the table to me, and I see she's looking not in Austria, but in Germany. "Hertzscheimer." I read the name out loud, probably mispronouncing it, but Gram doesn't correct me.

"That's where your grandfather and I were born. Where we grew up."

"Is that where my dad was born, too?" I ask her. Though I know it was what initially drew my parents together, their common German background, beyond that, it wasn't something either one of them had ever spoken much about to me.

She shakes her head. "No, sweetheart. Your dad was born in Bremen, I think. Our town was very small. We knew everyone. Once . . . You can't find it on a map anymore. They burned it down, after we left." Her hand shakes a little just from her talking about it. "And I haven't seen it written out like this in so many years. On a map. A real place!"

I pat her wrinkled hand, but she doesn't say anything else as she keeps flipping through the book, eventually moving away from her home. Toward Austria.

I always knew that my grandparents grew up in what eventually became communist East Germany, but it was something Gram always spoke of in general terms, with a fleeting look of sadness. Not something she'd ever shown me specifically on a map, until this morning. And aside from her slight accent and her delicious apple strudel, which she'd bake for Rosh Hashanah dinners when I was a kid, I never really gave her German heritage, or mine for that matter, much thought. "They really burned down your entire town?" I ask her, wondering about friends, relatives, she must've left behind. "You never told me that."

"I don't like to talk about it," she says, and she doesn't offer anything else as she keeps paging through the maps. "Ah, this is what it's referring to," Gram says.

"What?"

"The address, on your letter." Her curled finger is over another circle, with the word *Grotsburg*. The way the address had been written on the letter, I'd assumed Grotsburg was the name of the street, but here, on this map, it appears to be the name of a town. "In the smaller villages, we didn't put the street names on letters," Gram says, seemingly understanding my confusion. "No need back then." She clears her throat and closes the books. "We went to Austria, once. Did I ever tell you?"

"Grotsburg?" I ask. "You knew of it?"

"Oh, no. Vienna," she says. "I was a little girl, and my parents took me there on a holiday. We went to see an opera. *Die Frau ohne Schatten*. The Woman Without a Shadow. Terribly beautiful. I'll never forget it." The irony of her words sinks in, in light of my father. And I hope she's right. That she won't. That she'll live many more years, her memory completely intact. "It was destroyed during the war, you know. The Opera House." I shake my head. I didn't know. I probably should've, and maybe I did learn that once, but I've forgotten it, if I did. "They rebuilt it, but I bet it was never the same. Nothing ever was."

Gram finishes off her mimosa and stares off, toward the ocean. I look at her, sitting here like this. She got out of her town in Germany before it was destroyed, before the region fell under the iron curtain. She's as much a Southern Californian as I am, brunching by the beach, bundling up in wool when the temperature falls to a blustery, wintry sixty-five. She has a cottage and a life here. And I'm wondering if the Faber girls do, somewhere, too.

❋

Later that night at home, I pull out the map where Gram found Grotsburg and a current *World Atlas* that Daniel left behind, sitting on the shelf in what was once our mutual home office. I'm neither a geography nor history buff like him or my father, the only things they had in common, that they could discuss with ease. But now I'm happy to see the atlas still here. At least it saves me another trip to the library.

I compare the prewar map to the current one and find Vienna, still in the exact same spot, though with what Gram said about the Opera House, I consider how different it is on the ground, off the map. I trace with my finger to the west, but where Grotsburg is located on the map dated 1932, it simply doesn't exist on the current map. Just like Gram's home of Hertzscheimer in East Germany.

My eyes skip back and forth between the two maps, comparing the differences. Other tiny towns have disappeared, too. And as I look at the two maps, side by side like this, it feels like tangible evidence of the horrors in these countries during World War II and beyond. It hits me in a way I've never quite been able to conceptualize before. The dots on the map represent homes, businesses, people. Wiped off the map. Just like that.

Jason's suggestion to search the archives for the Fabers seems futile. There will be no archives for a town that is long gone. The Faber girls, and all records of them, were probably destroyed with the town. But somehow, was it possible they got out before then?

As I get into bed, Benjamin's words haunt me about how nothing good could've happened to the Faber girls at that time, in Austria. I fall into a deep and restless sleep, my dreams filled with towns burning, women whom I don't even know disappearing, their bodies turning to smoke.

Austria, 1938

FREDERICK?" Kristoff rushed to him, wanting to be sure his eyes weren't deceiving him. Frederick didn't answer, but as Kristoff stood just above him, Kristoff could see that he was breathing, his chest rising slowly up and down, though his beard appeared singed, and his left hand was wrapped in what seemed to be a makeshift bandage.

"I found him in the woods," Josef said quietly. And Kristoff felt a quick flash of jealousy that Josef, not he and Elena, had been the one to find Frederick. Then guilt, for even thinking that. Frederick was here. He was alive!

"He burned his hand in the fire?" Kristoff asked, trying to determine what kind of shape Frederick was in.

"No, frostbite," Josef said. How long had poor Frederick been out in the snow, the cold? He felt even guiltier. He and Elena had given up too easily on their own search. They should've kept looking.

"He asked for you," Josef said. "He kept asking for you." Josef cleared his throat and turned away. "As soon as I could make it back through the woods to come get you, I did." Elena had said Josef had a good heart. Maybe she was right.

Frederick stirred a little and Kristoff went to him, kneeled down beside him. "My boy?" Frederick said. He reached his good hand out, and Kristoff took it. "My home? My family?"

"Everything is fine," Kristoff said. "They're all safe. They'll be so happy to know you're alive."

"You can't tell them yet," Josef said.

"Of course I'll tell them." Kristoff couldn't let Mrs. Faber, Elena, and Miriam go on grieving for Frederick when he was right here.

"It would only put them in danger now," Josef said. "The Germans will come looking for him when the snow melts, and Minna will tell them what she believes is the truth, that Frederick is dead." Josef paused. "And besides, Minna and the girls would never leave without him, and we need a plan to get them away from here." Kristoff had said it himself, only a few minutes earlier: the girls needed to get out. He knew there was some truth to what Josef was saying, but it still felt unnecessarily cruel.

"He's right," Frederick said, and Kristoff looked back to him, amazed that he was here. Breathing. Talking.

"But you can't let them believe that you're dead," Kristoff said. He wanted to tell Frederick how Mrs. Faber's kind face seemed permanently puffy from crying; how Miriam had spent days just sitting still; and how Elena's face was carved with stoicism, but underneath, in her eyes, Kristoff could detect a new, ingrained sadness. But he didn't want to upset Frederick more, so he kept that to himself.

"We'll get them out of the country," Josef said. "And then Frederick will join them in a little while. When he's a bit more healed. They'll all be together soon enough. This is only temporary."

"But the Germans will never let Frederick go just like that—"

Josef cut him off. "We will make him new documents."

He thought about his conversation with Elena in the workshop the other night, the work she and Josef wanted to do, the uses she said they could have for the engraving tools. "You and Elena will forge them?" Kristoff asked.

"No!" Frederick shouted, and Kristoff and Josef both jumped, not expecting such force out of him, when he'd seemed so weak only moments earlier. "Elena can't!"

Josef shot Kristoff a dirty look that seemed to say: *This* is why I don't trust you. Or like you. Elena had taken so much care to hide her engraving endeavors from her father. She hadn't wanted him to know anything of her involvement in anything like this. By *we* Josef must've meant himself and Kristoff. Josef didn't want Elena to know that Frederick was alive, so how could she be involved in forging his papers? Josef wanted Kristoff to forge the papers, and perhaps that was really why he'd brought him here.

Josef kneeled down again to Frederick's level and put his hand on Frederick's shoulder, gently. "We'll get the girls and Mrs. Faber out of Austria first, and after you get a little stronger, Kristoff and I will get you out, too."

Kristoff felt Josef's words sink in. *Out of Austria.* Their country was no longer safe for them. Austria could no longer be the Fabers' home.

❀

That night, Elena came up to the attic. Miriam and Mrs. Faber had long been asleep, and it was late. The only light came from the moonglow slanting in through Kristoff's tiny window. Kristoff had been trying to sleep, but he couldn't stop thinking about Frederick, injured but alive, hidden, lying on the cold floor of the secret cabin in the woods. He'd gotten out of bed, to think, and it wasn't until Elena came into his room that he realized he'd been pacing again.

"I'm sorry," he said as she entered the room and walked toward the window to stand next to him. She would think he meant for the pacing, for keeping her awake. But really he meant it for so much more. *Your father is alive.* He wanted to tell her the truth so badly. But he kept his lips shut. Not because Josef had told him to, but because it was what Frederick wanted.

"The snow has melted enough to get to town," she said. "Father has a friend from art school who lives in America. I've written him a letter and asked if Mother and Miriam can come to live with him for a while. I'll go in the morning to the post."

"Elena," Kristoff said. "You can't go to town."

"I'm not afraid of the Germans. What will they do to me? Simply for mailing a letter?"

"You should be. Afraid, I mean." Josef had said the town was destroyed, so many men missing. The German soldiers had left behind a trail of death and destruction. Kristoff had read the newspaper that Josef had also given him earlier when he'd come to the workshop: thousands of Jews across Austria and Germany had been arrested the morning after *die Kristallnacht.* Their only crime, he surmised, was being Jewish.

"But what is there really to be afraid of but death?" Elena asked. "And I'm not afraid of that."

He was. He didn't want to imagine the world, his world, without

Elena's bright voice, her pink cheeks and pale skin as white as the edelweiss petals. "I'll mail your letter in the morning. Okay? I'll take it to town for you," he said.

"And what would make you any safer?" She folded her arms in front of her chest. She was wearing a long white formless nightgown, but her defiant stance gave it shape, so Kristoff could envision the curves of her body underneath.

He looked away. "I'm not a Jew," he said. The words sounded shameful, awful, and as he said them out loud he wished he could take them back. Though they were undeniably true.

Elena didn't respond for a few moments, until finally she relented with a reluctant, "All right." But she didn't immediately move to leave his room. She looked out the window, and Kristoff tentatively moved his hand over and reached for hers. He expected her to push him away again, to run out of his room the second he touched her. But this time, she didn't. She let him take her hand. She didn't let go; she didn't move.

They stood there together for a long time, holding hands, staring out the window into the night sky, into a new Austria that neither one of them understood nor would recognize for very much longer.

✻

In the morning, Kristoff set off through the woods for town with Elena's letter. It was addressed to *Mister Leser*, Frederick's friend, Kristoff assumed, though he had never heard of him before now. Elena had stamped it with both Austrian and German postage for the airmail, a dual franking, the way they had been doing since the occupation. The Austrian stamp was her father's most recent design, an Austrian hillside in the springtime. And Kristoff looked at it with sadness. Though the hill still existed, just beyond the Fabers' property, the stamp was a reminder to Kristoff of everything else that did not.

This morning was the first time he'd actually gone to town since *die Kristallnacht*, when he and Elena had stood at the edge of the woods and watched the fires. And now when he made it through the woods, past the clearing, into town, he saw that Josef was right. What was left was an ashy mess. A few buildings remained: Wien Allee, where the post office still stood, near the edge of town, was relatively untouched. But most of the rest of the town appeared to be destroyed. Buildings were missing windows, walls, roofs even, and debris littered the sidewalks. Broken glass cracked further under Kristoff's boots as he walked, and with each step he felt more and more like he wanted to scream over all the loss and destruction that surrounded him. It was all such a waste. All the beautiful buildings, lives, businesses that were broken, for no good reason.

As Kristoff approached the post office, he noticed a German soldier walking up and down the street, his boots clicking back and forth, his right hand resting easily on his gun in his holster. *He's patrolling*, Kristoff thought, but he wasn't sure for what. The town felt too empty to need any patrolling. Kristoff didn't see any other people, citizens of the town, with the exception of a few men out cleaning the sidewalks, picking up debris. He recognized Mr. Himmle, the shopkeeper who owned the market. Himmle looked up, his eyes met Kristoff's in recognition, and he quickly looked down, went back to work cleaning up. Kristoff began to feel nervous, though he wasn't doing anything wrong. Simply mailing a letter. Even in Österreich this was still legal.

He walked inside the post office, but instead of the girl who normally worked inside, a German soldier stood behind the counter. Kristoff wondered what had happened to the girl, but maybe it was better not to know. Probably nothing good. Was she Jewish? Kristoff couldn't remember. In fact, he wasn't sure of her name, just that she had always been here, working here, for as long as Kristoff had been coming. And Elena had mentioned once that they had been schoolmates until she'd left school to go help her ailing father at the post.

Kristoff's hands shook as he gave his letter to the soldier. The man looked at him, seeming surprised that he was here, that anyone was here. Who would be mailing a letter at a time like this? His raised stern black eyebrows seemed to be asking.

He handed the letter back to Kristoff.

"I would like to mail this, please," Kristoff heard himself saying, his voice sounding too high, reminding him of the stupid mouse in Miriam's bedroom wall.

The soldier handed him a booklet, the official gazette of the Reichspostministerium. He opened it up for Kristoff to read what he guessed was the important line: from the 31st October 1938 Austrian postage stamps would no longer be valid. Kristoff's eyes skimmed over the rest about how unused stamps could be exchanged for German ones at a three-to-two rate.

"I'm sorry." He heard himself apologizing to the soldier, and he hated the way his voice sounded, as if he truly were sorry. Not angry. Not filled with hate. "I'll purchase the correct postage, then? My mistake."

The soldier took Kristoff's money and covered up Frederick's beautiful stamps with German ones, Hitler's face. And Kristoff worried the soldier would question him more. What the letter said, whom it was being sent to and why. But after franking it correctly, he took the letter from Kristoff's hands without giving it any more notice.

❀

As Kristoff walked back toward the house, the sky was graying into dusk, and he thought about the new curfews the Germans had enacted for Jews. What would the soldier patrolling the streets have done if Elena had been out mailing the letter too late? Kristoff shivered as he crossed the clearing and escaped back into the unpatrolled woods. He felt an odd safety in their denseness, amidst the snowy trees, and he remembered what Josef had said about the cabin. No one knew it was there. The Germans wouldn't even know how to find it.

The Germans. It made him terribly sad to think of all of Frederick's hard work creating the stamps, engraving the plates, and how just by the new German decree they were suddenly worthless. He wouldn't tell Frederick (or Elena) about the stamps, though Elena would figure it out soon enough.

But as he reached the house, he forgot all about the stamps. Something was wrong: The front door was ajar. It was much too cold out, winter, nearly night. No one would've intentionally left the door open.

He ran inside the house, yelling for Mrs. Faber. Then Elena. Then Miriam. But no one answered him.

A teakettle boiled over on the stove, and Kristoff turned it off.

But the house was empty. The Fabers were gone.

Los Angeles, 1989

O N SUNDAY, I have an unremarkable visit with my father. I don't mention his stamp collection, nor the letter, nor my visit with Gram. My father knows it's me again, and seems to have no recollection of my evening visit earlier in the week. Of his warning that I could never come back. We talk about the weather—it feels chilly this November for Los Angeles. We talk about the movie I'm supposed to go see tonight for work, *Driving Miss Daisy*, and how it stars Jessica Tandy, and how we both enjoyed her in *Cocoon* a few years earlier. We talk about Thanksgiving, which is coming up before we know it, and then my father asks if we'll be back home before then. If I've found our plane tickets, to know when it is exactly we'll be flying back.

"I'm looking," I tell him, the way I always do now. I lean down and kiss his balding head, and I tell him I'll be back next Sunday.

"I know," he says, and as I leave I hope that maybe he does.

✳

When I get home, there's an unfamiliar car parked in my driveway, a white Ford. I park on the street, and walk up the driveway, where

I see Benjamin sitting inside the car. I knock on the driver's side window, and he jumps, and rolls it down halfway. "You weren't home," he says, sounding sheepish. "So I thought I'd wait till you got back."

"How long have you been sitting here?" I ask. He shrugs, and I guess it's been a while. "And I thought you were in San Francisco at a conference?"

He gets out of his car and then he follows me up the front path to the house. "I was in San Francisco. Just got back this morning," he says. "And I found something."

"Something?" I open the front door, and Benjamin follows me inside the house. It's a mess, in a way it never was when Daniel, who's a neat freak, lived here. My library books are all over the coffee table in the living room, and there's a pile of laundry on one end of the couch that I haven't put away yet. *At least it's clean laundry.* I shuffle the books into a pile and carry the laundry into the kitchen, where I set it on the counter, out of his sight.

"Nice house," Benjamin says, not seeming to notice the mess.

"Thanks." Benjamin is right—it's a beautiful house, my mess notwithstanding, a renovated craftsman that the previous owners had stripped down and rebuilt to look like a new modern eighties version of its former self. But I don't tell Benjamin that I've been thinking about selling it ever since Daniel left and then *graciously* handed it over to me.

"Coffee?" I ask Benjamin instead. He's made himself comfortable on my couch and is eyeing my library books, my maps of Austria.

"Sure," he says, and I put up a fresh pot before walking back into the living room and sitting down next to him. I'm suddenly aware of our closeness, and I shift down the couch a little, so our legs don't accidentally touch.

"So tell me about this something you found in San Francisco," I say.

"I showed your stamp around the whole conference," he says, but he's still glancing at my books, not looking at me. "No one had ever seen it before, with the flower, in the steeple like that, I mean." This does not sound like something. It sounds like nothing. He turns his attention away from the books and looks at me, and his face is more animated than usual. He's excited about whatever it is he found. "But then I started asking around about Faber, if anyone had a collection of his stamps, if anyone knew what happened to him after the *Anschluss*."

"He died," I say, remembering the dates for him in the philatelic handbook I'd checked out of the library.

"Right, but then how did his flower get into this steeple?"

"Well, it wasn't his," I say, which seems obvious. But Benjamin shrugs as if he isn't sure, and I wonder if it's possible that this stamp was made earlier than Benjamin thought. "Hold on, let me grab the coffee." I walk into the kitchen, fill two mugs, and bring them back into the living room. Benjamin takes his and thanks me.

"Anyway," he says. "I met this guy who's a really big World War Two–era collector. He actually had the original St. Stephen's Cathedral stamp in his collection. The one without the flower. Remember, I told you about it." He pulls a Polaroid out of his bag and shows me the picture he must've taken in San Francisco of the original stamp. This stamp looks so similar to the stamp on my letter, in my bag, that I almost wouldn't know it was different at all. Except I do. This one is missing the small flower petals at the top of the steeple.

"So what does this all mean? My father's stamp is a special edition or something?"

Benjamin takes a sip of his coffee. "I don't know about that yet. But that's not even the part that's interesting. This collector said a few years ago a woman contacted him. She was looking for Faber stamps. She wanted to know what he had, offered to buy them from him at a pretty steep cost. More than they were worth."

Benjamin speaks quickly; he's overly excited. But nothing he's saying means anything to me yet. "I don't understand," I say. "Why does that matter?"

"The woman who contacted him, she said she was Faber's daughter."

"*Fräulein Faber?*" I try to imagine this girl, now presumably an old woman and, very possibly, no longer a Fräulein at all. But she's alive, and she must've gotten out of Austria, somehow. "Where is she? Do you know?"

"Well, he said a few years ago she was in Cardiff."

I'd just driven by Cardiff-by-the-Sea, on the way to see Gram. "San Diego?" The thought of her here, so close, feels almost unbelievable.

"No, Cardiff in England. Wales."

And suddenly she's far away again. Across the country and then an ocean. I'd have to put so much postage on this letter to get it to her if I sent it today. And I'm not sure I could do that, just buy some airmail stamps and toss it carelessly in the mail, letting it wing its way across the world. What if it got lost?

"Jack's going to look up her contact information in his files when he gets home and said he'd get it to me next week. I want to write to her, ask her about this particular stamp, this letter you have." He finishes off his coffee and sets the mug down on my coffee table, next to my library books. "If that's okay with you, that is?" I nod. "If it's particularly valuable, she might be willing to pay good money for it. And, well, even if it's not, Jack said she way overpaid for all of his Fabers."

A gem, my father had always said. That's why I went to Benjamin in the first place. If there was just the slightest chance, I'd wanted to know. I was thinking about my father, the expense of his continued care, after all. But I can't sell this letter to this woman, for whom it was possibly originally intended, years ago. Even if she offered to pay top dollar for it, I couldn't take her money for a letter addressed to her.

Jason was so certain there's a story here. But is it possible the story isn't in the stamp at all, but in this old woman, living in Wales, who once was younger, in love, a girl living in Austria? How did she get from there to Wales, and what happened to the man she loved?

"I can't sell it to her if it's rightfully hers," I finally say to Benjamin. "I'll return it to her, but I'd like to write her a letter myself, ask her about her story. When you get her contact information from this Jack guy, can you give it to me?"

"Sure," Benjamin says, more affably than I would expect considering I've probably wasted his time, sent him on a fruitless chase for which he won't ever get paid. "But you'll ask her about the stamp, too? About the flower?" he insists.

"Why do you care, if I'm not going to sell it?" I'm not saying this unkindly, just matter-of-factly. What's in it for him now?

"I just want to know. I just want to understand it." For the first time, he meets my eyes. His eyes are deep blue, almost black, like the ocean in Santa Monica. They're both beautiful and a little sad, filled with more emotion than I would expect from him. And it strikes me that I don't really know him at all, that he's got a life outside of stamps and I'm a little curious what that is. "You know," he adds. "In case I ever come across something like this again." He offers me a half smile.

"Of course," I tell him. "Of course I'll ask her about the stamp." And I wonder if Benjamin wants to unravel the history, too. If, like me, he's suddenly more interested in her story.

Austria, 1938

THE TEAKETTLE WAS BOILING OVER, and Kristoff grabbed it off the stove. Hot water splashed onto his hand, burned his skin a little, but he barely felt it as he set the kettle down on the counter.

Where were the girls?

He ran through the house calling for them, up and down all three stories, but his voice echoed through empty halls, rooms. No one answered. He ran back to the front door and examined it again. Had it just blown open, from the wind, maybe? But no, there was a footprint in the center, a large booted footprint, and he imagined a German soldier kicking down the door, dragging Mrs. Faber, Miriam, and Elena away.

He sat down against the front door, out of breath, defeated. The skin on his hand had already blistered a little, and he stuck it in the snow to cool the burn. The girls were gone. *But they couldn't be.* Elena would never let that happen.

Maybe they ran when they heard the Germans coming? But where would they go? Where would Elena take them to stay safe? The secret cabin in the woods, where Frederick lay on the floor?

Elena would kill him if she found out he knew that Frederick was there—that is, if Josef didn't kill him first for not keeping a closer watch over the girls, for leaving to go into town in the first place. Or maybe they were just in the workshop? Kristoff hadn't checked there yet.

He stood, ran through the house, then out the back door across the snowy lawn. "Hallo?" he called into the workshop as he opened the door.

But inside, it was dark, empty. And he sat down in Frederick's old armchair, his whole body shaking with fear, with regret. "No, no, no," he said to himself. His voice echoed again, in the empty space.

He had no choice but to go to the cabin in the woods, to Frederick, and pray the girls were already there. Because the alternative, he realized, was having to tell Frederick that the girls were gone, that he didn't know where to find them, that there was a footprint in the shape of a German boot on his front door.

Kristoff heard a sound, a small squeak. He heard it again, but what was it? A hiccup? Was that . . . *Miriam?*

He lit a candle and gazed around the workshop, examining every inch of it with his eyes and the candlelight. But he didn't see them. "Miri, Elena?" he called out. "Are you here?" They didn't answer, so he tried again. "The Germans are gone. It's only me. Kristoff. I'm all alone. I promise. Are you here?"

Everything was silent and still for another moment, until he heard the creak of a floorboard, and the earth shifted below him slightly. The piece of flooring just next to him moved, Elena slid it back, and she and Miriam climbed out from under the ground.

He'd had no idea there was a crawl space beneath the workshop. "Father used to store engraving plates under here," Elena said, brushing herself off, wiping away dust and cobwebs and god knows what else. "It's not very big, but it was big enough to hide in."

"It was like being in our own tomb," Miriam said. She was a mess, her face streaked with dirt and tears.

Elena looked down at the floor, and didn't say anything else for a moment, as if Miri's words had rendered her mute. The thought of her own tomb. She had said just last night that her own death didn't scare her. But Miri's death? Kristoff knew that was another story.

"They took her away, didn't they?" Elena's voice trembled when she finally spoke, and she still didn't look up at him. "They were asking Mother for Father and I heard her say he was dead. But then I grabbed Miri and ran out here and we hid before I could hear anything else." She finally looked up. Kristoff could see every bit of her face in the glow of his candle. She wasn't crying, like Miri. Her green eyes were stoic, resolute. "But they took her, didn't they?"

"I don't know." Kristoff swallowed hard, feeling pretty certain that Elena was right, that they did. "The house was empty when I came back from town. The front door was still open. The stove was still on. The teakettle boiling over . . ." His voice trailed off. They all knew, with certainty, that Mrs. Faber wouldn't allow that to happen, if she was still here.

"Mother and Father both are gone. In just an instant." Miriam's voice rose. "We're all alone in the world. We're orphans."

"No." Kristoff held out his hand to Miri. "You're not. Come with me."

❊

Kristoff didn't think about Frederick's worry, or Josef's rage, as he walked through the woods with the girls toward the cabin. He thought only about Miriam and Elena, and how they needed to know their father was actually alive. It had been stupid to keep it from them in the first place. Josef had said it was to protect them, should the Germans come, but it had protected Mrs. Faber from nothing. The worst of it was, they'd taken her anyway and she still believed her husband was dead. Kristoff would never forgive himself for not telling her the truth, and he wasn't going to keep Frederick from Miri and Elena any longer.

"What are we doing here?" Elena asked when she realized they were headed toward the cabin. She stopped walking, put her hands on her hips, and grabbed on to Miri's arm hard enough so that she had to stop walking, too.

Kristoff didn't want to tell her about Frederick; he wanted to show her, the way Josef had shown him. He hoped that by seeing him alive, she would focus on that and not the secret that Kristoff had been keeping from her. "Just trust me," he said to her. She hesitated, and pulled Miri back, closer to her. "Please." He put his hand on Elena's shoulder, and finally she let go of Miri's arm and followed him again, to the cabin's door.

Kristoff walked in first and used the glow of the candle to illuminate Frederick, still lying on the floor. He appeared to be sleeping. But he opened his eyes and he looked straight at Kristoff, Elena, and Miri. "What have you done, my boy?" His voice came out raspy, as if he were almost choking on the words.

But Kristoff turned away, unwilling to see the disappointment on Frederick's tired face. Instead he looked at Miri. "You are not an orphan," he said, but she wasn't listening to him. She was too busy shouting, jumping, hugging Frederick to her.

❋

"There's a train leaving Vienna next week," Josef told Kristoff one evening as the two of them had walked back to the house to gather supplies to bring to the cabin for the Fabers. Days had passed, then weeks. There was still no sign of Mrs. Faber, but the Germans hadn't returned either. Josef had said the best they could hope for was that Mrs. Faber had been taken to the work camp in Mauthausen in Upper Austria, but if that was the best then Kristoff didn't want to consider the worst. The few times he went back into town he'd heard rumors of others who'd been taken away to Mauthausen or killed in the street. He heard whispers that a German soldier shot Mr. Himmle, right on Wien Allee, as Mr. Himmle tried to run after they'd put him under house arrest. Kristoff wasn't sure whether that was true or not, but Himmle's shop was being run by a German, and the supplies were much less abundant than they were when Mr. Himmle owned the market.

"A train?" Kristoff asked Josef as they walked together now, not sure what Josef was getting at.

"The British. They're beginning a *Kindertransport*, accepting children under the age of seventeen, sponsoring them to come to London. Live with foster families for a while. There was a notice from the Kultusgemeinde." Kristoff recognized that as the name of a Jewish organization based in Vienna. Their office had been a street over from the orphanage, and he'd walked by it many times as a boy. "They'll take both Miri and Elena." Josef was still talking. "I already got tickets for them."

"You got them tickets out, just like that?" Kristoff asked.

"They're giving priority to orphans," Josef said.

"But they're not orphans."

Josef stopped walking and turned to look at Kristoff sharply. He was still angry that Kristoff had brought the girls to Frederick. But would they have been safe at the house, still? Only until the Germans came back. And surely they would. "They *are* orphans," Josef said. "For all intents and purposes."

Kristoff wouldn't tell Josef that he couldn't bear the thought of Miri and Elena leaving, boarding a train, and then presumably a boat, all the way to London. Because they would be better off there. He knew they would be. But he also didn't want them to go. "Have you told Elena?" he asked Josef.

"No. I think you should. That's why I'm telling you."

"M-Me?" Kristoff stammered.

"She likes you. She'll listen to you."

"But I thought the two of you were . . ."

"Elena?" Josef laughed. "She thinks of me as a brother." He paused a second, enough for Kristoff to understand that Josef might not feel the same way about her. "Her and Miriam, both. My father and Frederick were old friends—they used to paint together."

"Your father is an artist?" Kristoff couldn't hide his shock that a gruff man like Josef had come from any sort of artistic upbringing.

"He was," Josef said, but he didn't offer anything further on what had happened to his father. "I've known Elena since we were little kids, running up the hillside together in the summers. Sledding down it in the winters." He cast his eyes down. Maybe he couldn't bear to remember happier times. Summers and winters of abundant freedoms.

They had reached the cabin, and Josef stopped walking before going inside. "I'll bring Miriam back to the house to gather up a bag, some things, so she'll be ready to go in a few days. You convince Elena," he said, as if it were just that easy.

❋

Kristoff asked Elena if she would walk with him in the woods, and though it was cold, snowing lightly again, she agreed. The cabin was tiny, one room, which thankfully had a fireplace to keep them all warm. But nothing else. And Kristoff could tell Elena hated being cooped up all day. He'd brought her a pile of English novels he'd found in her room and of course he'd brought them all clothing, food. But Elena was not the kind of girl who could spend her life in a tiny room, when there was so much else going on all around her.

They walked for a few moments in silence, matching strides, matching footprints in the snow, until Kristoff made himself speak. "Josef found a way out for you and Miri," he said, trying to keep his voice light, hopeful.

Elena stopped walking, turned, and faced him. "I'm not going anywhere."

She tilted her face upwards, and all her features were rigid, unyielding. She shivered a little, and Kristoff took his warm hand from his pocket and put it to her cheek. Her skin was freezing. "It's a train leaving Vienna next week," he said. "A *Kindertransport*, taking orphans to London to live with foster families, just for a little while, just till all of this passes."

For a moment she didn't say anything. She didn't move. Her skin warmed beneath his hand, and she was so still it seemed she was barely breathing. "Okay," she finally said.

It wasn't what he'd been expecting, and instead of feeling relieved he felt somewhat conflicted. He was happy that she'd agreed to go so quickly; sad that she'd agreed to leave him, just like that. "Good," he said, trying to sound calm and sensible. But it was an effort to keep his voice from shaking. "I'll figure out a way to get your father out of here, too."

"And you'll help Josef," she said. "You'll fight them, won't you, Kristoff?" How could an engraver, an artist, really fight a soldier? Many soldiers? The burin was no match for guns, fire, destruction. But he heard himself agreeing, telling her, of course he would. Of course he would fight.

She looked at him. Her cheeks were so pink from cold, her lips redder than usual. She had three freckles on the bridge of her nose that Kristoff had not paid much attention to before. And he fought the urge to reach over and trace them with his finger.

She was leaving. She hadn't even argued with him, not really. She was going to be safe, and though he was grateful, he couldn't move his hand from her cheek, couldn't take his eyes away from her face, from those beautiful lips, those freckles.

He leaned down, and he did what he'd been wanting to for months. He kissed her. Elena's lips were cold, and she jumped back a little. He'd caught her off guard, or maybe she'd never imagined kissing him the way he'd often imagined kissing her.

She reached her hands up, put them on his face. His cheeks were rough. He almost had a beard. He hadn't shaved in weeks, since *die Kristallnacht*. As if all memory of his prior routines had been erased in the fires that destroyed most of Grotsburg.

She ran her hands across his cheeks and then she leaned in and kissed him back. Her lips were soft but forceful. *Just like her.* The kiss lasted for only the briefest of seconds until she pulled away, put her hand to her own mouth. "What are we doing?" Her words came out soft, flat, lacking her usual conviction.

"I don't know," he said. "I'm sorry. I was . . . saying goodbye, I guess."

She stepped back, and put her hands in the pockets of her wool coat. "I don't like goodbyes," she said.

"So it wasn't a goodbye, then," he said. "It was a see you again, soon."

She didn't say anything else, and she didn't wait for him before she turned and started walking quickly back toward the cabin in the woods.

Los Angeles, 1989

I'M FREEZING MY ASS off here," Karen complains to me over the phone a few nights later. I haven't heard anything more from Benjamin, and I feel impatient to get Fräulein Faber's contact information from him. But I don't want to call and pester him about it either. So I've called my best friend, Karen, to catch her up instead, and she immediately launches into a diatribe about the miserable November weather in Connecticut.

"God is punishing you for abandoning me," I say, only half joking. I know it's not her fault that she's so far away, that her husband got a new job in Hartford at the same time Daniel decided he was leaving and I realized my father needed to move into the Willows. But Karen and I have been friends since kindergarten, and other than a short jaunt away from Los Angeles for separate colleges, we've always lived near each other until this past year.

"So have you signed the papers yet?" Karen switches topics quickly, the way she always does.

She's the one person (other than Jason now, I guess) whom I've been honest with the entire time about me and Daniel. "Not yet." I glance at the envelope still sitting on my kitchen counter. I haven't touched it, moved it, opened it, much less signed anything.

"You have to do it. You'll feel better when it's over. Final."

"Will I?" Karen is married to Mark, her high school sweetheart. They're the kind of couple who agree on everything, who sometimes answer in tandem and dress alike, purely by accident, just because they're *that* in step with each other. I used to see their sameness, their quiet domesticity as boring, when Daniel and I would revel in weekends in Napa, fancy dinners, and movie premieres compliments of the magazine. But once all that was gone, once my father's illness consumed me, maybe we could've used an iota of what Karen and Mark have.

"And once you get a new job," Karen is saying. "You've been looking, right?"

"Kind of," I say, and I tell Karen everything, all about the unusual stamp, the love letter, how Benjamin might have located one of the Faber girls. And how Jason wants to hire me to write the story for him, once I figure it out.

"So you're using all this to avoid thinking about your divorce." Karen says it matter-of-factly, not as a question. She used to work as a therapist before she had Jeffrey two years ago, and I'm used to her trying to therapy-speak me.

"I'm not," I insist. But maybe she's right, and that's exactly what I'm doing. Obsessing over someone else's love story, to avoid thinking about what a mess my own has become.

"So this Benjamin guy . . . Is he cute?" she asks.

I laugh a little. "No, Kar, it's nothing like that. He's just helping me with this stamp, that's all."

"But is he cute?"

I remember the way his eyes looked as he sat on my couch the other night. The way he smiled a little when he thought about the possible story behind the stamp. "I mean in a nerdy sort of way, I guess so."

"What's that old expression?" She lowers her voice. "The best way to get over one man is to get under another one."

"Karen! No! Seriously, he's just a stamp dealer."

She laughs, and I know she's joking. Or at least half joking. Then she yells for Jeffrey to stop doing whatever he's doing in the background. "Sorry," she says to me. "He's supposed to be in bed and instead he's trying to put his Halloween costume on Mittens. I have to go rescue the damn cat."

I laugh, too. "Of course," I say. "Call me later this week when you can talk."

She promises she will, and then we hang up. But our phone calls are all like this, stilted, interrupted, faraway and half finished. It's not just her move to Connecticut, but also the fact that she has Jeffrey, and I don't have any kids. Daniel and I had agreed that we weren't ready for kids, at first, and then just around the time I'd begun to think maybe it was time, my father got really bad. At night, Daniel was already asleep when I got home from my dad's, or if he wasn't, I was way too tired and emotionally drained to have sex, much less kids.

I guess I should be thankful that we didn't have kids together, although mostly I feel sadness at the idea that I might never get to be someone's mother like Karen is.

But I don't dwell on it now, and I get into bed with my legal pad. I start to draft out a letter I might send to Fräulein Faber. I don't care what Karen says about *why* I'm obsessing over this letter, I want to tell Fräulein Faber what she might've lost, what I've found among all the other nothingness in my father's vast collection. I want to learn and write about her love story, and I hope that, unlike mine, it has a happy ending.

❀

The next morning at work, instead of doing actual work, writing my review of *Driving Miss Daisy*, I finish up my letter. I'm antsy to connect with Fräulein Faber, and I can't concentrate on much else.

At eleven, I tell Janice I'm leaving for lunch and to tell Daniel I'll get him the review I owe him when I get back. But I'm not hungry, and I get in my car and drive out to Sherman Oaks instead.

The sky is clear today, the air has warmed up, the traffic is remarkably light on the freeway. I park in the shopping center in the same place I did the last time, when I unloaded what felt like my father's entire life, but this time I'm empty-handed as I walk into Benjamin's office.

I notice now there's a little bell above the door, and it clangs brightly as I open it. Benjamin sits behind his messy desk but looks up when he hears the bell. His TV is on, and I recognize Erica Kane (once my mother's favorite) on the screen.

"*All My Children?*" I ask him, and I can't help it, I laugh.

Benjamin turns the knob and shuts it off. "It's just whatever came on after the news. I was working, not really paying attention."

"Uh-huh." I laugh again.

"What are you doing here?" He stands up, almost defensively, and I feel a little bad that I laughed.

"Sorry," I say. "I was just getting impatient. I wanted to see if you'd heard from Jack yet."

He nods and sits back down behind his desk, riffling through one of the piles. "He gave me the contact information for the attorney they used in New York to negotiate the deal. I gave him a call this morning. But he said Mrs. Kleinfelter had recently taken ill."

"Mrs. Kleinfelter?"

"Her married name." *Of course.* She's no longer Fräulein Faber. "Anyway, he said she'd recently moved into a nursing home. It sounded like maybe she wasn't up for buying stamps any longer."

"But I don't want to *sell* her the stamp."

"I know." His voice softens as he seems to remember that this means something to me. "He's going to get me the name and address of the home. If you still want to write to her?"

"Did he tell you what's wrong with her?" I ask. "Why she's in the home?" Benjamin shakes his head. And I suddenly feel defeated. There's not going to be a story for me to write; she's not even going to be up for answering my letter, if she's in any kind of shape like my dad is.

❀

I don't go back to work after I leave Benjamin's office. I know I should, that I'm going to miss the deadline on my review, but I go home instead and call Janice, feigning a bout of the stomach flu. Or is it food poisoning from my nonexistent lunch? She tells me to feel better, and I feel only a little guilty for the lie after I hang up.

I uncork a bottle of wine, though it's just after three p.m., shove my library books onto the floor, sit on the couch, and put my feet up on the coffee table. I glance through the Help Wanted ads, seeing nothing remotely promising, and I flip on the TV. *General Hospital* is on. I haven't watched since college, but I sip my wine and jump right back in. Apparently Edward Quartermaine has died—I'm not sure how—and Lila converses with his ghost. Much more complicated than my own life, in the best possible way. I should probably change the channel, find something vaguely news-oriented, see what's happening in East Berlin. Or maybe it's just going to be Berlin again, the West and East will all be the same? But I don't change the channel. I don't move. I drink half the bottle of wine, and then I curl up on the couch, close my eyes, and fall asleep.

❀

I awake sometime later, to the sound of someone knocking on my door. It's dark in the living room. The television is still on, bright flashes of light and sound I can't comprehend at first. Somebody wants to buy a vowel. *Wheel of Fortune.*

I hear another knock on the door, and I drag myself off the couch. I look through the peephole, and I'm surprised to see Benjamin, standing on the other side, his hands awkwardly in the pockets of his brown Members Only jacket.

I open the door, and his hand is raised; he was about to knock again, but when the door opens, he freezes, and doesn't lower his hand for a moment as he eyes me up and down. My hair is probably a mess, and I reach up self-consciously in a futile attempt to smooth it down. I'm wrapped in the bright orange and green blanket Gram once crocheted for me, that I was curled up with on the couch. "Are you sick?" Benjamin asks. And I try to decide whether that's concern in his voice for me, or whether he's worried I might give him something contagious.

"Not really," I say, remembering the lie I told Janice about the stomach flu. "It's just been a long day."

He hesitates for a moment. "I'm sorry. It's kind of late. I just thought . . . Well, I thought you didn't sleep much, like me."

I consider Karen's question, about whether or not he's cute, and he kind of is, when he stammers like this, like I make him nervous. I blush thinking about her other comment, that I should have sex with him. But I push that ridiculous thought away and open the door wider. "Come on in," I say. "I really don't sleep much anymore. Just happened to have a little bit of wine and fall asleep on the couch."

Benjamin eyes the half-empty bottle of chardonnay on the coffee table, and I quickly pick it up and move it to the kitchen counter. "I do that sometimes," Benjamin admits, then looks a little sheepish, as if he's just admitted something too personal to me, something he shouldn't have said.

"Have a seat." I gesture toward the couch.

"No, I can't stay. I just wanted to give you this." He pulls an envelope out of the inside pocket of his coat.

I take it from him, and at first I think it's another letter, another piece of the Fräulein Faber puzzle, but there's no stamp, no address. The outside of the envelope is blank. "What's this?"

"Jack called me back with the address right after you left. And you just looked so upset. And then I figured, well . . . I thought maybe you have some time off for Thanksgiving next week. And I thought we could go visit Mrs. Kleinfelter in person."

"Wait, what?" At his office earlier he hadn't even seemed that interested in pursuing things any further. And anyway, it didn't seem like Mrs. Kleinfelter was in any shape to be pursued. "I can't just go to England next week," I say after a moment of shock. "It's . . . expensive."

"I have miles," Benjamin says. "I travel a lot. Go to a lot of philatelic conferences. I have a lot of miles."

"I couldn't take your miles."

"You already did," Benjamin says, pointing to the envelope in my hand.

I shake my head, still confused, though I peek inside the envelope and there is indeed an airline ticket to London with my name on it.

He clears his throat. "You don't have to go. I can trade your ticket back in. After you left my office, I just decided I should go. That it would be a good time for me to get away next week. And I wanted you to be able to come along." His cheeks get redder as he rambles on, and it's endearing that he's attempting to include me in this crazy scheme of his. "I mean it's fine if you can't or don't want to or you're busy . . . if you have plans for Thanksgiving or something."

I've spent every Thanksgiving of my adult life either at my dad's house or, for the past few years, at Daniel's mother's house. This year I'd planned a lunch at the Willows with my dad and then turkey and wine for one back here, which barely counts as plans. Not plans that can't be changed, anyway. "Don't you have plans for Thanksgiving?" I ask him. I find it hard to believe that he doesn't.

"I hate Thanksgiving," he says.

"Who hates Thanksgiving?"

He ignores my question. "I'm leaving on Tuesday. Coming back the following Sunday." Then he adds, "If you don't want to go, can I get the letter back from you so I can take it with me?"

But I don't want to give the letter back to him. I *do* want to go. I want to take the letter to Mrs. Kleinfelter myself, meet her in person, hear her story, and I hope that she's in good enough shape to tell it. "I'll go," I say. Benjamin opens his mouth, raises his eyebrows a little, surprised that I've taken him up on his offer, which also seems odd given that he showed up here with a plane ticket. "Thank you for doing this," I add. "Really. It means a lot to me. And I'll find a way to pay you back for the ticket, and your time, too."

"Not necessary." Benjamin turns around, and he's already halfway out the door. He seems more uncomfortable now than he was when I was calling his idea crazy a few minutes ago. He'd expected me to say no.

"But I want to," I say.

"You don't need to pay me. It really wasn't a big deal. I have a lot of miles, like I said."

I put my hand on his shoulder to stop him from running out, and he turns and looks back at me for a minute. "It is a big deal. To me," I say.

He averts his eyes, shakes my hand off, and starts walking down my path toward his car in the driveway. "I'll see you next week, at the airport," he calls behind him. Then he adds: "Don't forget to bring the letter."

Austria, 1938

AFTER ELENA AND MIRIAM left to get on the *Kindertransport*, Kristoff returned to the workshop. It had been only a few weeks since he'd been here last, but in that time a new law had been passed for the Aryanization of all Jewish businesses, and it felt like it had been forever since Kristoff had actually worked here, with Frederick. It was the middle of December, and the weather was colder than Kristoff could ever remember. It seemed the world had frozen, just after it had been scorched.

Kristoff held the burin in his hand and it felt like a foreign instrument all over again, the way it was when he first came to live here. He didn't feel like working with it, practicing, having the attention to detail and the concentration to force metal into tiny difficult lines. And besides, he had no real work to do, no stamps he should create even if he wanted to. So he put down the burin, got his charcoal and his sketch pad, and he began to sketch instead.

He imagined Miriam and Elena, on a long train ride across Austria, headed toward a new life in England. He sketched them until his hand began to cramp up from holding the charcoal for so long. He sketched and sketched for days, until the entire workshop was filled with his drawings of the girls, as if by drawing them he could conjure them back, here, with him.

❀

A few days after Miriam and Elena left, Kristoff received his first visit from Herr Bergmann, who came to the Fabers' home accompanied by two German soldiers.

Kristoff was in the workshop sketching when they arrived, and had just come back from bringing Frederick lunch at the cabin. When he was there, Frederick had told him that he wished to come home, to work again. *It's too dangerous*, Kristoff had told him, *and besides that, illegal now*. Frederick had said he didn't care. But as Kristoff saw the three Germans walking around the back side of the house, toward the workshop, he knew that he'd been right. He was relieved he'd talked Frederick out of coming back here, and then immediately terrified to face these men.

Kristoff quickly gathered all his drawings into a pile and turned them facedown, and then he opened the door to the workshop for the men before they knocked, or before they could kick it down. The truth was, he'd been expecting them. If not them, specifically, then someone. With Frederick out of commission, he had no idea who in Austria was engraving the stamps, and he didn't know how the German engravers and printers would be able to suddenly keep up with the overwhelming demand of having to frank a whole new annexed country's mail.

"Hallo." Kristoff waved and called out to the men, trying to keep his demeanor friendly, trying not to show that he was actually terrified and seething inside. That he hated these men and what they stood for. That he hated that they had taken Mrs. Faber away, somewhere. That Miriam and Elena had been forced to leave home, to run so far, so quickly, and that Frederick was living in a one-room cabin, hidden in the woods.

Herr Bergmann introduced himself as head of the Ministry of Postage, and he and the other men walked inside the workshop and began looking around, as if they belonged here. Herr Bergmann examined the engraving tools on the worktable. "Where are the Fabers?" he asked. His features were unflinching, devoid of any emotion. It seemed he was not asking after people, *a family* who used to live and work here, but about a cut of meat he might be ordering from the butcher.

"Frederick died in the fires a few weeks back. And Mrs. Faber . . ." Kristoff shrugged, hoping they would tell him where she was, but they didn't. Herr Bergmann simply nodded, in recognition. He knew that they had already come for her, and though Kristoff wanted to ask whether she was okay, whether she could come back here, he held his tongue out of fear.

"What about the children?" Herr Bergmann asked sharply.

Kristoff wasn't sure whether it would anger them to know about the *Kindertransport*, that Elena and Miriam had left the country. So he simply said that they had left, too, gone to Vienna, which was also the truth.

Herr Bergmann nodded again, seeming satisfied. "And you were the engraver's apprentice?"

"Yes," Kristoff said.

"And you know how to use the tools?"

"Yes," Kristoff said again.

"Good, then we have rid the place of Jews. And we have kept all the equipment and your expertise." He ran his hand across the worktable, over the burins and the chiseling tools. Kristoff swallowed hard, fighting back all the angry words he felt building up inside of him. "I've come here with a request for you. A job from the Führer himself. You should feel very honored," Herr Bergmann said.

Kristoff felt full of anger. He did not want to do anything Herr Bergmann—or Hitler—asked of him. But he knew they weren't actually asking. He couldn't say no. Perhaps that was why Herr Bergmann had brought the soldiers along, in case they'd found Kristoff uncooperative. "Yes?" Kristoff heard himself saying, trying his best to sound eager, though he was certain he was failing. That Herr Bergmann could see straight through him.

But he appeared not to have noticed. "The Führer would like to have some new German postage stamps, paying homage to the beautiful places that now belong to Germany. Scenes from Österreich, if you will."

"Scenes from Österreich?" Kristoff repeated. Pay homage to the beautiful places of Austria? It seemed at odds with burning them down, didn't it? But again, he didn't speak his mind.

"Yes, come up with some sketches. Landmarks, scenery. We have pride in Österreich. We want to show this on our stamps." He stared closely at Kristoff's face as he spoke, and Kristoff tried not to react to any of Herr Bergmann's words with the horror he was feeling. "I'll be back in a few weeks to see what you've come up with. The Führer himself will choose the ones he likes best and you will engrave those into plates to make into stamps." He paused and stroked his mustache. "We will compensate you, of course."

"Of course," Kristoff murmured. It made his stomach churn to think of drawing sketches for the Führer's approval. Taking money for it. That Hitler would see and touch and enjoy his sketches made him feel even more ill.

Herr Bergmann raised his hand in a salute. "Heil Hitler," he said, and the soldiers followed suit.

Kristoff raised his hand up and did the same, but after the men left, his stomach continued to heave, and he ran outside to be sick.

❊

It was hard to focus on the beauty of Austria, the awe Kristoff had once felt in Vienna as a boy. He'd used his sketch of Stephensdom in order to get his apprenticeship, and Frederick had told him then he had a good eye. He remembered once having sketched the Opera House from just across the plaza. It was a lazy summer day, and he'd taken his lunch from the orphanage—a stale piece of bread with apricot jam (because it was summer, and Sister Marta made her own apricot preserves especially for the boys). He'd sat in a patch of grass, his sketchbook on his lap, and had drawn all the beauty of the Opera House with this feeling of greatness filling up his bones: the vast blue summer sky above him, the sounds of chirping of birds and the smell of newly opened flowers, of his own freedom, surrounding him.

Sitting in the workshop, cold and alone, Kristoff wished that he could feel as happy and free as the memory of that day in Vienna. He wished that he didn't understand the pain of a synagogue burning, of Mrs. Faber being stolen from her home, of Frederick being forced to stay away from a profession that he loved, and most of all of Miriam and Elena having to run. *Elena*. He wished he had never met her. Never kissed her cold lips in the woods. The emptiness he felt now was never-ending, unyielding. Could he run from that, from here? Just abandon the engraving tools, the Fabers' house, Frederick and Josef. Just disappear onto the streets of Vienna that once had been his own. Could he get it back, that feeling of contentment and peace? Could he forget about Grotsburg, flames, engraving plates, burins, Elena's lips?

Every time he closed his eyes he saw her. He could still taste her, still smell the apricot of her hair. He knew he would not be able to forget about her, no matter where he went.

And anyway, Kristoff couldn't run away. He wasn't a runner. He did not abandon people who needed him, the way his mother once left him on the steps of the orphanage. As tempting as it was, he knew he couldn't leave Frederick's fate in Josef's hands. He couldn't abandon the Fabers' home and Frederick's workshop either. He'd promised Frederick he would look after it, keep it safe. Kristoff didn't break his promises.

And so Kristoff drew what Herr Bergmann asked of him. *Scenes from Österreich*. He drew them from memory, the beautiful buildings in Vienna, which he realized he had no idea now whether or not they were still standing. But he drew them as they were, the Austria he knew, the Austria he once loved.

※

Kristoff showed his sketches to Frederick a few days later. He carried his sketchbook with him, along with the food he brought to Frederick daily. As he walked through the woods he was careful to check if anyone was following him, since he didn't know exactly when Herr Bergmann and the soldiers might return. But no one was. Kristoff was all alone, living in more solitude than he ever had. The quiet haunted him, and he had trouble sleeping at night inside the Fabers' large empty house, all by himself.

Kristoff walked inside the tiny cabin, and found Frederick sitting on the floor this afternoon, leaning up against the wall, reading a book Kristoff had brought him earlier in the week. Kristoff had pulled a pile out of Frederick's former study, and the one Frederick was reading now was *Edelweiss* by Berthold Auerbach.

"Good book?" Kristoff asked as he walked inside and set the bread and hard cheese by Frederick.

Frederick's face looked so thin, his still-singed beard seemed to hang at an unnatural angle, and his hand that had gotten frostbite did not look so good. He'd unraveled the bandage and his fingertips had a greenish-bluish cast. It was his left hand, though, at least, and Frederick was right-handed. So he would be able to draw and engrave again. *Someday.*

"I've read this before," Frederick said, his voice quieter than usual, nostalgic, and perhaps in rereading it he was remembering another time, a happy time. "You know what Auerbach says of the edelweiss flower?" Kristoff shook his head. He had never come across this particular book in the orphanage. "He says, 'the possession of one is a proof of unusual daring.'" Frederick paused to take a bite of the stale bread.

Kristoff knew the special meaning of the edelweiss flower, how important it was in Austria, how it symbolized purity and love, nobility. How the flowers grew in the most unexpected and hard-to-reach places high up in the mountains. But he'd never before heard this particular expression.

"You know many men have died trying to go up to the rocky cliffs where the edelweiss grow. They want to show their love for a special fräulein, perhaps, give her such a beautiful, noble flower. And they are stupid, who knows." Frederick grimaced.

"Proof of unusual daring," Kristoff repeated.

"That's why I made the edelweiss stamp, you know?" Frederick's voice grew raspier. "I wanted to give my Minna an edelweiss flower of her own, but I didn't plan on dying doing it." His eyes filled with tears, and he turned away from Kristoff.

Kristoff leaned down, touched Frederick's shoulder gently. He wanted to comfort Frederick, to tell him that everything would be okay, but he wasn't sure it would be, and he couldn't bring himself to lie. "It was a beautiful stamp," he said instead. "A beautiful gift. I bet she loved it."

Frederick wiped his eyes a little with his good hand. "At least the girls will be safe now," he murmured. "The best things I ever created. Better than any stamp." Kristoff wondered what it would be like to create a person, a child, and he wasn't sure he ever would want to. That he would have it in himself to be a father knowing how terrible and cruel the world can be.

"If nothing else," Frederick said, "at least the girls will be safe in England." He put his book down, and finished off the food. "What's that?" he asked, suddenly noticing the sketch pad Kristoff had brought along with him, and Kristoff hesitated before handing it over and explaining what had happened with Herr Bergmann and the soldiers.

Frederick took the sketch pad and began to flip through. "These are very good," he said. "The Führer will be pleased with you."

"I hate that." Kristoff felt anger rising in him, his neck flushing with warmth in the cold cabin. "I hate him." He was nearly shouting. He felt nauseous again.

"I know," Frederick said calmly. He handed Kristoff back the sketch pad. "But better he should be pleased than you should disappoint him, my boy."

※

Kristoff thought about what Frederick had said on the freezing, lonely walk back to the house. So it was better to please a madman than to anger him? Better to do what he asked than to fight him? But he'd promised Elena in the woods, the day he'd kissed her.

You'll fight them, won't you, Kristoff?

Working with them, making the stamps they wanted, beautiful scenes from Österreich, seemed the exact opposite of fighting them.

Kristoff gathered firewood from the dwindling pile and walked inside the house to light a fire in the dining room. The table looked long and empty, almost foreboding. It was a Friday night, and the house was so cold, so empty. No one had a baked a challah—he didn't have the slightest inkling how to—and the house was devoid of all its former good, warm smells that Friday nights and the Sabbath had always brought.

Kristoff tried to remember where Mrs. Faber kept the Shabbat candles. He went into the kitchen and searched through the cupboards until he found them, and he walked back into the dining room, put them on the table, and lit them.

He'd memorized the Hebrew prayer from many Friday nights of listening to the Fabers say the words.

All the Jews are gone, Herr Bergmann had said.

And Kristoff's voice quivered a little as he spoke out loud: *Baruch atah, Adonai, Eloheinu . . .*

You'll fight them, won't you, Kristoff?

For the moment, that felt like a start.

Cardiff, 1989

I'M EXHAUSTED BY THE TIME Benjamin and I reach Wales. After two long flights and a train ride from London to Cardiff, I'm not sure what time it is or even what day at this point, but it's still light out, and my stomach tells me I've missed a meal. Or two. Everything I see out the train window appears stunning, magical, a world so far away from Southern California that we might as well not be on the same planet. The English countryside is quaint, foggy, and quite green, which turns eventually into the murky Bristol Channel, which we cross just before we get to Cardiff proper, a city of old European buildings, castles and spires, misty green lawns that seem to stretch for days.

On the plane I tried to make small talk with Benjamin. I asked him again why he didn't like Thanksgiving, and he only shrugged and said this week was a good time for him to get out of the country. Then he put on his headphones, turned on his Walkman, and opened his book, and I gathered he wasn't interested in talking any more. As the train finally arrives in Cardiff, I realize I might actually agree with him, that it is an amazing thing to be out of LA this week, where thousands of miles away from us, the people I used to love, I used to call my family, will soon be drinking too much wine and stuffing themselves on Daniel's mother's dry turkey and burned rosemary potatoes. I went to visit my dad yesterday before we left and told him I was going on a trip to the UK, that I wouldn't be with him for Thanksgiving, and though I felt guilty, he hadn't seemed to mind. He'd asked a lot of questions about where I was going, what I was doing, and I only told him I was flying to London and taking a train to Wales, without mentioning Mrs. Kleinfelter or the stamp.

"It's beautiful here," I say to Benjamin as the train slows to approach the station. He grunts a little, having fallen asleep on the train, and I'm amazed by his ability to sleep in these uncomfortable seats. He'd slept on the plane for a while as well, but I've been awake the entire long time.

"You've never been to Wales?" Benjamin asks, stretching, yawning.

I shake my head. "You?"

"Once," he says. "Years ago. With my wife."

"Your wife?" So Benjamin has a wife? I feel oddly disappointed at the thought. I'd assumed that by coming here, this week, he has no one, like me. That we had something in common. I took care of booking our rooms at the Cardiff Marriott through the travel agent who'd booked a trip to Hawaii for me and Daniel a few years ago, and I made sure to request separate rooms, deciding to worry about the pounds-to-dollars conversion later, when I get my Visa bill. But I can't imagine his wife is happy about this, even with separate rooms. "You didn't want to spend Thanksgiving with her?" I ask him.

"She's dead now," he says, and he puts his hand to his mouth as if he's shocked he mentioned her at all. He hadn't meant to, I realize. The never-ending travel and bizarre sleeps of the past two days had made him say something to me he probably wouldn't have back in LA.

"I'm sorry," I say, and I really am. "I had no idea."

The train comes to a stop and Benjamin stands, grabbing both of our bags from the luggage rack overhead.

"I can take mine," I say.

"I've got it." He walks toward the front quickly, his arms laden with the bags, and it feels less a gesture of kindness than a need to occupy himself with something else, to run away from me, much the same way he ran out of my house last week.

❀

I fall asleep after a room service plate of Glamorgan sausage, which is tasty in spite of the fact that it tastes nothing like any sausage I've ever eaten before. The reputation that the Brits have for bad food seems to be wrong. Or maybe I'm just starving.

I sleep better than I have at home for weeks, months. I don't dream, and I don't wake up until I hear a knock on the door the following morning, Benjamin's voice calling for me.

It's daytime; the room is somewhat light, and I hear raindrops against the window. I get out of bed, throw on a robe over my nightgown, and answer the door. "What time is it?" I ask him. I'm not exactly sure what day it is either. Wednesday? Thursday?

"It's ten o'clock," Benjamin says, walking into my room. He

holds two Styrofoam cups and hands me one. I take a sip expecting coffee, but it's tea, strong and bitter, and I make a face. "I thought you'd be up," Benjamin says. "Sorry I woke you." His voice is soft, sweet, kind. I remember what he said yesterday about his wife being dead, and I'm sad for him.

"No, it's okay. I'm glad you did." Now that I'm awake I feel eager to do what we've come for, to go deliver this letter to its intended recipient at long last. "Just give me ten minutes to get dressed." I put the Styrofoam cup down. "And I have to find some coffee. They do have coffee in Wales, right?"

Benjamin laughs, says he's sure they do, and that he'll meet me in the lobby. He looks different than he did yesterday, more relaxed. He turns and walks out slowly and I'm glad that he seems to be done running away from me.

❋

Half an hour later, we're in a cab on our way to the nursing home. Benjamin located some coffee while I got dressed, and I drink it on the way even though it's bitter, terrible, acidic. I should have stuck with the tea.

Mrs. Kleinfelter's nursing home is a place called Raintree, and it's by the River Taff, not too far from the hotel, but far enough we can't walk. And I wouldn't want to anyway in the rain. My hair is already four times its normal size, and I forgot to pack an umbrella. Benjamin has come more prepared and he offers to share.

Raintree is located in a brick building that I bet has been here already for two hundred years or more, because it looks old, and also dank, dirty, shabbily upkept. It's a far cry from Santa Monica, and the Willows. And though the inside is a bit newer and shinier-looking, it smells too strongly of Lysol, and the reception area in front shines a putrid yellow from the terrible fluorescent lights buzzing overhead.

"We're here to see Mrs. Kleinfelter," I tell the nurse at reception.

"Americans, are you?" She scowls a little. It's possible Benjamin and I are the first Americans to visit Raintree. Maybe ever.

"Yes," Benjamin answers. "We're visiting from California." I elbow him, wanting him to stay quiet. Whatever bad things we Californians think about British food, the Brits probably hate everything about us "LA types" ten times more.

"You're family?" she asks.

I'm not sure if she'll let us back, if we say no. So I quickly say yes before Benjamin can answer truthfully. "Distantly," I add. The nurse raises her thin-penciled brown eyebrows and I'm not sure if that's to register her surprise or disbelief. "Well good on you, then, for making the trip," she finally says. "Twelve-C." Then she adds, with a dry laugh, "Best of British to ya."

"Is she lucid today?" I ask tentatively, hoping Mrs. Kleinfelter is in better shape than my father.

The nurse laughs again. "She's full of beans, she is." I'm not sure what to make of that, but I'll see for myself soon enough, so I just murmur a thanks. She points down the hallway, presumably toward the direction of 12C.

I feel a sudden deep sadness for Mrs. Kleinfelter as we walk down the dimly lit yellow hallway, which smells faintly of urine. I get glimpses inside tiny hospital-looking dark rooms along the way. The inside of this place is even more depressing than the outside.

We stop when we reach 12C. The door is slightly ajar and I can hear the sounds of the television on inside. I feel nervous, and my hands shake as I reach inside my bag to pull out the letter I've been walking around with for weeks. *A gem*. But maybe it's not. And maybe she won't remember, even if it is.

Benjamin steps forward and knocks lightly on the door. "Mrs. Kleinfelter?" he calls into the room.

"I already told ya, I'm not taking any more of those pills," she yells.

Benjamin pushes the door open more, and takes a step inside. I do the same, my breath suspended in my chest, unable to speak for a moment, as Benjamin says, "We don't have any pills for you."

Mrs. Kleinfelter sits in a wheelchair by the window, her left leg braced and extended outward, somewhat unnaturally. She has gray hair, long, wispy, pulled mostly back into a braid, but it's still speckled with brown, a remainder of her youth. She doesn't seem as old as I've pictured her in my mind. Younger than Gram. Maybe younger than my father.

She looks at Benjamin, then at me, and she frowns. "You got the wrong bloody room, I tell you then."

"No." I finally find my voice, and I step forward. "I'm Katie. You don't know me, but I think I have something that might have been meant for you once." My hands are still shaking as I take the letter from its plastic sleeve and hand it over to her. "My father has been a stamp collector his whole life, and I came across this letter when I was going through his collection."

As soon as I say "stamp," she seems to perk up a little, and she takes the letter from my hand and gestures to the metal nightstand. "Get me my glasses." Benjamin does, and she puts them on, and holds the envelope close up to her face.

"You were Fräulein Faber once, right?" I ask, hoping we haven't come all this way only to have her say we're in the wrong place.

She lowers the letter, places it in her lap. "I was Fräulein Faber. Once." She hands the letter back to me, and she frowns. "But you're wrong. This letter wasn't meant for me. It was meant for my sister."

Austria, 1938

M Y SISTER HELD on to my hand as we walked through the woods, leaving our home, everything we had ever known behind. We had both packed small sacks with our belongings. She'd packed some clothes and some books and I'd packed clothes and a few art supplies I'd taken from Kristoff's room in the attic. I wasn't sure if he'd miss them after I was gone. I imagined him puzzled, looking through his stash only to find it smaller than he'd remembered, but would he ever think of me as the culprit? Would he ever think of me again, at all? Probably not. I was just the little girl who annoyed him with my nonsense, as my mother had called it. *Stop pestering Kristoff with your girlish nonsense.* She'd meant that pesky mouse in the wall, that I'd invented so Kristoff would come into my room and talk to me. So I was thirteen and Kristoff was eighteen or nineteen, but what was five years? Father was seven years older than Mother, anyway. Not that Kristoff ever looked twice at me when Elena was in the room, too.

"Miri, keep up," Elena said to me. The snow was so deep and the air was so cold, but I wanted to walk through the woods slowly, to remember all of it forever: the feel of the snow seeping through my worn boots, the sharp smell of the fir trees, the pale gray color of the winter sky. Elena had told me that we were going to England together on a train, a *Kindertransport*, that we would be happier and safer in England, and that it was all only temporary. But that morning, as we trod through the snow, I suspected she was lying about all of it.

"What if we just stay?" I asked her as we reached the Bauers' farm. I remembered coming here as a little girl when Herr and Frau Bauer were still alive. We didn't have close relatives—Father's family had disowned him years before I was born when he'd married Mother out of order from his older sisters, and Mother's relatives were almost all dead. So the Bauers were like our family, and we'd celebrated many Passovers and Rosh Hashanahs at their farm, up until a few years ago when Herr and Frau Bauer both fell ill and passed within a few months of each other.

Josef was a few years older than Elena and always bigger than us. When we were kids he used to chase us around the chicken coop. Once, I fell in the mud and started crying and Josef, probably no more than ten, taunted me: *hampelmann*. My mother told me Frau Bauer later washed his mouth out with soap for being so rude to an innocent little girl. And I'd felt pleased that I'd elicited such a punishment for him, big bad ten-year-old Josef.

But Josef was a man now, so serious and worried, the way Herr Bauer used to look. Always frowning. He was frowning as he stood there outside the main house, waiting for us. "You're late," he barked at Elena.

But she didn't apologize. My sister apologized for nothing. Ever.

That's the way she always was. "We'll make up the time on the road," she said instead, jutting out her chin, as if to make herself a little taller in Josef's large presence.

Josef knew a man with a car, who was willing to drive Jews, to hide us in the backseat the two hundred kilometers to Vienna, Elena had told me this morning before we left. I hadn't asked how he knew this man, or what should happen to us all if we were caught. I couldn't stop thinking of my mother, being pulled out of our house by German soldiers while Elena and I hid in the floor in Father's workshop. I tried not to imagine what happened next, where she was now. But I knew it wasn't England.

Josef reached into his coat pocket and handed Elena an envelope. Our tickets, I assumed. "You are only sixteen," he said to her, gruffly. "They are only taking children younger than seventeen, so if anyone asks . . ." Really Elena was almost eighteen, but she was short, and beautiful enough so that no man would question her, I was sure.

She took the tickets from Josef and put them in her bag, and she ushered me into the backseat of the stranger's car and told me to crouch down low. She went to get in, too, but Josef grabbed her, folded her tiny body up into a hug. "Be safe," he commanded her, but she didn't answer. She pulled herself away and got into the car with me. I tried not to cry; I tried to be brave the way Father would tell me to if he were here.

"What if we just stayed," I said again as the car jolted forward and we rolled on the floor of the backseat. Elena held on, clutching the side of the car. "We could hide in the cabin with Father for a little while longer." I was desperate to get out of the car. My stomach roiled, and I thought I might be sick. And Elena would kill me if I got sick all over her.

"Miri," Elena said harshly. "This is what we have to do. Be quiet so the man can get us to Vienna safely."

❋

The last time I'd been to Vienna was the summer I'd turned ten. Father and Mother took us into the city to see an opera. We'd all dressed in our best clothing—Mother had bought me a new dress for the occasion, which rarely ever happened, since mostly I was forced to wear Elena's old clothing when she grew out of it. That dress had a lace bodice with a skirt that was the prettiest shade of blue I had ever seen. And I'd thought Vienna the grandest and most beautiful city in the entire world.

"What was the name of the opera?" I asked Elena as Josef's driver let us out at the train station and then sped off, into the rush of the city.

"What?" The station was crowded, so many children. Elena stood up on her tiptoes, trying to see through the crowds. The children surrounding us appeared mostly younger than me, their clothing more tattered. One little boy whom I guessed to be maybe eight or nine was holding on to a baby, who was crying, and the boy looked bewildered; he didn't understand how to comfort the baby. I wondered what had happened to the baby's mother, and why this silly boy was in charge. But after everything we heard and read about *die Kristallnacht*, I grew afraid that the baby's mother was dead, gone. Murdered.

I looked away. "The opera we saw, when we came to Vienna with Mother and Father," I asked Elena. "What was the name of it?"

"Miri." She said my name with an air of exasperation, and she held on tighter to my arm, afraid she'd lose me in this crowd of lost and forlorn children, though I was much too old to be a child who could get lost. "Why does your mind always have to wander into such silliness? I'm trying to figure out where to get on the train."

"I just want one perfect memory," I said softly, and I wasn't sure she heard me, because she didn't say anything else about it. But that was all I wanted, one complete, perfect memory of my family, in Vienna, when it was wonderful still, when it was whole, when we were whole, dressed up in beautiful new clothing, listening to beautiful new music.

"Come on." Elena tugged on my arm and pulled me forward, yanking me through the crowd, bumping me into other children who were younger, sadder. She stopped when we reached the line that had begun to form to board the train.

The train was already at the station, and the children who had tickets were showing them to a uniformed train worker. The children in front of us got on board, one by one. Some of them were crying, and no one hugged them, or told them to stop. Elena pulled us into the line, and she took the tickets from her bag.

We inched forward slowly, and though it was very cold here, nearly as cold as it had been in the woods in Grotsburg, I found myself sweating, a trickle of sweat running under my braid, down my back. I unbuttoned my coat a little, and no one noticed, told me not to.

When at last we reached the front of the line, Elena handed our tickets to the uniformed man, and he barely glanced at them; no one asked her age or mine. He just ushered us on board, where Elena pulled us to a seat and then exhaled.

"Miri," she said to me as I sat down. "I want you to promise me something." I was still sweating. I unbuttoned my coat the rest of the way. "No matter what happens, no matter what I do, I want you to stay on this train, follow their instructions, and go on to England. Promise me." She shook my shoulders a little.

"Okay," I said. "I promise. We'll go together."

She didn't say anything else, and she turned so she wasn't looking at me any longer. She reached for my hand, and I held on to her. Our fingers laced tightly. When I was a little girl, Mother always had Elena hold on to my hand whenever we went anywhere. Her fingers were always so much bigger than mine, except now, they were exactly the same size. Elena still saw me as a little girl. But I wasn't.

The train began to move, slowly pulling out from the station, and Elena let go of me. "Elena," I said, but I already knew what she was doing, already understood what was happening. "Don't!" I cried out.

But she didn't turn back. She pushed her way through all the children and made it to the door we'd come on at.

I blinked, and then she was gone.

Wales, 1989

IUDITTA," MIRIAM SAYS, snapping her fingers, as if it has just come to her again. "That was the name of the opera we saw that night in Vienna." Her expression is far away. Maybe she's remembering that night, exactly as she once wished to, whole, perfect.

"So you listened to Elena?" Benjamin asks her, not tuning in to her quiet moment of nostalgia. I nudge him a little; I don't want him to make her angry. I don't want her to stop talking, to ask us to leave. I want to hear the rest of her story.

"Yes," she says. "I listened to Elena. I took the train all the way across the Netherlands and Belgium. Then I boarded a ship to Harwich. I was taken in by the Winslows, who lived in Bristol, and they let me stay with them until the end of the war. I was one of the lucky ones."

"And Elena?" I ask, feeling a sinking dread for Miriam's sister, the actual recipient of this letter, so Miriam says.

She shakes her head. "After that day on the train, I never saw my sister again." She wipes at her eyes. This poor woman. She was forced out of her home as a teenager, sent to England, abandoned by her sister on a train. And all these years later, we just barged into her depressing room in Raintree and unearthed it all again.

"What happened to Elena?" Benjamin is asking. "Where did she go?"

"Presumably she went back to Grotsburg. She probably would've said she was going back to fight the Germans." She laughs, bitterly. "But I think she really went back for Kristoff. She was in love with him, you know. And love makes us do the stupidest things." Then she adds, "She loved him more than she loved me."

"I'm sure that wasn't true," I say. Benjamin looks at his shoes, and I wonder if he's thinking about his wife. Daniel and I never had the kind of love that made us do anything even remotely stupid, and maybe that was half our problem.

"I went back to Austria, once. Years after the war. In the sixties. My Herbie went with me. But it was all gone by then." She folds her hands in her lap and looks down at them. I nod, remembering the differences between the old map and the modern-day one Gram pointed out to me. "I searched after the war, and eventually found my mother died in Mauthausen. But my father, Elena, Kristoff, even Josef. I was never able to find out what happened to them." She shrugs. "It's why I've been looking for my father's stamps all these years. I always thought if Elena had made it, survived the war, if she was alive, *somewhere*, then certainly she'd be looking for pieces of our father, too. And she'd be looking for me, don't you think? But every collector I've talked to has never heard of her or gotten any inquiries from anyone like her."

"And this wasn't one of your father's stamps?" Benjamin asks, handing the letter back to her once again. "You're certain?"

"Yes. I've never seen it before," she says. "And it's a Deutsches

Reich stamp. So it couldn't have been him." Couldn't have been him because her father was a Jew, and he wouldn't have been allowed to engrave stamps anymore after Hitler took over Austria. "It could've been Kristoff," she says. "But I don't know. He was only an apprentice when I lived there. I'm not sure he could've pulled this off."

"Kristoff wasn't Jewish, then?" She shakes her head, and her face turns, like she might start to cry. "I can't imagine how terrible this must have all been for you," I say.

"I suppose it was," she says. "But I don't remember it that way. We had a very nice life. We were always happy. Right up until *die Kristallnacht*." She pauses, lost in the recollection of it. "Then I was only in Austria for a few more weeks after that. And in England, the Winslows doted on me. They were never able to have children and here a teenage girl fell into their lap. They were my second parents for many years. God rest their souls." She laughs a little. "It's funny you showed up to see me here, of all places. This place is like my penance, you know?"

"Penance?" I raise my eyebrows, not understanding.

"I spent so many pounds buying up my father's stamps all these years. Then I fell and broke my bloody hip and the surgery went all wrong. Doctor said I might never walk again. And because I spent so much of our savings on stamps, we just really couldn't afford any private care at home to help with the rehabilitation. So here I am, public health's finest." Her words come out in a rush, and for a second, it seems like she really might cry, but then she smiles instead. "Poor Herbie is just all broken up about it. I'm the tough one of the two of us. I'll muddle through it." She laughs. "And besides, I won't be here forever."

I smile at the idea of her poor broken-up Herbie, and at her insistence that this place is only temporary. Thank god.

"So here you are." Miriam hands me back the letter. "I can't buy it from you. One, because I really don't have the money to do it. And two, because it isn't mine. It was never meant for me."

"But are you sure?" Benjamin asks. "You wouldn't want to open it up and see? Be certain?" He seems impatient, the way I have for weeks, to know what's written inside. But I can't believe he's actually asked her to open it and diminish any possible value of the stamp, which has been his concern all along. I shoot him a look.

"Oh, I'm quite certain," Miriam says. "It's not mine. No one would've been sending me a love letter in Grotsburg in 1939." She pauses. "The edelweiss is an expression of love, you know. *Proof of unusual daring*, my father used to say. That's how you proved you loved a girl. You ventured to the most dangerous mountaintops to find an edelweiss to give her." She sighs. "And the only Fräulein Faber who Kristoff Mueller ever noticed, ever loved, was my sister."

❀

On the cab ride back to the hotel, Benjamin and I are both quiet. Before we left Miriam, she told us that if we had any more luck finding out what happened to Elena or the rest of her family than she ever had, that we must contact her immediately. I gave her my card, and I also promised her that we would keep in touch, but deep down I feel that Elena is most likely long dead. That we've come all this way to deliver this letter, to learn about this stamp, and we've found nothing but a spunky old woman with a broken hip, in debt from chasing too hard after her past. *At least she has Herbie.* At her age, I'll be divorced and all alone.

"You hungry?" Benjamin asks as we get out of the cab at the hotel. The rain has slowed to a drizzle. Not enough to need Benjamin's umbrella any longer, but just enough for my hair to get even puffier. I fluff my bangs a little with my fingers, but the effort's futile at this point. I'm not hungry, but I don't want to go back to my room yet either, so I nod. In all the singularity Daniel's departure has brought me—cups of coffee, glasses of wine, and king-size beds for one—somehow none of it has seemed as lonely as staying in a hotel room alone.

Instead of going into the hotel, we walk around the block to a small restaurant, go inside, and grab a booth. Benjamin orders a rarebit sandwich, and not being certain what that is and thinking it sounds too close to *rabbit*, I stick with the Glamorgan sausage again.

"You know that's not really sausage," Benjamin says, after the waitress takes our orders. I don't say anything, not willing to admit that I don't. "Leeks," he says. "And cheese."

"Well, I had some last night from room service, and it was delicious."

Benjamin looks genuinely puzzled at the fact that anyone could enjoy leeks in a sausage form, and I don't know if I'll like it again now that I'm not starving. But I do.

Benjamin's rarebit looks good, too, once I realize that a rarebit sandwich is something akin to a grilled cheese. Everything I have ever thought about British food is wrong. Where are the bangers and mash? The stale bread and dark ale? Wales seems like a beautiful world unto itself, and I wish I were here on vacation, with Daniel. *No, don't think about him.* He'll soon be walking up his mother's bougainvillea-lined front path without me, going inside her beautiful estate in Hidden Hills, sitting around her big dining room table with all his cousins, aunts, uncles . . .

Stop it, I tell myself. I want to erase all the images of Daniel from my head. All the Thanksgiving pasts. And I raise my cup of tea, which has been served ever so delicately in flowered china, despite the fact that this restaurant has a distinct dive-diner atmosphere. "Happy Thanksgiving," I say to Benjamin. That's what this is, our Thanksgiving meal. A rarebit sandwich, Glamorgan sausage, and tea.

Benjamin ignores me, and takes another bite of his sandwich. He's told me multiple times that he hates Thanksgiving. That's why he wanted to come here, this week. And I feel like an idiot.

"Sorry," I say. "How about Happy Rainy Day in Cardiff, then?"

"Isn't that just every day?" But he smiles a little, and raises his cup of tea to clink mine.

"I'm sorry you wasted your airline miles on this," I say, after I drink a little more tea.

"So that's it, then?" He finishes off his sandwich and wipes his hands with a thin paper napkin from the dispenser on the side of the table. "You're done? Giving up?"

I shake my head. "Poor Miriam doesn't know what happened to her sister. I can't give up. I'm just not sure what to do next."

Elena took Miriam all the way to safety and then she jumped off a train just on the precipice of being safe herself. I could never do anything like that. I'd be terrified of jumping, of the ground moving beneath my feet. Of the Germans who would've made my home unsafe. But from Miriam's description, Elena was nothing like me. She was fearless, beautiful, unapologetic. So what happened to her, then? Did she make it back to Grotsburg, to her father's apprentice, Kristoff, whom she loved? Or did the Germans arrest her before she ever got back there?

❀

Benjamin and I split the check and then walk back to the hotel, in silence. It's no longer raining, the sun is almost out, and once we hit the lobby Benjamin grunts a goodbye and darts off. Running away from me again. But he was acting even more distant than usual on the walk back. And I'm glad to be rid of him.

I don't feel like going upstairs yet, and I decide to go back out and explore Cardiff instead. I'm here, why not? Why do I need Daniel, any man for that matter, to explore a new city?

I meander through the streets, taking in the beautiful lush greenery, the dank, earthy smells, all the way to the university: beautiful brick and ivy buildings. And then on the way back, I walk toward the giant stone-walled Cardiff Castle, which sits atop a grassy hill, and I climb what feels like a hundred steps to wander inside the castle.

I explore for a long time, reveling in the thick damp air that clings to me, in the feeling of my own silent steps, the weight of my aloneness. I walk and I walk until my feet are sore and blistered, and I don't make it back to the hotel until it's nearly dark.

Austria, 1938

KRISTOFF STARED at the flames of Mrs. Faber's Shabbat candles on the dining room table: two little flickers of light. That was all. And yet if Herr Bergmann were to choose this moment to return, Kristoff knew he could be arrested, killed. Still, he spoke the prayer aloud, defiantly: *Baruch atah, Adonai, Eloheinu melech ha'olom* . . .

"You're saying it wrong." Her voice came out of the darkness, softly, and at first, Kristoff thought he imagined it. So he kept on reciting the prayer until he finished with a *shel Shabbat*. "It's not 'me-like,' it's 'mellick.'" Her voice was louder this time.

"Elena?" He whispered her name into the darkness, afraid if he spoke it any louder she would disappear, a figment of his imagination, a ghost. Because she couldn't be here. She'd gone on the *Kindertransport* with Miri last week.

He heard a noise, the dining chairs were moving, and she crawled out from underneath the table. "I heard someone come into the house, and I wasn't sure whether it was you, until I heard you butchering our prayer." She stood, waved her cupped hands in front of the candles, and whispered the prayer herself once, quickly.

Then she turned to face him and she raised her eyebrows a little. "So . . . what? You're a Jew now, Kristoff?"

"Elena?" He said her name a little louder, as loud as he dared, and he reached out to put his hand on her face, if only to feel that it was really her, that she was real. Her skin was just as soft, almost as cold as it had been that day in the snowy woods when he'd kissed her. His lips grew warm, at just the memory of it. "Why are you here?" he asked her. "You're not supposed to be here." He moved his hand from her face, to her shoulder, so glad to touch her, to feel her close, but he was afraid for her, too. "You're supposed to be in England."

"I got Miri on the train. She'll be safe."

"But what about you?"

"I told you. I don't care about myself." She pulled away from him, lest she might feel from the warmth of his hand on her shoulder that he cared, that she should care, too. "Someone has to fight, Kristoff. If we all run away, who will be left to fight them?"

"Me," he said, though even as he spoke the word it felt like a lie. What was Elena going to think of the sketches he'd already done at Herr Bergmann's request?

"But I don't want to run away," Elena said. "This is my home." Her voice broke a little on the word *home*, as if realizing the possibility that this house, the place she'd spent her entire life, and Kristoff had spent the best year of his, might never truly be home again. Frederick was hiding in squalor, Miri on her way to England, Mrs. Faber missing.

"There has to be another train out," Kristoff said. "You'll get on the next one. I'll take you to Vienna myself."

She laughed a little and folded her arms across her chest. She would do whatever she pleased. She always did. She turned and began to walk toward the back door.

"Elena, wait," he called after her, and she stopped for a moment and turned back toward him. "Where are you going?" She didn't answer, and kept walking toward the door. "The Germans have been here. They're coming back. I'm supposed to be designing some new Österreich stamps for them."

"The Germans," she spat back at him. "And if they could only see you now, with your Shabbat candles." She walked out the back door, letting it slam hard behind her. Her words hurt him, a new physical pain in his stomach that he hadn't been expecting.

It took him a moment to recover. He grabbed a lantern, used a Shabbat candle to light it, and blew out the candles (though he knew that you were not supposed to do that). He fanned the smoke with his hands to make sure they were out, and he took the lantern and ran out after her.

At first he could see her footsteps in the snow. He followed them, into the woods, past the turnoff for the small cabin where Frederick was. He lost track of her footsteps, as snow was coming down, filling in her tracks, but he knew if she hadn't gone straight to her father, she must've gone to Josef first. At least he hoped she had. He hoped she wasn't stupid or defiant enough to walk into town.

He reached the edge of the Bauers' property, and he could see that inside the house, the lights were on. He saw the shape of Josef's back, reaching down, scooping Elena up in a hug, and, feeling somewhat disgusted, and embarrassed, Kristoff turned and went back toward the house.

He lay awake in bed for a long time, listening for the sounds of the back door or the steps creaking, but he never heard them, and eventually, he fell asleep.

He awoke sometime later, his room filled with darkness. The middle of the night. But Elena was back; he could sense that she was here, in his room. He felt his bed shift as she climbed in and lay down next to him. Her face was close enough to his that he could feel the warmth of her breath on his earlobe. *She was real.* He was afraid to speak, afraid to move. Elena was in his bed.

"Can I just stay here? Just tonight?" she asked.

"Yes." The word escaped him hoarsely, barely audible.

Her body sighed against the mattress, and she shifted closer into him. He moved his arm, put it around her tiny shoulders, pulled her even closer, and she lay her head against his chest. Her warm cheek rested against his heart. When she fell asleep, her body went limp and her breathing evened, but he didn't let her go. He wouldn't ever let her go again. He promised himself.

✳

When he awoke the next day, sunlight streaming in through his window, he was all alone. Was Elena being in his bed a dream? Had he willed Elena here by sheer force of his imagination, his wanting? But he could still feel the weight of Elena's cheek on his chest, conjure the slight scent of apricots in her hair. *He had not imagined her.*

He got dressed and walked out to Frederick's workshop, where he found Elena sitting at the table, flipping through the sketches he'd made in anticipation of Herr Bergmann's imminent return.

"These are very good," she said, not looking up to acknowledge his presence, or to explain her visit to his bed last night. Not that she needed to. He was glad she had come to him. Though he felt shy around her now. "But do you think your metal skills are good enough to engrave them? All this detail . . ." Elena's finger gently traced the many intricate details, the small windows and arches he'd sketched from memory on the Opera House.

"I don't know." Truthfully, he wasn't sure he could engrave these well. But he hadn't thought that far ahead. He'd worried only about the sketches. About Herr Bergmann coming back and liking them enough to think Kristoff was valuable to the Germans, that Kristoff deserved to be keeper of this house, the engraving workshop and tools, his station as a stamp engraver in Austria. Kristoff had promised Frederick he'd keep this place safe, and it seemed working with the Germans was the only real way to do this. "I will have to," he finally said.

"Hmmm," she murmured, and she closed the sketchbook. "I talked to Josef last night about getting my father out of the country." Her voice turned brusque, as if she were conducting business. Any emotion she'd felt in the darkness in his room in the middle of the night had seemingly disappeared without a trace.

Kristoff nodded, wondering how Josef had felt about seeing Elena, back here. And Frederick, too. He dreaded the conversation he'd have with either one of them himself later. Josef, certainly, would blame him.

"I want to get him to America to go stay with his friend."

"America? Not England, to be with Miri?"

"He'd have nowhere to go in England. They're only taking children. He has a friend in America, and Miri can join him there, once he's settled. And Mother, too, eventually." She paused, and Kristoff understood that this was the real reason why she'd come back. She got Miri to safety and she wanted to do the same for both her parents. "I want to make him some papers, a visa with a different name, make him a non-Jew."

"Forgery," Kristoff said. Elena and Josef's plan for the engraving tools all along. The last time Elena brought it up, it had seemed like something vague, distant. Now it felt so close, dangerous, and Kristoff felt sick to his stomach. But he couldn't think of another way to help Frederick. The Germans thought Frederick was dead, and even if they didn't, Jews were no longer allowed to leave the country without paying the high German tax, which Frederick wouldn't have the money for, especially since he'd need to pay his passageway to America. "We'll be killed if we get caught," he said.

"And my father will die if he stays in that cabin for much longer." Elena spoke without hesitation. "He needs a doctor, for his hand. And he needs real food. And fresh air."

Elena was right. He didn't know how much longer Frederick truly could survive hiding out in the tiny cabin. And Elena had left Miri on a train to come back here, to fight; Kristoff couldn't be a coward. "If you or Josef can get a copy of actual exit papers, a visa, I'll help. I can draw out replicas for Frederick with a new name," he said.

Elena smiled at him, and jutted her chin out a little. "And I can engrave the plates." He remembered how Frederick had criticized her engraving plates once, believing them to be Kristoff's. Not precise enough. Too fast, too sloppy. But to the untrained eye, Kristoff thought they would look better, in fact, than his.

"How will we print them?" he asked.

Frederick had always taken his stamp engraving plates to Vienna to be printed by Herr Schweitzer, but that wouldn't do for this, and besides, who knew if Herr Schweitzer's place had been burned to the ground? Even if it was still there, Herr Schweitzer was certainly no longer running it. "Josef has a friend who's willing to do it," she said.

Of course. Josef always had an answer for everything, and Kristoff tried not to feel annoyed. He looked at Elena, and her face seemed softer, the way it had felt against his chest in his bed last night. "We're going to make papers for you, too," he said. "You want to stay and fight, but you also need a way out. I'm not going to let you fight to your death." She just stared at him, her expression unwavering. "I'm not," he repeated.

Wales, 1989

I ALMOST WALK RIGHT BY Benjamin sitting in the lounge bar when I get back to the hotel. But he notices me and calls out: "Kate, over here." It's strange that he's suddenly calling me Kate, which hardly anyone ever does, except my father. But he waves me over, and I drag my blistered feet in his direction.

He's drinking a mug of dark ale, probably not his first, because his cheeks are ruddier than usual, and that might explain the newly familiar way he called for me, too. "Have a drink with me," he says, motioning for me to sit down. I do, and I order a glass of white wine.

"Wine? In Wales?" Benjamin laughs when the waitress brings over my glass.

"I'm not much of a beer drinker." I take a slow sip.

"Me neither." He raises his mug of ale. "But when in Wales." He laughs again.

"How many of those have you had?" I ask.

He doesn't answer, and anyway it's not my business. "I came up to your room to look for you," he says instead. "But you weren't there."

"I decided to walk around, explore the city a little." I tell him about the beautiful castle, the hundreds of steps and the ancient stone walls.

"You know what you should do?" He's slurring his words the tiniest bit. "You should write travel guides."

"What?" I laugh a little and take another sip of my wine.

"You're a writer, right? Instead of those movie reviews you should write travel books."

I'm not sure how Benjamin knows what I write (has he looked up my reviews?) or how desperately I need to find a new job. Maybe he doesn't. Maybe he's just had too much to drink. "Anyway," I say. "You said you came up to my room. You were looking for me?"

"I was thinking . . . Faber's apprentice, Kristoff. I've never heard of him before."

"So?"

"So let's say he did make this stamp. Maybe he made others for the Third Reich, too."

I shrug; I still don't understand what he's getting at.

"Miriam said she thought he wrote this letter, maybe made this stamp, that her sister went back to Austria for him. He wasn't Jewish. Maybe he made a lot of stamps. Maybe he survived the war?" He pauses and finishes off his ale. "Maybe we've been looking for the wrong person. Maybe we don't want to find Elena, Fräulein Faber. Maybe we should be trying to find Kristoff?"

"So you didn't waste your miles, then, did you?" I'm not sure Benjamin and I ever would've known about Kristoff if it hadn't been for Miriam sharing her story with us earlier.

Benjamin sips his ale and then keeps talking. "I know this professor at Oxford who specializes in World War Two–era history."

"Oxford? How far is that from here?"

"Not far. A train ride."

"Can we go there, ask him about Kristoff and our letter?" I hear my voice rising with excitement, though I've misspoken: the letter is not *ours*. It's mine, or my father's or Elena's or even Kristoff's. But it is certainly not ours, Benjamin's and mine.

But Benjamin doesn't seem to notice. "Yes," he says. "I gave him a call before I came down here. We can go tomorrow, if you want." I nod, I do. Benjamin motions for the waitress, and when she walks over, he asks for another Double Dragon. I'm starving from all the walking around, and I ask if she can bring me a rarebit sandwich.

We don't say much while we wait, but as the waitress brings everything over to our table, I ask him if he's ever been to Oxford before.

Benjamin doesn't answer me at first, and I take a huge bite of my sandwich—I'm so hungry I want to inhale the greasy cheese and bread. So there's no turkey or pumpkin pie, but my sandwich is delicious, and Thanksgiving—and my regular life—seems so far away. As I sit here in the dingy hotel pub in Cardiff, this is all that feels real.

"Yes," Benjamin finally answers me. "I've been to Oxford before."

"With your wife?" I venture cautiously, when he doesn't explain more.

"You ever been married?" he asks.

I hesitate before I answer him truthfully. "I'm in the midst of a divorce," I say, and it's the first time I've ever said that particular phrase out loud. I flinch a little.

"I'm sorry to hear that." He sounds genuinely sorry. "What happened?"

"I don't know. I wish I could just pick this one specific day or a fight and say, okay, this was the end of my marriage. But we hardly ever fought. My father's memory got worse and worse, and I was spending a lot of time at his house, helping him out. I guess Daniel and I, we just grew apart. And then he left me. I honestly can't really explain it."

"And that's just life, isn't it? All the small stupid things we can't explain." He drinks his new ale down. "It's been two years this week . . . since Sara and Davis were killed." His face contorts on the two names.

I want to know more, to understand this man sitting across from me, who has shown me nothing but kindness the past few weeks. But I also don't want to pry for details he's unwilling to share, so I just settle for saying that I'm sorry. I reach my hand across the table and put it on his arm. "That's why you hate Thanksgiving?" I wish he'd gone exploring the city with me, climbed up the stone steps in the fortress of the castle, the dampness of a thousand years invading his senses the way it had mine.

"It's a brutal holiday. Everyone has a family, everyone has something to be thankful for. And I have the anniversary of a fatal wreck on the 405." He sighs and finishes off his ale, but now he seems oddly sober, weary. "Sara used to fucking love it, too. It was her favorite time of the year." The harshness of the curse word sounds all wrong in Benjamin's even tone. I try to imagine him with a wife, this vibrant woman who loved things deeply. Maybe Benjamin was a completely different person then, two years ago. Maybe he was vibrant and loved Thanksgiving, too.

176 · Jillian Cantor

"And Davis?" I ask, tentatively.

Benjamin doesn't answer for a moment, like he might ignore my question. But then he says, "My son. They were hit by a drunk driver who was going the wrong way. Killed on impact. He would've turned three next month." His words are so terrible that they cut me; I feel like I'm bleeding.

Two years ago Benjamin was someone's husband, and someone's father. He was so much more than just this quirky guy whose whole world is stamps, who has collected thousands of frequent-flier miles traveling around to philatelic conferences. He was part of a family, and then, suddenly, he wasn't. "That's really awful," I finally say. "I'm so sorry."

"Yeah," he says. "Me too." He raises his hand; he wants to order another ale, but then seems to change his mind and pushes the empty mug across the table, away from him. "I don't usually talk about it. I don't know why I'm telling you all this."

"Oxford," I remind him gently. "You went with Sara once?" I wonder if he's always been a stamp dealer, or if stamps became a hobby he indulged, turned into a business, in his grief.

He nods. "Sara did her master's there, before I met her. We went back to visit once, before Davis was born, and I met Dr. Grimes then."

Is that why Benjamin really wants to go to Oxford tomorrow? Is this entire trip not so much a fact-finding mission or Benjamin's escape at all, as he'd claimed, or even about my stamp, but instead a connection to his past, the woman he once loved?

I finish off my wine, and push the glass toward the center of the table by Benjamin's empty one. "I should probably go up to bed," I say. "If we're going to go to Oxford in the morning, we'll want to get an early start."

"Right," Benjamin says. But neither one of us moves for a moment. He looks so sad sitting here. I want to say something more to comfort him, but I don't know what that would be. Finally Benjamin stands, and so do I.

We walk together toward the elevator, and when it stops first on the third floor, my floor, Benjamin puts his hand on the door to stop it from closing behind me. "Can I come with you?" His words tumble out in a rush. "We could watch a movie or play cards or . . . something? I just don't want to be alone right now." He stares at his beat-up sneakers.

"Sure," I hear myself saying before I can really think it through.

He lets go of the door and gets off the elevator, following me to my room.

He is not coming to my room to have sex with me, I think as we walk down the hallway. He's lonely. He doesn't want to be alone. The ghosts of his dead wife and son are hanging over him this week, all these miles from home. Benjamin's kind of grief must be a never-ending pain.

I put my key in the door, and we go inside. The room is dark, and the maid has come in my absence, so when I turn the lamp on I see the bed is made, the clothes I'd strewn on the floor tidied and placed in a pile on top of my suitcase.

I look around and realize there's nowhere to sit but the bed or the floor. Benjamin sits on the bed, but I walk over to the television to turn it on, avoiding any inevitable awkwardness for another moment. Benjamin picks up the clicker from the nightstand and begins switching channels before settling on the BBC. A reporter in West Berlin is talking about the *Mauerspechte*, wall woodpeckers, people who live in East Germany and who are finally allowed out from behind the iron curtain. They are literally pecking away at the wall, chiseling it, piece by piece. The reporter zeroes in on a woman in a khaki raincoat who is chipping at the wall with a pickax.

I sit down on the bed, because my feet are aching, and I want to take off my sneakers and put my feet up. I sit as far to the other side as I can, not wanting to get too close, not wanting to accidentally bump elbows or hands with Benjamin.

"The wall came down," he says. "But there it still is."

The woman the BBC is focusing on is petite, blonde. Her raincoat is too big. She swings the pickax as hard as she can, and small pieces of the wall turn to dust all around her. The reporter asks her why she is hitting the wall so hard, and she replies in German, which they translate on the screen. *Because it kept me from my family.*

If any station in the United States is showing something similar, Gram would be taking such joy from watching a moment like this, the wall being slowly, slowly chipped away by this tiny little woman who was oppressed by it, isolated behind it, for so very long. Who now, it seems, can finally be with her family again.

"It's beautiful to watch her, isn't it?" I say. Benjamin doesn't say anything. But his hand moves slowly across the bed, reaches for mine, and I take it. Our fingers interlace; his hand is twice the size of mine, but I fold my fingers into his, so we are linked, connected, fit together, like the pieces of a jigsaw puzzle. I turn a little and his eyes are closed. I close mine, too, and we both fall asleep like that, holding on to each other's hands.

Austria, 1939

HERR BERGMANN RETURNED IN the first days of the new year, his arrival so sudden that Elena barely had time to hide in the floor space in the workshop before he walked in, without knocking. As if Frederick's old workshop really belonged to the Deutsches Reich now. And maybe, Kristoff thought, it did.

Kristoff didn't have time to hide the nearly finished plates Elena had been working on for her father's exit papers. Or, rather, the exit papers for another man, a made-up Christian man, Herr Charles Darnay, which happened to also be the name of one of Elena's favorite Dickens characters. *It might as well mean something*, she'd said to Kristoff, of the new chosen name for her father. *Charles is the one who's saved in* A Tale of Two Cities, *just as Father will be when we finish his papers.* And Kristoff prayed Herr Bergmann wouldn't notice the plates, question them, examine them.

"I trust you have had ample time to make sketches for the Führer?" Herr Bergmann's tone was brusque, and Kristoff didn't want to think what would happen if Herr Bergmann—or the Führer himself—should not be satisfied with his sketches. Or if they were to hear the gentle noises of Elena breathing as she hid beneath the floor below them. Or understand the evidence of their forgery in progress laid out right on the worktable.

"*Jawohl, Herr Bergmann,*" Kristoff said. He picked up his sketch pad, and tried not to look at the forgery plates. *If I don't look*, he thought, *Herr Bergmann will have no reason to notice.* He couldn't stop his hands from shaking as he handed over the sketches.

Herr Bergmann flipped through the way Elena had only a few weeks earlier. He made an approving clucking noise with his tongue, nodding his head briskly. "I think the Führer will be pleased," he said at last. "You are quite skilled."

Kristoff kept his head down, not sure whether to answer, but Herr Bergmann shoved the sketchbook back toward him, and Kristoff looked up, took it. The page was open to his drawing of Stephensdom, a variation on the drawing he'd shown to Frederick when Frederick had first decided to bring him on as an apprentice. "Begin with this one. It is a very nice picture of Österreich," Herr Bergmann said. "You have all the tools you need here to make an engraving plate for this?"

"*Jawohl,*" Kristoff repeated. It was hard to breathe, and he felt certain Herr Bergmann could sense it, see it, the way Kristoff could sense Elena underneath the floor.

But Herr Bergmann didn't notice. He had nothing to suspect, and he seemed to have taken Kristoff at his word that all the Fabers were long gone. He pulled an envelope from his coat pocket and handed it to Kristoff. "I trust you will find this acceptable payment." Kristoff didn't look inside the envelope but he nodded all the same. "Good. Then I should return in a few weeks to get your engraved plate." He turned to leave but then stopped, turned back, and put his large imposing hand on Kristoff's shoulder. "It is a great honor to make a stamp for the Deutsches Reich."

He raised up his other hand to his forehead in salute, but he didn't move his left hand from Kristoff's shoulder until Kristoff stood up tall and saluted back. "Heil Hitler," Kristoff finally said, with as much enthusiasm as he could muster.

Herr Bergmann smiled, revealing a gold bottom tooth, and then he turned and left as swiftly as he'd come.

❋

Kristoff watched him walk away and disappear around the side of the house, but he waited, listening carefully for the motor of the car before he called to Elena, telling her it was safe.

"Heil Hitler?" she hurled at him, as she pulled herself up out of the ground, dusting off her clothes. Miriam had once called the floor space a tomb, akin to her own grave. Elena, though, didn't seem upset about that. Instead, she folded her arms across her chest and glared at him.

"I don't know what you want me to say." He walked to her, put his hand on her shoulder, but she yanked away. "Elena, I had to say it or he wasn't going to leave." He couldn't tell whether she was truly mad at him or she just hated the futility of their situation.

Kristoff handed her the envelope that Herr Bergmann had handed him moments earlier. "What's this?" She looked inside, her delicate fingers riffling through the reichsmarks. She made a small sound of disgust and handed the envelope back to him. "I don't want their money."

"Put it toward your father's ticket to America," he said, handing it back to her again. "What better way to get back at them than to use their money to help your father out?"

"I could think of better ways," she huffed, but she accepted it and stuffed the envelope into the pocket of the old pair of her father's pants she was wearing. She'd been wearing her father's clothes to work in each day, and he wasn't sure whether it was because she didn't want to get her own clothes dirty or because she felt her father's clothes, silly as it seemed, might make her a better engraver. Even dressed in these old clothes, stray bits of her hair falling out of her braid, dirt from the floor space smudged across her cheek, she looked so beautiful.

They'd never spoken about that night when she'd crawled into his bed, when he'd slept with his arms around her, her apricot hair just inches from his nose, and she'd never visited his bedroom again. The past few weeks they'd tiptoed around each other, each living in the house, working side by side in the workshop, but they spoke only casually or in passing or about the papers they were making.

Kristoff longed to touch her, pull her toward him. But he didn't move. "It'll be dark soon," he said, instead. "It's Friday."

"It's not *your* Sabbath." Her tone sounded accusatory. She was still mad.

"Well, what if I think it is now?" Why couldn't it be? He was an orphan, after all. Who knew what his true past, his true heritage was?

"It doesn't work that way," Elena said. "You can't just decide to be a Jew, and besides, why would you want to . . . here?" She held her hands up, and it looked like she was gesturing to the cozy space of the workshop, but he knew she meant Grotsburg. Austria. Europe. Here and now. Where being a Jew was the most reviled and dangerous thing on God's earth. Jews were no longer allowed to own businesses, attend German schools, not to mention the billion-mark fine Hitler had levied against them for the property destroyed during *die Kristallnacht*.

Kristoff wanted to tell her that no place had ever felt like his home the way this place had. No family had ever felt like his family the way the Fabers had. But instead he said, "I want you to understand, I'm not one of them."

"But you're not one of us either," she said. Then she walked out of the workshop and walked into the main house.

As the winter darkness overtook the yard that evening, Kristoff stood at the workshop's door, and he could see the glow of two small candles flickering on the other side of the house's kitchen window.

❀

Kristoff stayed in the workshop for a while that night, trying to reproduce his Stephensdom drawing into the metal, but Elena was right. His drawing had so many small lines, and he couldn't force the burin to behave with the preciseness that he wanted. After a few hours he grew frustrated, gave up, and went back into the house.

Elena had left him some bread in the kitchen—not challah, because eggs were too scarce and too expensive these days. A dry flat brown bread that she had baked this morning, a poor replacement. But she'd left some out here on a plate for him, a small peace offering. He took the plate of it from the counter, smeared it with a bit of the apricot jam they'd been rationing, and took it into the dining room. He added another log to the fire to warm it up, and looked around the room, and under the table, making sure Elena wasn't hiding in earshot. She wasn't.

And before he ate his bread, he said the Shabbat prayer quickly, quietly, to himself.

※

A few hours later, Kristoff paced in the attic, unable to sleep. He worried about how he was ever going to make his engraving plate look right and stay in Herr Bergmann's good graces.

Suddenly, Elena opened the door to his room without knocking, much the way Herr Bergmann had barged into the workshop earlier. She walked in and sat down at the edge of his bed. "Kristoff." She said his name gently. She was no longer angry.

Kristoff stopped pacing and stood in one spot, close enough to her that he could almost reach out and touch her, but not quite. "Thank you for the bread," he said. "It was good."

"It wasn't," she said, matter-of-factly. "But it was the best I could do with what I had to work with." She folded her hands in her lap, twisting her fingers together. "I couldn't sleep. I shouldn't have been so cross with you earlier, in the workshop. You've done so much to help us, my father." She looked down at her hands. "I know you're not one of them, that you have no choice but to work with them."

Kristoff took another step forward, and they were close enough that they practically had to touch. "You know I would never do anything to hurt you." He reached out for her, put his hands on her shoulders. She shivered a little, stood, and before she could leave, run from his room back down the stairs, he pulled her to him. He wrapped his arms around her, holding on tightly. If there was ever one perfect moment in his life, this was it. The feel of Elena in his arms, the smell of her, the warmth of her cheek against him.

"We're going to fight them," Elena said. "And we'll win. Together."

To Kristoff it sounded like she was saying they would be together, that she wanted to be with him, that whatever they would do, they would do together. Though he knew that wasn't exactly what she said, he heard himself saying back to her, "I want to always be together, you and I."

She stood up on her toes, leaned her face in close to him, and kissed him.

At the first touch of her lips, he couldn't breathe. He'd thought of this moment, over and over, since that day in the woods, in the snow, when they'd shared a goodbye kiss. *I don't like goodbyes*, she'd said. That had been a kiss of desperation, filled with the overwhelming sadness that he might never see her again. But this kiss was slower, softer, sweeter. A beginning, not an ending.

Kristoff moved his hands to the top of her nightgown and fumbled with the button. She put her hand up, on his, he thought, wanting him to stop. So he did. He moved his hands to his sides, stopped kissing her, and took a step back. He was breathing hard, and her cheeks were flushed. "I'm sorry," he said. He wasn't sorry.

She unbuttoned her nightgown quickly, efficiently, pulled it over her head, and let it fall in a heap on the floor. She'd been completely naked underneath the gown. And seeing her like this, all the pale beautiful skin, the gentle slopes of her bare breasts, he gasped a little. "You don't like what you see?" She had that edge to her voice that she always had, that toughness that made her stubborn and stupid and brilliant and beautiful. That made her want to fight. She was stunning like this. Every line and curve of her body a perfection that he was certain he could never achieve should he try to draw her sometime later, from memory.

He reached his hand out again, placed his thumb on her collarbone and traced it gently across, the way he would draw the line if his thumb were charcoal, her skin the white paper of a sketch pad. He traced from her shoulder to the top of her chest, and then he paused before continuing down. He had never touched a woman like this before. And yet his hand kept moving, as if he knew how, as if somehow touching her were as effortless as drawing her. "You're so beautiful," he said, his voice hoarse.

He lifted her up on the bed, and he felt her body relax against his arms. He didn't think about anything else. Not the Germans, the stamps, the imminent danger all of them were in. Only of Elena. The smooth texture of her skin against his hands.

"Kristoff." She spoke his name not as a command nor a question, but as a certainty. This was what she wanted, as much as he did.

Oxford, 1989

THE TRAIN RIDE TO OXFORD is a blur of green across the English countryside. I sit by the window and watch rolling hills and tiny towns go by, while Benjamin sits next to me with a Dodgers cap low enough to shield his eyes. He was gone from my room when I woke up this morning, but he'd left a note that he'd called and there was a train we could take at 9:00, that I should meet him in the lobby at 8:30. Neither one of us mentioned the events of last night nor spoke much on the cab ride to Cardiff Central. He's a little hungover, I'm guessing, so I let him be, and we don't talk much for the two-hour train ride either. I stare out the window, transfixed by all the greenery.

By the time we reach Oxford it's drizzling again, but we walk the short distance from the train. Despite the rain, I'm in awe at the beauty of the campus. The buildings are a pale brick, with domes and towers and spires. I feel like I'm on the set of a fairy tale, not a university, and I half expect King Arthur or Sir Gawain to come riding by on a horse any moment. But I see only the usual-looking college students milling around, dressed in sweatshirts and jeans tight-rolled at the bottom, girls with perms and teased-up bangs.

They could be the UCLA students I see walking around in West-wood all the time.

Benjamin raises his hat a little and tells me that Dr. Grimes was Sara's thesis advisor, many years ago. He walks next to me, but he seems careful not to stand too close, to accidentally brush up against my shoulder, much less take my hand the way he did last night.

"So your wife studied World War Two history?" I'm still trying to picture Benjamin married, much less to a scholar.

He nods, pulls a piece of paper out of the pocket of his brown leather jacket, and looks down to double-check the address. "This way," he says. "On George Street."

I follow him toward a triangular building, which looks more like a church than a university office building, but a sign in the hall-way as we walk inside indicates that we've reached the right place, home to the faculty of history.

Dr. Grimes's office is up a set of stairs, on the second floor, and Benjamin walks ahead of me, taking the steps slowly. Is Benjamin thinking of Sara as he walks these steps, thinking about the way her feet must've traced them many years ago? I am. I create this picture of her in my head—she's small, with brown hair, an angled bob, and shocking green eyes.

"Ben Grossman, how the hell are you?" Dr. Grimes has walked out of his office, to meet us at the top of the stairs, as if he'd been expecting us, and I guess Benjamin told him which train we'd be on. He's older and much more rotund than I'd imagined him. He's balding and wears a tweed jacket that looks about two sizes too big. He reaches out to shake my hand.

"I'm Katie," I tell him.

"Pleasure to meet you, Katie."

"This is the client I was telling you about over the phone," Benjamin says, and Dr. Grimes invites us into his office. Inside, the light is dim, the space overcrowded with too many bookshelves covered in what appears to be a disorganized mess of thousands of books. He moves a few off two chairs across from his desk. We sit, and I pull Elena's letter out of my bag and hand it across the desk to him.

"I brought him up to speed over the phone," Benjamin says to me as Dr. Grimes grabs a pair of glasses off his desk and examines the letter and the stamp carefully.

"The flower." He traces his stubby finger gently across it through the plastic. "It's remarkable the way they snuck it in there, isn't it? Barely even visible at all." He stands to get a book off one of the shelves behind his desk. Though it all appears such a mess to me, he seems to know exactly where, and what he's looking for.

He lays the book on his desk, finds the right page, and then points to what he wants us to read. "See here," he says. The top of the page reads "Nazi Stamp Conspiracy," and there's a picture of a German stamp, with an unfamiliar man's profile.

I skim over the words, but he begins to explain before I can get a sense from the book.

"During the war, people were trying everything to fight the Germans. You couldn't fight them with force, see. So you fought them with things just beneath their noses. At first people used letters to send secret messages. They'd alter the words in poems or such, but then the Germans caught on. So they started finding other ways to send messages using letters."

"Stamps?" I ask, wondering if Benjamin knows any of this. It's kind of mind-blowing to a total stamp amateur like me.

"Yes, stamps," Dr. Grimes says, putting his finger back on the book. "This one you see here on this page was part of a plot to overthrow Hitler dreamed up by the SOE—the Special Ops—here in Great Britain. They had thousands of fake stamps printed up with Himmler's face on them, instead of Hitler's. Himmler was a Nazi, very high up. Everyone knew he wanted to overthrow Hitler, become Führer himself. So someone in the SOE came up with the idea to make fake stamps with his picture. They smuggled them into circulation in Germany and thought it would create infighting in the regime. Hitler would think Himmler was trying to overthrow him—they thought they could bring the entire regime down." He pauses and flips to something else in the book. "Only problem was, nothing happened. No one noticed." He puts his finger on a different page, and I see an image of the Hitler stamp I'd seen in my own philatelic guide I'd checked out of the library. Only in this version, Hitler's face looks like a skeleton. "Then there was Operation Cornflakes," he says. "These beauties were attached to letters of propaganda, inscribed with the words *Futsches Reich*—ruined Reich, instead of the usual *Deutsches Reich*. Thousands of them were dropped out of planes in an effort to garner support for the resistance movements. Create an uprising on the ground."

"So our stamp?" I ask him. "Was that a part of all this?"

Dr. Grimes shrugs. "I have never seen your particular stamp before. But to create a fake in Europe during—"

"So you think this is fake?" I interrupt him.

He nods. "And in my opinion, there were only a few good reasons to create a stamp like this there and then." Benjamin and I both stare at him, unmoving, wanting to hear what he's about to say next. "If you had something to say and no other way to say it. If you were fighting the Germans and you didn't want them to know it. What better way to do it than to mail an innocuous letter with a hidden message embedded in the stamp? It's brilliant, really."

"But a flower?" I ask. "On a love letter?"

"Sure," Dr. Grimes says. "It all seems so very innocent. But I suspect this isn't a real love letter. The upside-down placement of the stamp, perhaps that was a message, too. And maybe they tried to pass it off as a silly love letter—because who would question that?"

Miriam claimed her sister loved Kristoff, that she left her chance at safety, a new life in England, to go back and be with him, and I want Dr. Grimes to be wrong. I want this to really be a love letter. I want Elena and Kristoff to have found each other again, to have loved each other. I want this stamp, this letter, to be proof of that.

I glance at Benjamin, and he's grinning, looking more animated than I've ever seen him. "Of course," he says, his voice rising with excitement. "That all makes sense."

"So what could the flower have meant?" I'm still skeptical. "It's just a flower."

Dr. Grimes holds up his hand. "It is not just any flower, my dear. It's an edelweiss. A symbol of love and purity in Germany and Austria, but it's also a nearly impossible flower to attain. It only grows in the scraggiest, rockiest terrain. Men used to die climbing up mountains to try to get them for their lovers. And the ones who didn't? The flower became a symbol of overcoming adversity."

I lean across his desk and look at the stamp again, observing the flower the way Dr. Grimes just described it. A symbol of overcoming adversity. Miriam told us yesterday that it was *proof of unusual daring*. "And what about Kristoff Mueller, Frederick Faber's apprentice?" Benjamin asks. "Have you ever heard of him?"

Dr. Grimes leans back and folds his arms across his wide stomach. "I'm afraid not." He thinks for another moment. "But the Nazi-issued stamps were issued by the ministry, not necessarily accredited to particular engravers, artists, the way they are today or were before the war. And I haven't heard of him since, have you, Ben?"

"No," Benjamin says. "He most likely wasn't still engraving stamps after the war."

"He very well may have created many stamps for the Nazis," Dr. Grimes says. "Or he might not have. Perhaps this was his only one." He lowers his voice. "If he was forging stamps, working for the resistance, there's a fair chance he was caught at some point. Killed."

"But if he wasn't?" I say, wanting both Benjamin and Dr. Grimes to be wrong.

"I like your optimism, Katie," Dr. Grimes says, somewhat grimly. "But if he wasn't, well, then I suppose anything could've happened to him. He could be anywhere at all by now, dead or very much alive."

❀

It's pouring when Benjamin and I walk out of Dr. Grimes's office and back onto campus. The heavy rain obscures the beauty of all the bricks, and the dampness cuts straight through my thin jacket, a coldness I can feel in my bones. I shiver and feel a wash of homesickness for LA's perpetual sunshine. Benjamin notices and moves like he's going to reach for my arm, but then seems to change his mind and reaches for his umbrella in his backpack instead, opens it, holds it over my head, and ducks under the umbrella with me.

"Do you think Dr. Grimes was right?" I ask Benjamin, once we're back on the train, heading toward Cardiff.

"About what?" Benjamin says.

"That maybe it isn't a love letter at all?"

"Does it matter?"

"I guess not," I say, but for some reason it feels like it does.

"I thought you were asking if I thought he was right about this letter being a part of the resistance." His voice rises a little with excitement. "I think he could be, and then think, we would actually have *something* here."

It sounds like he's talking about money, about the value of the stamp. But I don't think he is. He feels excitement about the possibility of discovering something new, some previously unknown piece of history, the war. There is a story here, love story or no.

"When we get back to LA, I'm going to start to search for Kristoff," I say. I'll work with all the information Jason gave me, the organizations he knew of. Is this the story I'll write for him, about Kristoff and the resistance and a secret message in a stamp?

"Me too," Benjamin says. "If he was a stamp engraver, someone in the philately world might've heard of him before."

But what Dr. Grimes said about the dangers in working for the Nazis, and in working against them, makes me wonder if anything will turn up at all. Or if Kristoff is nothing more than a ghost.

Austria, 1939

A S THEY PLANNED TO get Frederick out of the country, Kristoff had trouble concentrating on his engraving plate for Herr Bergmann, especially when Elena was working next to him, finishing up the plates for her father's papers. Once those were off to Josef's friend who was a printer in Vienna, Elena offered to give Kristoff's stamp drawing a try in the metal, and he gladly agreed, certain she was a better engraver than he was, that she would make a better plate. If only Herr Bergmann, or the Führer, were to know that their stamp plate was being made by a Jew, and a woman. Kristoff took pleasure in the thought that they wouldn't know. As if this tiny thing, this small act of rebellion would change anything. Kristoff knew it wouldn't, but still, it gave him the slightest feeling of satisfaction.

In the daylight, in the workshop, he and Elena barely spoke, unless it was about the work they were doing. Short, blunt sentences. Pass this, or hand over that. All focus was on the task at hand. And every day Kristoff would wonder whether Elena would return to his room, his bed, again later that night.

But she always did. She followed him up the steps to the attic after supper, and slipped underneath his covers and clung to him. Sometimes they wouldn't talk at all, but they would make love and slip into an easy sleep. And other times, nights when Elena said they had to be careful because they didn't want a child, they talked for hours in the darkness. It felt like an entirely different world from the workshop during the day. At night, in his bed, they were no longer in Nazi-occupied Austria, but somewhere perfect and safe. Just the two of them.

Elena told him she had never planned on learning her father's trade, nor had any interest in engraving as a little girl. She'd always dreamed of studying literature at the university and writing books like the ones she loved to read. She told him that her favorite English book was *Little Women*. Frederick had brought her a copy back from America many years earlier when she was a little girl, still too young to read it in English, but eventually she learned and had read the book several times. "I'm like Amy," she told him, after describing all the sisters to him.

"But isn't she the youngest?" Kristoff asked, confused.

"Yes, but also the most passionate, the most artistic. She gets what she wants. And she gets to be with Laurie in the end."

"Am I Laurie?" he asked lightly, wanting her to say he was. That he was the person she wanted, in the end.

She laughed, rolled over, and kissed him. He put his hands on her cheeks, kissed her back. He could kiss her forever. Or at least, all night. Or at least until it was late, and their bodies were too tired to stay awake any longer.

Elena sometimes fell asleep mid-sentence. She was so exhausted but she wouldn't give in to sleep until her body couldn't hold out any longer. Kristoff pushed sleep away, always waiting for her to fall asleep first, to savor every last moment with her.

"I love you," he would whisper into her hair, after he was sure she was sleeping. He was still afraid to say it when she was awake, afraid that she might not respond, might not love him back. That she might disappear one night into the woods on the way to see her father, or Josef, just like that.

❀

By the time his papers were ready and all the arrangements had been made for him to sail to America, Frederick had lost a considerable amount of weight. He looked frail, older, almost unrecognizable. Josef said it was good he looked so different; the Germans wouldn't recognize him either. But Kristoff worried that Frederick wouldn't survive the long journey to America, even if he would fool the Germans. But now it seemed they had no other choice. Frederick had to go or surely he would die here, living like this.

On the day before Frederick was set to leave, Elena was at the Bauer farm working out the last-minute details with Josef, and Kristoff took the stamp engraving plate he and Elena had been working on for the Germans and went to show it to Frederick in the cabin.

Kristoff hadn't seen Frederick alone since before Elena came back, and part of him felt a little nervous going to see him today. Would Frederick immediately sense how he felt about Elena? Kristoff doubted that he would approve of his daughter spending every night in Kristoff's bed.

"My boy, your lines are still sloppy," Frederick said as he looked at the engraving plate. His voice was hoarse, but he spoke to Kristoff as he always had. He didn't sound angry. So Kristoff didn't mention that some of these were Elena's sloppy lines, that she was involved in making a stamp for the Deutsches Reich with him. Frederick patted him lightly on the shoulder. "But overall this is very good. You have a lot of power, making a stamp for the Germans."

"I have no power at all," Kristoff said. "I don't want to be doing this. But I have no choice."

"But sometimes the only way to fight the enemy is to become them," Frederick said.

Kristoff nodded, though he despised the very idea of *becoming* them.

Frederick handed the engraving plate back and didn't say anything else for a few moments. He stared at Kristoff, eyes wide, sunken against his sharp cheekbones, as if he could see everything Kristoff was trying to hide from him, everything they weren't talking about. And Kristoff felt exposed. He should say something, but he wasn't sure what. Should he apologize? But he wasn't sorry. He loved Elena.

"You will take good care of her?" Frederick finally said. He grabbed on to Kristoff's arm. His grip was weak, but Kristoff didn't pull away.

"I will," he said.

Frederick let go of his arm, let out a little sigh, and sat back against the wall. "You will bring her an edelweiss?" His voice was filled with a sad sort of resignation.

Kristoff remembered Frederick's story of why he'd created his edelweiss stamp so many years ago: a gift for his love, for Mrs. Faber. He felt an overwhelming sadness that Mrs. Faber wasn't here with Frederick, that he would have to leave for America alone, without her, without even knowing what had happened to her. Frederick had tried so hard to give her everything, and she'd been ripped away from him, just like that, violently and with no meaning. It had been months since Mrs. Faber had been taken, and the more time that passed the less likely it felt to Kristoff that she was okay, or that they would see her again anytime soon. Kristoff had read about Hitler's speech at the end of last year, where he declared if a war were to break out it would mean extermination for all of Europe's Jews, and that, coupled with the rumors that the work camp in Mauthausen, Upper Austria, was growing larger by the day, kept Kristoff from sleeping many nights, even after Elena had drifted off.

"You will make sure Elena stays safe," Frederick said now, his voice thick with regret. Maybe he blamed himself for what had happened to Mrs. Faber, though it wasn't his fault. None of it was. Kristoff wanted to tell him this, but then Frederick said, his voice louder, sounding desperate, "Promise me."

"I promise." Kristoff would not let what happened to Mrs. Faber happen to Elena. He wouldn't.

❋

The next morning, Kristoff and Elena helped Frederick through the woods to the Bauer farm, where a car was waiting. The driver was someone Kristoff had never met before but who Elena said was Henrik Schwann, a boy she'd known from school. Henrik wasn't a Jew like Elena and Josef. Not a Nazi either—a combination that was harder and harder to find these days near Grotsburg. Schwann was going to drive Frederick—no, Charles Darnay—across the border into Germany, then to Bremen, where Frederick would board a ship bound for New York City in three days, if all went well. Frederick's friend Mr. Leser would come for him in New York. So many hours, days, weeks of travel. But it was all arranged. In a few weeks' time, Frederick would be safe.

"I wish you were coming with me." Frederick clung to Elena's arm an extra moment, before he got into the car. They all knew it was impossible and they had already told Frederick as much in the past weeks, several times. Elena didn't have papers for herself yet, nor money to pay for another ticket. But Josef stepped back, allowing Elena and her father a moment, and Kristoff did, too.

"Soon," she promised Frederick. "We'll come to America as soon we can." She hugged him tightly. Tears formed in her eyes, and Kristoff looked away, pretending not to notice, knowing Elena would be angry at him for observing any part of her weakness. Not that he blamed her; he wanted to cry, too. "I'll find Mother and get Miri and then we'll all come together to meet you. Very soon," she promised him again.

"You know how to find Gideon Leser?" Frederick said. "You'll come to America and find him. And me."

Kristoff remembered the letter Elena had written and that he had mailed to Mr. Leser, and he heard Elena promise that she did know how to find him. Elena let her father go, and he got into the car. "I'll see you soon," she called after Frederick as the car drove away, leaving behind only tracks in the snow. Elena refused to say goodbye, just as she had once with Kristoff.

Josef put his arm around Elena and Kristoff flinched a little, though he knew Elena was upset; Josef was only reacting to that. They were all upset. "We've done a good thing," Josef said, trying to comfort her. "We've saved him."

Elena appeared to be holding back tears, but she nodded. Kristoff couldn't stop staring at Josef's arm, perched across Elena's shoulders, the way his fingers squeezed her shoulder like she belonged to him.

"But there's another *Kindertransport* to London next week, taking children, and I'm going to put you on it myself," Josef said to Elena.

Elena shrugged out of his grasp. "I am not a child," Elena hissed.

"You came back to help your father, and you did. And now you need to help yourself." Josef's voice was calm, steady.

"I'm not going anywhere." She turned to Kristoff, as if she just remembered he was here. Josef looked at him, too, and narrowed his eyes.

Kristoff needed Elena. He didn't want to let her go, not from his bed nor from his work. And he needed her help to make the stamps that would keep them alive. But he had also promised Frederick he'd keep her safe. He knew he couldn't do that if she stayed, and he would never be able to live with himself if the Germans found out she was here and came for her, dragged her away, too. "I . . ." he began, but he couldn't finish his thought.

Elena spun on her heel, turned back toward Josef. "Yes, I helped my father," she said. "But what about my mother? And there are others. So many others. Kristoff and I, we can make more papers. Help more people get out of Austria."

"You forge more papers, you'll get caught eventually," Josef said. "They would shoot you in a second."

Kristoff had the sudden image of the snow-white skin of Elena's chest being ripped apart, bloodied, and he couldn't breathe. "You should listen to Josef, go to London," he heard himself saying.

Elena looked at him again, and her face fell as if she really had been wounded. Not by a German gun, but by him. She narrowed her eyes at him, and looked back and forth between the two of them. "You're both *dummkopf*." She turned away and stormed off into the woods.

Kristoff moved to go after her, but Josef held him back. "Let her cool off," he said. "You'll talk to her later, when she's not so upset about her father leaving."

"She'll never go to London," Kristoff said quietly, wishing he had kept his mouth shut. Elena was better off here, next to him, than she was running through the woods alone. "She won't leave without her mother. And she wants to fight. We're never going to talk her out of it."

Josef nodded. He already understood this, but, well, it was worth a try. He asked Kristoff to wait while he got something from the house. He returned a few moments later and pulled a gun from his coat pocket, placed it in Kristoff's hand. The icy smooth metal stung against Kristoff's bare skin, and the object surprised him, its weight, its inherent coldness. He had never held a gun before; he had never wanted to. "Why are you giving me this?" Kristoff asked.

"There are things you can't do with the engraving tools," Josef said.

It was one thing to forge a visa, make an illegal engraving plate.

It was another to think about fighting the German soldiers with guns. "I don't want this." Kristoff tried to hand the gun back to Josef.

"You need it," Josef said, pushing the gun back toward him.

Kristoff knew Herr Bergmann could barge into the workshop unannounced. He imagined what should happen if he were to pick up the pistol, aim it squarely at his large forehead, and pull the trigger. He pictured Herr Bergmann's gun coming up faster, aimed right at Elena's forehead.

The gun felt too heavy in his hand; he began to sweat, to feel nauseous. He turned and vomited his breakfast in the snow.

"Jesus," Josef said as he took the gun back. "You don't have the stomach for this. Maybe you're the one who should get on the *Kindertransport*."

Kristoff wiped his mouth with the back of his hand. Josef shook his head in disgust and tucked the gun into the waist of his pants.

Los Angeles, 1989

WHEN I WALK BACK into my house, I feel like I've been gone for weeks, not days, and my head feels heavy with a crushing, suffocating jet lag, worse than any hangover in recent memory. I feel this odd sense of emptiness, too; I'm alone again. Benjamin and I parted ways at LAX, and I'd grown used to his company this past week.

"We'll talk soon," he said to me at the airport. He leaned in as if he was going to hug me but seemed to change his mind halfway, and he reached out his hand to shake mine instead. As we shook, I looked at our hands intertwined, like the night when we fell asleep in my bed in Cardiff holding hands. We'd both since pretended that had never happened. And at the airport we'd left each other with that handshake that lingered just a few seconds too long.

I check my machine on my way to bed, and I'm surprised to see I have seven messages. The first five are from the Willows—my father, they say, has been inconsolable, ranting about my mother. I sit down on the couch as I listen, my hands trembling. I can't believe I left him to go halfway across the world, and he needed me. That I became so wrapped up in someone else's life, someone else's potential story and family, that I abandoned my own. Here he'd been, thousands of miles away, falling apart. But those messages are from the first two days I was gone, and then they stop, so I hope that means he improved, not that the Willows just gave up on calling me. It's nearly ten, too late to call over there; I'll have to wait until morning to figure it out.

The next message is from Daniel, saying only that he needs to talk to me, his voice devoid of emotion or any specifics about what he needs to talk about, and I'm too tired right now to care. And then lastly, there's a message from Gram, just checking in, she said. Because I missed our Saturday call. Had I forgotten to tell her I was going to Wales? It came up so fast, maybe I did. But it's too late to call her, too.

My exhaustion is countered with restlessness, helplessness, new worry for my father. But my exhaustion wins out, and I fall into a quick and deep sleep on my couch, under Gram's crocheted afghan.

❄

I wake up at four a.m., not sure where I am at first, thinking I'm still back in Cardiff. But the air is much too warm and dry, Benjamin isn't here, and I remember that I'm home, in Westwood, that my father has been struggling all week in the Willows.

I take a shower and get dressed, have two cups of coffee, but I still can't shake the heavy sinking feeling of dread mixed with jet lag. I want to run to the Willows, make sure my father is okay, but visiting hours don't start until eight. And it's still only six. I want to call Gram back, too, but I don't want to wake her.

My phone rings just as I think that, and I run to get it, sure it's her. No one else would call me this early. I want to ask her if she heard anything about my father, and also tell her everything that happened on my trip. But when I pick up, Benjamin's voice rings through the line so clearly, and it catches me off guard. "Hey," he says, in that way that feels familiar to me now, as if he's calling me from just down the hall, wanting to figure out plans for the day in Wales. As if we know each other well enough for an informal, intimate, early-morning greeting. "I figured you'd be up."

"I am," I say. "My body has no idea where I am, or what time it is."

He laughs a little. "Yeah. I fell asleep so early last night and then was wide-awake in the middle of the night. Completely backwards for me." I smile at the similarity in our routines. "You want to get breakfast?" he asks quickly, like the idea surprises him, even as he says it. "I mean, since we're both up we could get some coffee, figure out our next steps."

"I have to stop and see my father before work. There was some trouble at the Willows while we were gone."

"Oh, I'm sorry," he says. "Well, we don't have to—"

"But I can't go until eight," I interrupt him, not wanting him to rescind his offer. I want to see him this morning, want to talk more about how we'll find Kristoff before I have to face the real world again, head-on: the Willows, my father, work and Daniel. "Maybe we can meet in Santa Monica, so I'll already be over there."

"Okay," he says. "Not sure we can find you your favorite leek sausage in Santa Monica, though." His voice sounds so stoic, the way it always does, but I think he's trying to make a joke.

"I'll live," I tell him.

❋

An hour later, I'm sitting across from Benjamin inside Pete's Cafe, which is just across the street from the Willows. Benjamin looks tired, his brown curls rumpled this morning, but his blue eyes seem lighter than they had in Cardiff. Maybe it's just the swath of sunshine beginning to rise over the hills, slanting in through the window by our table. "So you have an idea for what we should do next?" I ask him.

He shrugs his shoulders, looking a little sheepish. "Not really. I just . . . got used to seeing you, I guess. I didn't really want to have breakfast alone."

"You were in Katie-withdrawal?" I try to keep my tone light, joking. But the truth is, I'd gotten used to seeing him, too, and I'm happy to see him again this morning.

"Something like that," he says.

I can't meet his eyes, and I turn back and look out the window. The sky is pink and purple, and I have a new appreciation for the color, for something other than gray. LA is a beauty like nothing else, smog and all.

"You should tell your dad about Miriam. And Kristoff," Benjamin says. I turn back to look at him, and he's gulping down his eggs, like he hasn't eaten in months.

I don't feel very hungry and I push my eggs around on my plate with my fork. "He made me promise to leave this stamp alone, to get his collection back from you. I don't want to upset him again."

"But you said he's been a philatelist all his life," Benjamin says.

"He'd love this. It's what we all want, to discover something new, something important."

A gem. It's why my father was collecting stamps all these years, dragging me to rummage sales and thrift shops every Sunday morning of my childhood.

It's hard to admit it to myself, but I don't think my father could appreciate any of this anymore. If there is a story here, maybe it's mine. The stamp is mine. The story is mine. Mine and Benjamin's. *Ours*. And isn't that what my father wanted all along—for me to inherit his collection? To do . . . something with it. To understand it. Maybe this is it.

Benjamin finishes off his eggs. I glance at my watch and see it's almost eight, and I take a five out of my purse and put it on the table. "I should head over there," I say. "I'll . . ." I was going to say, *I'll see you later*, but I'm not really sure what I'm supposed to say. When I'll see him again.

Benjamin leans across the table, puts his hand on top of mine. "Call me if you figure anything out, okay?" His voice sounds a little hoarse, and he hesitates like he has something else to say. I like the feeling of his hand on mine, and I sit there another minute, wait for him to keep on talking. But whatever it is, he doesn't say it. He pats my hand a little and pulls away, and maybe I've imagined any intimacy in his gesture. Maybe he was just being kind.

❀

As I walk into the Willows, I'm wishing I'd been able to linger at breakfast longer, talk to Benjamin more, sit there with his hand on mine another few minutes.

"Mrs. Nelson!" Sally exclaims from her place behind the front desk, and her voice brings me back, here, to my father, who hasn't been having a good week. I wave to her, and she waves back, her giant sparkling diamond catching the light of the chandelier in the grand foyer of the entrance. There's such a contrast between this place and Raintree. At least my father isn't in any place like that.

"Mrs. Nelson, it's great to see you," Sally says as I sign in at the desk.

"You should really call me Katie," I tell her. And though she smiles warmly, I don't explain any further. I want to talk about my dad, not myself, right now. "How's he doing?" I ask her.

"He's been having some bad days," she admits. "But the holidays are rough for all of our residents."

"I got the messages. I'm so sorry. I was out of the country."

She raises her eyebrows. She hadn't pegged me as the type who ever went anywhere. "Oh, what a shame to have to go over Thanksgiving like that."

Benjamin had said he needed to leave the country for Thanksgiving, and I'm glad that I did, too, that I spent it with him. But I still feel awful for not having been here when my father needed me. "How bad is he?" I ask Sally. I know it must be pretty bad for them to have called me, left me all those messages. That has never happened before. And though it feels longer, it has only been a week since I've been here last, my usual interval. Logically I know I haven't done anything horrible or wrong, but I still can't shake the feelings of guilt, remorse.

"He was inconsolable for a few days. Really lost in the past," Sally says. "So you were in England?" I nod. "He was going on and on about England and about your mother, so I guess that makes more sense now. I didn't realize." She pauses. "We thought you were here in LA. That's why we called you. Sometimes it helps to see a real, living family member. Brings them out of it." I suddenly feel inconsolable myself and I can't stop tears from forming in my eyes. "Hey there, Katie." Sally reaches across the desk and puts her hand on my arm. "He doesn't seem bad today. And he'll be happy to see you." She gives me a gentle nudge toward the hallway, and I thank her and walk back.

When I reach his doorway, I stop and just breathe for a moment before going in. He's in his chair by the window, already dressed for the day, looking oddly dapper in his plaid button-down and khaki pants. He's wearing a hat today, too, an old brown bowler that he used to wear on the weekends when I was a kid, and now it hides his balding gray head, makes him look younger.

"Daddy," I say, not meaning to call him that, but not being able to stop it from coming out of my mouth either. He looks up, sees me, and his face registers surprise. I want him to know me so badly. I want to do what Benjamin suggested at breakfast and tell him about our trip, the stamp, his stamp, that it may have been used to send secret messages during the war, that it may or may not have been part of a love affair between a stamp engraver's apprentice and a young woman who seems stronger than I can imagine.

"You're back," he says, and he gestures that it's okay for me to come in, have a seat, but he doesn't offer a boisterous Kate the Great greeting. So I'm not sure if he knows it's me who's back or if he mistakes me for my mother now.

"I'm back," I say, sitting down next to him. "I missed you. I'm sorry I wasn't here for Thanksgiving."

"You were gone for so long," he says, contemplatively, turning to stare out the window.

"Only a week," I say. "And England and Wales were beautiful. You would've loved them."

"You should've stayed there," he says, not unkindly but matter-of-factly. But I still feel the sting of rejection. He doesn't want me. *He doesn't know you*, I remind myself.

"Of course I wasn't going to stay there. I'd never just leave you like that," I tell him.

He nods. *He knows.* Somewhere inside of his disease-riddled brain he knows me. He has to.

He turns back and looks at me and puts his hands on my arms. I exhale, because I see him, this man I've always loved and trusted. My dad. And I'm pretty sure he sees me, too. "You have to find Gid," he says.

My grandfather's name catches me off guard. He's been dead for many years, and I haven't heard my father mention him in a long time. "Dad," I say softly. Then repeat it louder, hoping my voice will snap him out of it, bring him back to the present. "It's me, Katie, your daughter. Kate the Great."

"Kate," he says, and I can't tell if his voice is filled with recognition or curiosity. I'd bought him a book of stamps at Heathrow, just before we left. I have them in my purse, but I don't take them out because I'm unsure if his English souvenir might set him off further.

I hear a soft knock on the open door, and when I look over, Sally is standing in the hallway. "Ted," she addresses my father. "Art class starts in five minutes." She smiles at me; she's told me before that art class is his favorite. "You don't want to miss that, do you? And I bet your daughter has to get to work."

He turns to me, puts his hand on my cheek gently. "I'll paint you something," he says.

"Wouldn't that be lovely," Sally says with a little bit too much cheer as she walks into the room to escort my father to his class. But then she turns to me and mouths, "I'll save it for you."

❋

The last place I feel like going after I leave the Willows is work, but I have to. I haven't been there in a week.

I'm almost happy to be stuck in traffic on my way to the office, and my mind wanders to my grandfather. I haven't thought about him, really thought about him, for a long while. But hearing my father say his name brought him back this morning.

My grandfather worked in a civilian job, as a translator, for the navy at the base on Coronado Island, and he'd been proud to have a government job for a country he often felt saved him and my grandmother. As a teenager, I used to find him highly embarrassing. He would sing in public (in German, no less), or insist on taking me to the mall and buying me clothes. (What teenager wants to be seen at the mall with her grandfather? I was always thankful that no one knew me in San Diego for these little trips.)

My father and my grandfather had been close. But it's still disconcerting, the way my father brought him up again, this morning, wanting me to find him. I try to understand what it must be like for my father, dead people alive again, real, right here. Old abandoned distant memories feeling like they're in front of him, palpable, new. He doesn't remember so many things that have happened to the people he's loved, good and bad. Does it ease the pain of having lost someone if you can't even remember that they're gone?

⁂

When I finally get into the office I find a pile of assignments on my desk from Daniel, with a handwritten note echoing what he left on my machine: *Need to talk.—D.*

The last thing I feel like doing is talking to him. As I walked alone through Cardiff Castle last week, I almost started to feel like myself again, this woman I once was before Daniel. He waves at me now from his office, trying to get my attention, and I gesture to my phone, miming that I have an important call to make. Then I pick up the phone and dial Gram.

"Oh, Katie, I'm so glad it's you. I tried you so many times last week and couldn't get ahold of you. I was getting worried."

"I'm sorry. I went away," I say. "I didn't get to tell you. It was kind of sudden."

"Sudden? Is everything okay, sweetheart?"

"Yeah, everything is fine. You know how I was looking into that letter? I just had the opportunity to go to the UK for a few days."

"The UK? Oh, how wonderful," Gram says. "Well, that's exactly why I was calling you, your little letter." Her voice rises, excited. "I found something I think you might be interested in. Do you want to come down here this weekend and I'll show you?"

I glance toward Daniel's office. He's gotten on the phone, so he's not paying attention to me any longer. "I could come down this afternoon," I say.

"But don't you have to work?"

I lower my voice. "I think I have to quit my job." And I feel relieved once I admit this truth, out loud. I do. I need to quit. And not at some point. Right now. Daniel and I are over. I need to move on in every part of my life. I quickly catch Gram up on the divorce and tell her the rest of the story. It feels so good to be honest with her, finally.

"Oh, honey." She doesn't say anything for a minute, and I can't tell whether she's sad or disappointed or even confused. Then she says, "I'll go to the store and pick up some wine before you get here and we'll talk. Drive safe, okay?"

After we hang up, I glance toward Daniel in his office, one last time. The phone is tucked between his shoulder and his ear and he's talking, animatedly. I might leave him in the lurch by quitting without any notice, and I feel a little bad about that. But not bad enough to stay. I really want to see whatever it is Gram found that has to do with Elena's letter. I want to write that story, not what Daniel has laid out, assigned, on my desk, here.

I hastily scribble out a letter of resignation and leave it in Daniel's inbox. I take only my Rolodex with me from my desk, and then I wave to Janice, and walk out the door of *LA Lifestyles*, without looking back.

✻

I feel oddly free, happy, once I'm back in my car, and I pop my favorite cassette into the tape deck, and turn the Bangles up, loud.

Maybe "Walk Like an Egyptian" should feel like an odd anthem, but it's all mine now, and I belt it out, slightly off-key. I reach the freeway and make a snap decision to head in the wrong direction first, toward Benjamin's office. I have no idea what Gram thinks she found. It could be nothing. But Benjamin brought me all the way to England on his frequent-flier miles. The least I can do is bring him to Coronado.

Austria, 1939

WHEN HERR BERGMANN RETURNED, Kristoff gave him the engraving plate, a plate Elena had put as much, if not more, engraving work into as he had. But Herr Bergmann, none the wiser, took the plate and handed Kristoff another envelope of reichsmarks. Kristoff would save them to pay for Elena's escape to America. *Soon*, he hoped. He hadn't told Elena, but he'd begun drawing up papers for her, or rather, Amata Marsch, a Germanized version of her favorite character from *Little Women*. He would convince her to engrave them soon, or he would do it himself and have Josef get them printed. Kristoff had also written a letter to Gideon Leser, asking both about Charles Darnay's arrival and for assistance in sending Elena to America. But he had not as yet worked up the courage to send it. Putting a stamp on it, putting it through the post, meant the Germans could read it, should they choose to. And that could get them all killed.

Kristoff and Elena were working on his new assignment from the Führer and Herr Bergmann, a stamp of the Opera House, as winter turned into spring, spring into summer. The Nazis advanced and took Czechoslovakia, and they demanded Jews everywhere turn over all their gold and silver. But edelweiss still bloomed in the hills of Grotsburg. And the Stephensdom stamp went into circulation in all of Austria. Kristoff thought that he should feel at least a small bit of pride when he first saw the stamp on an envelope. His stamp. The one he made with Elena. Their stamp. And yet, instead what he felt when he saw it was sadness, fear, longing. He couldn't muster any pride at all.

※

After Frederick left, Kristoff, Elena, Josef, and Frederick's driver, Henrik Schwann (who swore he'd delivered Frederick safely to Bremen) began meeting in the cabin in the woods, late at night, once a week. Elena said if four people could get their Austria back, it would be them. And though Kristoff wasn't sure he believed that, he went along, if only to be with Elena, to know what she was planning.

Kristoff often brought his sketch pad along to their meetings and sketched idly, while the other three tossed around ideas. Their ideas were ridiculous mostly—Schwann took a mathematics course one day a week at Universität Wien and he would bring up the sympathetic students he met there. Somehow this discussion always led to Schwann wanting to stage an uprising, get guns to Jews, and though he was nineteen, the same age as Kristoff, Kristoff felt he seemed younger, so much still like a little boy, playing a dangerous game. Kristoff didn't talk much when these ideas were discussed. He just sketched, and the sketching calmed him. He didn't want Elena to see his fear when Schwann spoke of guns with such a stupid bravado.

One night Josef cleared his throat and tapped Kristoff on the shoulder so Kristoff would look up from his sketching. "I have cousins, in Vienna," Josef said, looking right at Kristoff. "Elisa and Robert. Robert used to teach physics at Universität, but since *die Kristallnacht* Robert lost his job, they've been kicked out of their home; they have no money. And Elisa is now expecting a child."

Kristoff shook his head, not understanding why Josef was telling him this.

"They need papers," Elena said, sounding a little breathless.

"Yes." Josef answered Elena, but held on to Kristoff's gaze. "They need papers. They don't have the money to pay the high Jewish exit tax. And they have to get out of Austria before their baby is born."

Kristoff looked away from Josef, feeling sick. There was so much danger in forging more papers. Josef had said it himself that morning Kristoff had vomited in the snow.

"Kristoff and I will make them papers," Elena said, before Kristoff could say anything, one way or another. "Won't we, Kristoff?" She put her hand on his arm and gazed up at him. Her eyes were wide, excited. How could he say no to her? And how could he refuse to help Josef's poor cousins, their unborn child?

He finally nodded and Josef sighed a little. "But these will be it," Kristoff said. "We won't keep on doing this. We can't."

No one said anything, and Kristoff's words seemed to echo in the cabin, already sounding false, even to him.

✳

The next morning, Kristoff awoke first. Now that it was summer, the air in the attic was warm, and they slept naked, their bodies so familiar to each other that it almost seemed stranger that they would sleep clothed. Elena's bare leg wound around his, and he gently moved her leg to the side so he could get out of bed without waking her.

He went to the workshop to work more on Elena's papers before she came in and questioned him. He felt a new urgency to have an escape route for her after his promise in the cabin last night to forge new papers for Josef's cousins. Should their work be discovered, Elena would need a way out, and quickly.

He worked in quiet for nearly an hour, and when he saw Elena coming toward the workshop from the kitchen, he hid his progress in the workbench drawer.

Elena walked into the workshop barefoot, wearing one of Kristoff's shirts, which was much too long and hung over her tiny body like a dress. She had two cups of coffee in her hands and put one down on the workbench in front of Kristoff. He leaned down and kissed her as a thank-you. And she kissed him back, slowly, deeply.

"Let's leave now." Kristoff grabbed Elena's hand, impulsively. "We'll go to America and find your father and we can live there and get married."

Elena laughed a little; she thought he was joking.

"Really," he said. "I'm serious."

She let go of his hands. "I can't leave Austria without my mother. And besides, who would I be if we ran away? Who would we be?"

"I don't care," he said, frustrated. Her face turned, and she looked down at her feet. "All right, I do care," he said, trying to keep his tone even. "But I just want you to be safe. I want us to be together."

She looked back up, her face softened. Her eyes were the color of ripe pears. "We will," she said. She reached up and touched his cheek with her forefinger; he hadn't shaved in days, and her finger bristled against tiny hairs. "Someday."

"Someday," he echoed back, realizing how much weight this one word held, the most they'd promised each other. A future.

He took her hand from his cheek and kissed it softly, rubbing his lips across her knuckles, then opening her hand, kissing her palm.

"I should get dressed," she said. "Then we can get to work on the new papers for Josef's cousins."

He wanted to stop her. He wanted to show her how Amata Marsch's papers were almost finished. The Führer could be an ocean away from them; *they* could be safe in America. Everyone else in Austria be damned. But he remembered Frederick's sad voice, the way he'd looked when he'd said Mrs. Faber's name. Josef's poor cousins who were going to bring a baby into the world soon. The image of the smoking ruin of the synagogue in Grotsburg. If they abandoned Austria now, he knew Elena was right, they were giving up on Mrs. Faber and all the people in trouble here, needing help. They were giving up on their country. And deep down Kristoff knew Elena might never sail across the ocean and abandon her mother, her home.

Coronado, 1989

BENJAMIN HAS NEVER BEEN to Coronado before, and as I pull onto Gram's street, he remarks about how quaint it is, how New England it feels. "So different from LA," he says, and I kind of wish we were here just to hang out and have a drink by the water.

Gram does a double take when she opens the door and sees Benjamin standing next to me. She raises her eyebrows, and I realize she has the wrong idea. "This is Benjamin Grossman. The *stamp dealer* who's been helping me figure everything out," I say before she can comment. Then I lean in and kiss her cheek, giving her a second to process and hoping she doesn't say anything too embarrassing.

"Oh, Mr. Grossman, pleasure to meet you." Gram holds her hand out to shake, and Benjamin takes it and offers her a slight smile. "Come on in, both of you. I was just having a cup of tea. Either of you want one?" We both shake our heads. "Oh, I forget who I'm talking to, Miss Coffee Snob over here. Want me to make a pot of coffee, sweetheart? Or I did buy wine, as promised." She shoots me a somewhat mischievous grin and casts another look at Benjamin. "Grossman?" she muses. "Where is your family from?"

"Coffee would be great," I say quickly.

"Lithuania," Benjamin answers her. "My grandparents came over when they were very young, so I don't know too much more than that."

She nods, pleased that he's indulged her with an answer. "We're all from Germany. Back when Germany was still a country of Jews. I suppose Katie has told you?"

"A little," I say. In the car I'd given Benjamin only the *Reader's Digest* version of my grandparents' past. Not that I know much more myself.

"Mr. Grossman, some coffee for you, too?"

"Please," he says. "And call me Benjamin."

Gram smiles at him and makes her way into her tiny galley kitchen, where she pours water into her Mr. Coffee. "So after you left, Katie, I kept thinking about your letter. Something was gnawing at me. Something familiar."

"About Grotsburg?" I ask. "She helped me find their town on the old Austrian map," I tell Benjamin.

"No," Gram says. "The woman's name on the letter. *Faber.* I just kept thinking I'd seen it somewhere before." She adds the coffee grinds, turns the pot on, and wipes her hands on a dish towel. She walks over to her tiny kitchen table and grabs a plastic box that appears to be filled with papers. "I went up to the attic last week. I keep a bunch of your grandfather's correspondence up there I didn't want to part with after he died. Letters his mother had sent us from

Germany before the war, things like that." She pulls a letter out of the box and hands it to me.

The envelope is old, yellowed, crumbly in my fingers. It's addressed to my grandfather, and has several canceled German (I think?) stamps on the top. "Third Reich airmail stamps," Benjamin says, pointing. "1939."

"This is from his mother?" I ask Gram, trying to conjure a mental picture of her and failing. My grandfather never talked to me about his family, his history, his life before he'd come to America, and now I regret that I'd never asked. But it just wasn't something we talked about. And I realize I'm not even sure what my German great-grandmother's name was.

"Not that one, no," Gram says. "But it was in the box with her letters. Go ahead, open it up."

Benjamin peers over my shoulder as I gingerly take out the crumbling letter from inside. "It's written in German?" It looks indecipherable to me.

Gram pulls her reading glasses up to her eyes. "Your grandfather went to art school in Berlin."

"I never knew that," I say.

"Well, his time there was cut short when we moved to America, and it seemed his passion for drawing went away once we got here, too. After we left I never heard him speak of it again. Until this letter came for him, years later. A friend of his from art school got trapped in Austria after the Nazi occupation and his daughter wrote to Gid, wanting his help in getting her father out."

I'm trying to piece together everything she's telling me about my grandfather long before I ever knew him, long before he was mine. He went to art school in Berlin, as a young man? A friend of his got trapped in Austria by the Nazis? Though I knew they were born in Germany, I always thought of my grandparents as American Jews, untouched by the war, since they were here long before it started. But Gram told me her entire town in Germany had burned, and now I think of the people they must've left behind. "I guess I don't really know much of anything about your lives before you came here," I say. "I feel bad that I never asked."

"It's okay, sweetheart," Gram says. "He never talked about it. Neither one of us did. We wanted it that way." She reaches up and touches my hair, the way she has since I was a little girl, and she smiles at me, in that way that a grandmother loves her granddaughter, with a pure and blind sort of perfection, the way she has always loved me and still does, even now that I'm a grown woman, newly unemployed, and nearly divorced.

Her hand moves from my hair, and her curling forefinger traces down the letter to the bottom. "Here, look at the signature on the letter, sweetheart." It reads, *Hochachtungsvoll, Elena Faber.* "Respectfully yours, Elena Faber," Gram says.

My hands shake as I put the letter down on the table. "So Grandpa Gid knew Frederick Faber? *That* was his friend from art school?" I ask.

At the same time, Benjamin says, "So did you help him get out?"

"Yes and yes," Gram says, looking at me, then Benjamin. "Only Herr Faber changed his name before he got here. I don't know, I guess they forged his papers so he could get out of Austria. When he came here, I just knew him as Charlie. I don't think I ever saw this letter before. Your grandfather just told me about his friend, and I'm sure he called him Frederick or Faber back then, but when he got here, to me, he was Charlie Darnay." She walks back into the kitchen to get mugs for the coffee. "That's why I didn't immediately connect everything when you showed me your letter a few weeks ago."

"So Frederick Faber didn't die in Austria?" Benjamin's eyes are open wide, his voice filled with excitement, discovery. "Frederick came here? He was living in California under a different name?" Gram nods, and Benjamin turns to me. "I bet that's how your father got the letter in his collection," he says. "From Frederick—or Charlie—himself."

"No," Gram says. "Poor Charlie wasn't in very good shape when he got here. He passed away only a year or so later. Before we ever knew your father," she says to me. "Marissa was just maybe a freshman in high school when Charlie passed. And she didn't meet your father until just after she graduated, a few years later. Your father never met Charlie." The coffee finishes brewing, she pours two mugs, and hands one to me and one to Benjamin.

"But maybe your dad found the letter here," Benjamin says. "Otherwise it seems like such a coincidence for him to have this in his collection, only to have what . . . found it in a thrift shop, randomly?"

"We didn't see Charlie much. I really didn't know him well, to tell you the truth," Gram says. "He was Gid's friend, and Gid found him a place to live and went to see him from time to time during that year. I had Charlie over for dinner a few times when he first got here, but then . . ." She holds her hands up in the air and her voice trails off. She isn't sure why she didn't know him. And it was all so long ago. Maybe she can't even remember.

"What about Elena?" I ask. "Did you ever hear from her again?"

"No," Gram says. "Like I said, I didn't think of her or the name until you showed me your letter a few weeks ago. And that's the only one I found from her among Gid's things. If there were others, they're gone now."

"So she never came here, after the war?"

"Maybe she did," Gram says. "But I never knew anything about it."

❋

Benjamin and I are quiet on the car ride back. The sky is growing dark, but there's still traffic, and I'm concentrating hard on the freeway. I'm thinking about Elena's letter, and not just the one I've been carrying around for weeks, the one intended for her, but also the one she wrote, to *my* grandfather to try to save her father. I've been picturing Elena as this beautiful stranger, trapped by the Nazis, but she's not that different from me, not that distant. I just had the good fortune of my grandparents making it to America before the Nazis rose to power. Of being born a little later, in a safe place.

"I don't believe in coincidences," Benjamin finally says when we are almost back, through Orange County. The traffic slows, and ahead of us, I see the glow of a million orange taillights on the 5, bumper to bumper, heading right into LA.

"What do you mean?"

"Your father having this letter in his collection. Your grandfather knowing Frederick Faber, helping him come to America. I mean maybe our letter was in your grandfather's stash of things, too, and your father got ahold of it at some point. Or maybe your grandfather told him about Frederick."

I'd just assumed my father had found the letter in a thrift shop, by chance, the way he'd collected so many of his stamps. But given what Gram just told us about my family's connection to the Fabers, Benjamin might be right. "Maybe that's why he got so upset when I showed him the letter a few weeks ago. It meant something to him, or to my grandfather. And he was talking about my grandfather the other day," I say. "Maybe it's all connected in his mind somehow." I just wish I knew how.

"Could you ask him?" Benjamin says. "Would he remember?"

"I don't know." Before he moved into the Willows, my father was spectacular when telling me about the past. "He's been so edgy lately. And he got so upset the one time I showed him the letter that I'm almost afraid to bring it up again."

"Yeah," Benjamin says. "Your father was worried you would get in trouble for having the letter?" I nod. "Maybe he took it from your grandfather without his permission."

"That doesn't sound like him. He loved my grandfather like a father. His father died when he was very young, so Grandpa Gid was all he had. I can't imagine he would've stolen anything from him."

We approach the exit for my house, and I consider inviting Benjamin to come over, have a drink. I enjoyed our breakfast early this morning, so many hours ago that it almost feels like days. And I can't stop thinking about the easy way we fell asleep that night in Wales, holding hands.

"Thanks for bringing me with you today," Benjamin says. "I haven't been south of LA in a while. I've been avoiding this part of the freeway since . . ." His voice trails off, and he turns to look out the window. But he doesn't have to finish his thought, I know he means since the accident that killed his family.

"Thanks for coming," I say, and I drive right past my exit, without bringing up my house, the drink. It's a stupid idea. Benjamin is still grieving for his wife; he's only here with me now for the stamp. I drop him back at his office and then I head home, alone.

Austria, 1939

THE COMFORT Josef and Schwann found in guns, Kristoff found in charcoal, paints, paper, and even the burin, so it wasn't a terrible job to work day in and day out, drawing up and engraving plates for papers with Elena, as long as he didn't let himself think about what would happen if Herr Bergmann were to find out.

When the new papers were nearly finished, almost ready for Josef to take to his printer friend, they discussed at their meeting how they would deliver them to Robert and Elisa in Vienna. It was too dangerous to mail them when the Germans opened and censored so much mail, too dangerous to hand deliver them either. Like all the remaining Jews in Vienna, they were no longer allowed to be tenants, and they'd been forced into a Jewish home, where they were closely watched by soldiers, ready to arrest them for the smallest reason.

"Everything is too dangerous." Elena held her hands up in the air, sounding frustrated, though Kristoff realized not with them, but with their situation. He sketched an edelweiss, and thought again about the promise he'd made to Frederick, that he would give her this flower, but that he would not be stupid doing it.

Kristoff stared at his sketch, his flower, as the others continued to talk. It resembled Frederick's stamp, the stamp Kristoff had admired as a boy. Frederick, weak in the cabin, had said that this was his way of showing his love. His proof of unusual daring. *The only way to fight the enemy is to become them*, Frederick had said to him.

And then Kristoff had an idea. They had the means to send Robert and Elisa a message that their papers were ready, a way right here in front of him the entire time.

"The stamps," he said out loud. They were all still talking over him, arguing, really, about what was dangerous and what wasn't. "Stamps," Kristoff said louder, loud enough so they stopped bickering to look at him.

"What about them?" Josef asked, folding his arms in front of his chest.

"The Stephensdom stamp is already in circulation. What if I altered it a little, put a message in the picture to let them know their papers are ready? You could mail them a boring letter talking about the weather, so even if the Germans read it, they'd have no idea what we're doing. The key would be the stamp. And the cathedral. You could take the papers there to give to them. The Germans won't be watching a church."

Elena looked at him. Her face turned in surprise, then delight. She reached out and laced her fingers through his. Kristoff thought she hadn't wanted Josef and Schwann to know of their affection. But she pulled him closer to her, wrapped her arms around him in a hug. He put down his sketch pad so he could hold on to her. Josef glanced between them, but he didn't say anything for a few moments. Finally he said, "You would be risking everything. If the Germans notice the alteration in the stamp, they'll know for certain that it's your work."

"I know," Kristoff said.

"They'll kill you," Josef said.

"Yes." Kristoff swallowed hard. He remembered the way Josef had looked at him that morning he'd vomited in the snow, after Josef had handed him a gun, the way Josef had continued to look at him since, as if he were a liability, a child. *I should've put you on the Kindertransport*, he'd said then, disgusted. But now he looked at Kristoff differently, as if he were seeing him, for the first time, as a man.

❄

The next morning in the workshop, Elena still seemed giddy with excitement over Kristoff's idea. She couldn't sit still. She paced; she practically bounced. Kristoff held his sketchbook on his lap, worrying he'd made a promise he couldn't keep. Every intricate line of Stephensdom seemed to taunt him. He wanted to hide an edelweiss in there, but it had to be hidden enough that the Germans wouldn't notice as the letter went through the post, obvious enough so that Elisa and Robert would. He tried sketching the petals loosely, lightly, in the spirals of the turret, and he handed the sketch pad to Elena to ask for her opinion.

She stopped moving to look at it. "I don't see . . . oh." She reached her hand up, traced the outline of the petals. "Just like my father's," she said, tears welling up in her eyes.

He pulled the sketchbook from her hands and put it down on the worktable. He reached for her, pulled her tightly to him. "Your father is safe now," he said into her hair. "And we're going to leave soon, too."

"Kristoff, I can never leave my mother behind. I—"

He kissed her to keep her from finishing her sentence, from protesting further. "Let me show you something." He walked over to the shelf where he'd hidden his work on Amata Marsch's papers, behind old textbooks of Frederick's. "I'm making you papers, too. I'm almost finished." As he handed the plates over to her, he felt nervous that she would get angry. But instead she started to laugh. "What's funny?" he asked, feeling a little hurt. Was she laughing at him? At these papers he'd worked so hard on for her?

She walked to the hidden floor space, removed the board, and pulled out an engraving plate. "I'm making *you* papers, too." She handed him the plate, the fake name she'd chosen for him, Theodor Laurenz, a perfect match to his Amata Marsch.

"I'm your Laurie," he said, and for the first time, Kristoff saw a real future for them, beyond this nightmare, beyond these beautiful stolen moments they'd been sharing. "I love you," he said, daring to say it when she wasn't in his bed already asleep, but in the daylight, when they were both wide-awake, when he was looking straight into her eyes, which in the light of the workshop appeared a greenish silver, with the luster of coins.

She put her plate down on the worktable, stood up on her tiptoes, and put her face right next to his. She kissed him once, tenderly. He knew how she felt. She didn't have to say it.

But then she did: "I love you, too."

Los Angeles, 1989

THE NEXT MORNING when I first wake up, it takes me a minute to remember everything that happened yesterday: the letter Gram found, Frederick Faber's connection to my family, and Benjamin's insistence that he doesn't believe in coincidences. Also, I quit my job; I don't have to go to work today. I get out of bed, get dressed, and head into the kitchen to make some coffee, feeling both overwhelmingly relieved and terrified to be unemployed.

I want to go back to the Willows, see my dad again, talk to him about what Gram found. But he was so out of it yesterday that I can't bring myself to do it just yet, so I start going through the files Jason gave me over drinks a few weeks ago, which have been sitting on my kitchen table ever since. I page through his notes, the various organizations he found that can help loved ones track down people lost during the war. The first one, the Holocaust Society of LA, seems closest, most accessible, so I decide to start by giving them a call.

I talk to a woman named Jackie Goldberg who says she can

search the database she's been working on for the past few years, compiling names of Holocaust victims, survivors. She tells me her database is still incomplete, but she's happy to check for Elena and Kristoff.

"He wasn't even Jewish," I tell her of Kristoff. "He's probably a long shot."

"Well, it's *all* a long shot," she responds, and sighs. "There were so many victims buried in mass graves, and then there are survivors who still don't want to be found or who've changed their names." Like Frederick Faber, whom Gram only knew as Charlie.

"So how do you do it?" I ask her. "It must be incredibly frustrating work."

"It is," she says. "But how can we not do it? We have to, don't we?"

It's funny how she says *we*, and I tell her I'm not doing anything, really, just looking for the writer and recipient of one letter. Just telling one story.

"Okay," she says. But she sounds skeptical, like she doesn't believe me, and then she says she'll get back to me if and when she finds something.

❋

I barely hang up the phone before I hear a knock at my door. I glance out the front window and Daniel's silver BMW is parked in the street.

"Katie," he calls for me through the door. "I know you're home. I see your car. Open up." I remember my hastily scribbled resignation note before I left the office yesterday, and even though I'd love to run back to my bedroom, crawl back under the covers, and ignore him, I should get this over with. So I go and open the door.

Daniel looks at me, surprised, as if he hadn't actually expected me to open up, despite what he called when he knocked. "Come on in," I say, but he hesitates for a moment, looks inside, past me, his eyes scanning the living room, the way you might study a place that once belonged to you, but doesn't anymore. It's like the way I felt when I went back to my father's house for the summer after my freshman year in college, just after my mother had died, when it was a place that looked like home but didn't feel that way anymore.

"You changed the curtains." He finally steps inside and points to the window, just behind the couch. Yes, I'd replaced the expensive curtains his mother had bought us for an anniversary gift with some cheap ones I'd found at Kmart. They have bluebirds on them, and they match the pale blue paint on the wall. I'd thrown the old velour curtains out, an act that had filled me with a small moment of satisfaction at the time.

"So I guess you got my resignation?" I ask, sidestepping his comment about the curtains.

He nods. His face is serious, but he doesn't look mad. "You don't have to resign, Katie. We can still work together."

"I don't think I can," I say.

"Okay," he says, like he gets it, but I'm not sure he does. After all, he moved on, moved out, months ago. "But that's not actually why I'm here." He sits down on the couch. "I was trying to get your attention yesterday, but you left before I could." He looks down and runs his hand across the brown fabric of the couch as if it's new, foreign, like the curtains, though he's the one who picked this couch out at Sears. "The Willows called me last week. I guess they couldn't get ahold of you?"

"What?" It wasn't what I was expecting him to say. The Willows and Daniel, my father and Daniel, are compartmentalized in my mind, like they don't even exist in the same universe.

"I guess I was on their emergency contact list," he says.

Now I feel guilty for avoiding him yesterday if this is what he wanted to tell me. "Sorry," I say. "I filled out the paperwork before we . . . I'll take you off next time I'm over there." I pause. "I went away for Thanksgiving. That's why they couldn't get ahold of me. Why you couldn't either."

"Away?" He raises his eyebrows, contemplating where I might possibly have gone. But I don't explain. It's not his business anymore, where I went, who I went with. "Well, I went to see him. Your dad, I mean. When they called me."

"You did?" Now I'm surprised. "Why?"

He shrugs. "They said they couldn't reach you, and I was next on the list. I didn't know what else to do. I wasn't sure how bad it was. I mean . . . I didn't want anything bad to happen to him, whether we're still married or not." Daniel never offered to help with my father when he was still here. For a good year before he left me, he completely ignored my father, his illness, and when caring for my father became my entire life, I ignored Daniel in return. But I also know that no matter what has happened with us, Daniel really is a nice guy, inherently gracious. And maybe that's why it's been so hard for me to accept, understand, that we're over, that our marriage fell apart.

"Thank you," I say. "It means a lot to me that you did that."

"You know what your dad said to me?" Daniel asks. I shake my head. He laughs a little. "He told me he let the love of his life go, and that I was an idiot to let you go."

I walk over and sit down on the couch next to him. "He doesn't know what he's saying half the time. He probably wasn't talking about you and me. He doesn't even know about us." I can't say any more, because I don't want to cry. Not for Daniel, for what we lost or let go or gave up on or how we grew apart. Because all of that already feels done, gone. But for my dad, and how he's still here but really, he isn't still here at all. "He's gotten pretty bad lately," I say. "You shouldn't take anything he said to heart."

Daniel nods like he understands. "He just came back from art class when I was there and he showed me the picture he made, of your mom. So maybe you're right, maybe he was actually talking about the two of them, but still . . ." His voice trails off, and he looks at me, our eyes meet. Daniel has good eyes, a pale blue, and I remember how thrilled I felt that first night I met him, when he looked at me as if I were something special, someone important. How I told my dad I already loved him, before I really even knew him.

But that was so long ago. So much has changed for me, for us. And maybe our love wasn't the lasting kind. Elena jumped off a train, risking her own life to save her father and to be with Kristoff. Everything must've been so hard, so dangerous, and yet she loved Kristoff so much, she risked everything for him. And Benjamin. Awkward, sweet Benjamin lost his family and he's still broken, two years later. Daniel and I never had love like that. Things got a little hard; we drifted apart; Daniel left. And here we both are, not all that much worse for the wear.

"He gave me the picture he made of your mom," Daniel finally says. "I have it. It's in my trunk. I've been driving around with it all week, wanting to give it to you, wanting to talk to you about it." He pauses, maybe waiting for me to say something else or suggest that maybe my father was right, that Daniel *was* an idiot to let me go, as I would've certainly said to him a few months ago. But I don't say anything. I don't really have anything more to say. "I'll go get the painting," he says. "I'll be right back."

As Daniel goes out to his car, I stand up and walk into the kitchen. I take the envelope with the silly flower stamps off the counter, slice it open, and pull out the divorce papers. I grab a pen and sign in the spots that are marked. When Daniel walks back inside, my father's picture rolled up under his arm, I hold out the papers to him. "What's this?" he asks, quickly followed by a flash of recognition on his face. "You don't have to do this now. You can mail them."

What stamps would I choose to send the papers back to him? I'm not sure exactly what's right to signal the end of a marriage. Maybe flowers weren't even the worst choice, as the end of our marriage is banal, ordinary, and not at all ugly, like these flower stamps themselves. "No," I say. "Take them. I'm sorry it took me so long."

He accepts the papers and hands me the painting. I unroll it, and a beautiful woman, who is most definitely not my mother, unfolds before me. My mom had olive skin, long brown curls, blue eyes, like me. This woman is green-eyed, with pale brown wavy hair that is nearly blonde. Their faces don't look alike. I never would've mistaken her for my mother. "This isn't my mom," I say. "They were probably just copying a painting of some random woman in their art class." I laugh a little.

"Well, I never met her," Daniel says. I glance at the picture of her that's sitting on the mantel of our—my—nonfunctioning fireplace. My favorite one. It's black-and-white, a candid shot taken on the beach in Coronado. I'm about five years old and she's holding on to me. That picture has sat on the mantel since the day Daniel and I moved in here together, but I guess he never paid close attention.

Daniel keeps talking; he's apologizing for his mistake, but I'm not really listening to him anymore. Something catches my eye in the painting, the waves of the woman's pale brown hair. It looks almost like . . . It can't be.

I hold the painting up closer to the sunlight coming in through the front window to examine it. And it's there; I'm not imagining it. The petals of the edelweiss unfold from the woman's hair, hidden, secret, just the way they are on the stamp.

Austria, 1939

I N SEPTEMBER, the Nazis invaded Poland, and France and England declared war. When Kristoff heard the news from Josef, he felt oddly relieved. Because now there were other people fighting the Germans, real soldiers. Not just them.

"Maybe we can stop this," Kristoff said to Elena, as they worked together in the workshop one morning in September. "The French and the British will defeat the Germans." Despite Kristoff's insistence that Robert and Elisa's forged papers would be their last, they were currently working on two new sets of papers: one set for married friends of Josef's cousins who'd heard about what they'd done through Robert, and the other for the Jewish friend of a student Schwann had met at Universität. And Josef had gotten fifty copies of Kristoff's new edelweiss Stephensdom stamp printed, a bad sign that everyone but Kristoff planned to keep on forging many more papers.

In addition to the papers, Kristoff and Elena were also finishing up a new engraving plate for Herr Bergmann. He would be back any day for it, and Kristoff awoke each morning dreading his return.

"That's wishful thinking, Kristoff," Elena said, about his hopes for the rest of Europe to save Austria. She sighed. He knew his continual worry exhausted her. "And I told you, you don't have to help with any of this if you don't want to."

"It's not that I don't want to." He would like to see all the Jews get safely out of Austria. More, have all the Nazis gone, have Austria and the Fabers' house be beautiful and full of light again. "I just don't think Josef was wrong when he said that if we keep doing this, we'll get caught. We'll all be killed."

Elena shook her head. "That was before your brilliant stamps."

"But if a German soldier were to ever notice the edelweiss . . ." He remembered what Josef said to him. *You would be killed if they found out.* Kristoff took it to heart, in a literal way that gave him a perpetual ache in his chest.

"They won't bother with the stamps," Elena said, sounding so certain. He wanted to believe her.

"But you don't know that. And you can't fight the Germans if you're dead," he said. It was a futile argument, one they had often. Kristoff wanted to make a concrete escape plan for Elena, for both of them; Elena refused to even discuss it.

Elena put down the burin, and held out her hand to him. A peace offering. She didn't want to fight. Outside it had turned to dusk, and the light in the workshop was growing dim. When they left the workshop at night they were no longer Elena and Kristoff, who tirelessly worked all day with the metal to help defeat the Germans in their own small way. They were just two people who loved each other. Who wanted to love each other for as long as they could.

❋

Each time they finished forging papers and Kristoff thought he could try to convince Elena to go, Josef came to them with another request, each story sadder than the last, each person more desperate to get out of Austria. And there was no way Kristoff could say no. Instead he and Elena worked longer hours, worked later into the night, grew faster at making the papers. Each time when they were done Josef would get them printed and mail a silly letter that discussed the weather or the condition of the sheep this season on the Bauer farm, and then he would address it and put Kristoff's edelweiss stamp in the corner. Josef would drop the letter in the post and Schwann would take the forged papers to Vienna, to Stephensdom to meet the recipients there.

Kristoff often felt he was holding his breath, waiting for the Germans to come take them away, arrest them for their crimes. He considered asking Josef for the gun back, but the truth was he wasn't sure what he would do with it, how to use it. And anyway, he was certain that he would lose in a gunfight.

❋

One morning in October they awoke to the sounds of pounding on the front door, and Kristoff jumped up in bed, his heart nearly stopped. *Germans.*

Josef had told them just last week that he'd heard in Vienna that hundreds of Jews had been deported, rumored to have been sent to the Polish ghetto. Their work was even more important now, Josef had said. Or, Kristoff had thought, they were about to be caught.

The pounding came again, and Kristoff was sure. They had discovered his stamp.

Then he heard the sound of Josef's voice, calling for Elena, and he rested on the edge of his bed for a moment, nearly collapsing with relief.

When Elena heard Josef call her name, she hastily pulled on Kristoff's long shirt, and he threw on his pants before they ran downstairs to answer the door together.

Josef stepped inside, looked right at Elena, and she wrapped Kristoff's shirt tighter around herself, as if suddenly she was embarrassed, too exposed. "What?" she demanded, sounding defensive.

"I got this in the post," he said. He held a lettercard out; his hands were shaking, so unlike him, and Kristoff's heart beat so fast, certain still they'd been exposed in some way, that it was all over. *How fast could we run?* he wondered. "It's from your mother," Josef said to Elena, his voice breaking a little.

"What?" Elena asked, taking it from him. "How?"

"Read it," Josef said. Kristoff peered over her shoulder and saw the lettercard said *Konzentrationslager Mauthausen* at the top. Underneath that were typed instructions for communicating and corresponding with the prisoner. *The prisoner?* But Mrs. Faber had done nothing wrong other than living her life, being Jewish in Austria. The right side of the lettercard was addressed to Josef, and it was franked with one of Kristoff's very own Stephensdom stamps—the authentic German-sponsored ones.

"The stamp," he said, and he felt overwhelmed with despair to think that it had been used by Mrs. Faber, like this, as a *prisoner*.

Elena turned the card over. On the back there was a note to Josef, and Elena traced the letters, as if by tracing her mother's handwriting she could feel her, imagine her again as real, breathing. She read the words out loud: *"Dear Josef, I am writing to ask you about my girls. I am well and a good worker. I am eating and the weather is not too cold yet. My daily spirits are good. But I think and pray all day every day about my girls, that they are safe. Please tell me that they are. Please write me back when you get this. Yours, Minna Faber."*

Elena held the lettercard to her chest, inhaled deeply. Her mother was alive, and she was all right, for now. "I'll write her today," Elena said.

"You can't," Josef said. "They censor all the mail and the Germans think you're gone. You can't write her."

"But I have to," Elena exclaimed. "I have to let Mother know that Miri is in England, and that Father is alive and in America, and that I'm here. I'm still fighting for her. For Austria."

She looked to Kristoff for support, but he agreed with Josef. "I'm sorry," he said. "Josef is right."

"I'll write her," Josef said. "I'll tell her you and Miri left for London. That you're both safe."

"But that's a lie! And what about Father? She thinks he's dead."

"It's better for all of us, better for her if the truth about your father stays our secret for now. The Germans believe him to be dead," Josef said. "It's better they keep on believing that."

Josef put his arm around her shoulders in a way that bothered Kristoff, but he didn't move. "Look," Josef said. "She's alive. She says she is strong. That is all good news."

"Yes," Elena tentatively agreed.

"I'll write her back today and tell her not to worry, to keep herself safe," Josef said. "That is the most important thing, for all of us. Staying safe."

For once, Kristoff agreed with him.

❋

"Tell me a story about our future," Elena said to Kristoff a few nights later. They lay in his bed, in the darkness. Elena's naked thigh tangled around his; her skin felt cold, and he pulled the blanket tighter around them both. The air was getting chillier in the attic now that it was fall.

"Well," Kristoff said. "We'll go to America, find your father. We'll get a little house. Smaller than this one, maybe, but it will be all our own."

"Near the water," Elena said, her voice soft, dreamy. "I've always wanted to be near water."

"Near the water." Kristoff did not know the geography of America well enough, but he vowed to study a map the next day to find a location Elena would love. He kissed the top of her head, inhaling her apricot hair.

Elena curled into him and her body relaxed a little. "We'll be reunited with Mother and Miri, too. And then we'll have a baby, a little girl," she said. "Or maybe two. A girl and a boy."

"A girl and a boy," Kristoff murmured, trying to imagine what it would be like not to feel this constant weight in his stomach. This continual overwhelming dread. He tried to imagine feeling light, free. He tried to picture Elena the same, as a mother, with their children. And what would their children look like? He saw them both with Elena's pear eyes and light brown waves. Two beautiful little people running amidst the skim of the sea, throwing shiny pebbles into the waves. Elena's laughter would echo in the rush of the water.

Neither one of them said anything else for a while, both lost in their own dreams. Kristoff realized he had never wanted anything more than he wanted this vision he'd said out loud for Elena.

"I want you to love someone else," Elena finally said, her voice lolling, half asleep. "If something happens to me, you'll have all of that with someone else."

"I'll never love anyone else," Kristoff said. "I don't want to. I only want it with you."

But Elena didn't say anything more. Her breathing evened. After nights of staying up late, working, she was finally sound asleep.

Los Angeles, 1989

IF BENJAMIN'S RIGHT, that it can't be a coincidence that my father has this stamp in his collection, then he must've known about Gram and Grandpa Gid's connection to Frederick Faber, somehow. And it must be something still ingrained in his memory. A piece of the past that comes through the sieve, even as so much else falls away. Why else would he have put the edelweiss in his own artwork?

I'm driving to the Willows, armed with the picture Daniel brought me, the unfamiliar woman with the edelweiss hidden in her hair. I'm hoping my father will tell me something today. I'm hoping that maybe he holds the key, somewhere deep in his mind, the knowledge of what happened to Kristoff and Elena.

"Oh good, you got it." Sally points to the picture under my arm when I walk in. "I gave it to your husband when he was here last week."

"Ex-husband," I say. It feels freeing to tell the truth, and Karen was right, I do feel better now that it's final.

Sally only acknowledges my correction with a nod and doesn't ask me any more about it. Really, why would she? "Ted's pretty good this morning," she says instead. I exhale, shaking off some of the nervousness I'd felt on the drive over here. It feels crazy to always be so nervous coming to see him, my own dad. But I don't know that I'll ever get over the uncertainty of never knowing how terribly our visit might go. "Oh." I realize Sally is still talking. "I have half a dozen more of those if you want them, too?" She points again to the picture I'm holding.

"My dad's drawings?"

She nods. "They're all the same, though. Every time he's been going to art class lately he draws your mom," she says. "It's really very sweet."

"This isn't my mom."

"Really? Oh . . . I. Well, that's why I saved them all for you."

"Why did you think it was my mom?" I ask, curious. It's strange that she and Daniel both had the same incorrect reaction to the picture.

She hesitates for a minute. "He just kept telling me that he was drawing 'his love.' I just assumed . . . But maybe . . ." She stammers a little like she's dug herself into a hole and she's not sure how to get out of it. She smiles sadly at me. "You should go on back," she says. "I'll get the other pictures out of the storage closet and you can decide if you want them before you leave."

❀

As I walk down the hallway toward his room, I look again at the picture I'm carrying. *His love.* Is he really so far gone that he can't remember my mother's face? I'm kind of heartbroken that it's just me and Gram keeping her alive, with our own foggy memories of her. Or is it possible that my father, this man I've always loved, always respected and trusted, had an affair? Loved an entirely different woman?

"Kate the Great!" He spies me in the doorway. His voice is boisterous. The man I've known forever. *He's still here.*

"Hi, Dad." I try to force some cheer as I walk into his room, but my voice comes out flat, like the cardboard Christmas ornaments hanging in the hallway just outside his room.

"What's wrong, honey?" he asks. I want to tell him everything. In this short moment where he seems to be himself I want to tell him the entire story of the last few months of my life: Daniel leaving and all the things Benjamin and I discovered. For some reason, most of all I want to tell him about the color of the bricks at Oxford, the way the air smelled like mud, and the way Benjamin has become as attached to the stamp and its story as I have.

But I simplify. "Daniel and I got divorced," I say.

He nods. This news doesn't surprise him. I try to judge whether Daniel told him when he was here (and whether he would actually remember this a week later) or whether he just always thought this would happen. That it was inevitable. "You're okay?" he finally says.

"I think so," I answer truthfully. "Maybe I'm just meant to be alone."

My father puts his hand on my shoulder, and I realize this is the most real conversation we've had in months. I want to savor it, breathe it in, stretch it out and make it last for days.

"You know, honey," he says, "you'll find someone else." I shrug. "There's not just one true love for every person. I never believed that. You can fall in love, and then that ends. And then you can fall in love all over again, with someone new."

"Like you did with Mom?" I unravel the picture from under my arm and push it toward him. "Your love?" I point to the woman he drew. "You fell out of love with Mom once, and in love with her?"

He frowns, reaches his finger out, and traces the woman's face on his painting. "This was a long time ago," he finally says. "There are things you never knew about me. Things that happened long before you."

I'm trying to process what he's saying, and it all feels so obvious, and yet so unexpected. It never really occurred to me to consider a life of his, a love of his, before me, before my mom. That he was once a person other than my dad. *A long time ago.* No wonder he has been reliving it lately as his short-term memories have begun to fade away. As his disease progresses, he's moving back into the past, living there. "What things?" I ask him. I want to know his stories while he still grasps them. I want to understand him before he's completely gone. It was why I took the stamps to be appraised in the first place. I'm just not ready to let him go yet.

"There are things you don't know about me, Rissa," he says, his voice breaking a little on my mother's name. I don't correct him, because I want to listen, want to know what he's remembering. "I was a different person once," he says.

Gram told me that she never knew Frederick Faber, she only knew Charlie. *He was a different person here*, she said.

"And you can't be mad about that." Was she mad? Did he tell my mother about this other woman once, and she got upset?

"I'm not mad," I say. My father's fingers linger on the woman's hair. He traces every line, every detail, the petals I'd noticed last night. "An edelweiss?" I say tentatively.

"Proof of unusual daring," my father says.

Proof of unusual daring, my father used to say, Miriam had told me and Benjamin in her depressing room in Raintree. "What did you say?" I ask him.

He attempts to clarify: "Proof that I loved her."

Elena loved Kristoff, Miriam had said. *And the only woman Kristoff ever noticed was Elena . . . The stamp could've been Kristoff's.*

It can't be a coincidence, Benjamin had insisted last night.

I look at him again, this man I've known my entire life. My father. Ted. What if everything I thought I knew about his past, before me, was wrong? How old was he in 1939? I try to do the math quickly in my head. Twenty. Twenty-one? He stares at his picture with longing, with loss, with . . . love? *I was a different person once.* And then I don't see my father at all.

"Kristoff?" The name escapes me with disbelief, even as I say it. I don't honestly expect any reaction. My father was born in Germany, Bremen, Gram thought. My father was a history teacher who collects stamps, not engraves them.

But he looks up, meets my eyes, and smiles a little, as if he's been waiting for me to say it forever.

Austria, 1939

B Y THE BEGINNING OF NOVEMBER, Elena and I had forged nearly twenty sets of papers. When Josef brought our most recent six to the workshop after being printed, I admired our work.

Parts of Poland had just been annexed by Germany, and everything felt like it was slipping away. We were losing ground. The French and British had not stopped Hitler as I'd hoped. Elena and I were working harder, working faster. I knew it would all come crashing down on us; we'd be captured, sent to a camp, murdered. I was always waiting for it. Knowing it was coming. Though maybe I didn't fully believe it. Maybe that was why I kept doing the work, kept going to bed every night and waking up each day and making papers, all side by side with Elena. Or maybe it was just that I loved her so much, I didn't know how to leave her, how to let her go, how to save her.

"And I have these for you, too." Josef reached into his satchel that night, and he handed me the papers I'd asked him to print for me, for us. Elena's papers and mine. Amata Marsch's and Theodor

Laurenz's papers. Amy and Laurie would be together, just like in Elena's favorite book.

"What's this?" Elena plucked them from my hands. "Kristoff?" She turned to me and scowled. "I'm not—"

"I know," I said. "I just want to be ready. In case we have to leave quickly." The truth was, I planned to convince her later, when we were alone, that we needed to go as soon as possible. Her mother was okay, but also out of our reach. She'd said in her letter that more than anything she wished for her girls' safety, and I hoped her words would be enough for me to convince Elena that it was time for us to let go, to leave Austria.

"Elena, he's not wrong," Josef said. "We have been playing a game, winning for a while. But eventually the Germans will notice the stamp, they'll come for Kristoff."

Elena sat down on the stool and looked up at me, offering a small sigh, then a nod. It was too easy, the way she'd agreed to leave on the *Kindertransport* that day in the woods, what felt like ages ago now. I didn't believe we'd changed her mind that fast, but I didn't want to discuss it any more in front of Josef. I would talk to her later, when we were alone.

Josef put down his satchel and pulled our forged stamps from their hiding spot in the floor, to take out what he needed for six more letters. He pulled out the stamps, looked them over, frowned. "What is it?" I asked him, wondering if he noticed some imperfection in the stamps.

"Nothing," he said. "It's nothing."

"Are you sure?" I asked him. "Is there something wrong with them?" *Those stamps*. It was the first time, the only time, I felt pride in a stamp I made. It belonged so much to both of us. Me and Elena. That was our beautiful creation.

"No. There's nothing wrong with them." He pulled out the six he needed and put the rest back into the hiding space in the floor.

❋

We planned to mail the six new letters out at separate times, sorted in among other regular mail, lest Josef look too suspicious carrying a pile of letters all with fake stamps into the post. Josef wanted him, Schwann, and me to each take two letters at separate times.

"I'll take one, too," Elena said. "Kristoff and I will split up."

"No," I said. As far as the Germans knew, Elena was gone. And even if they weren't to recognize her, I didn't like the idea of her going into town all alone.

"Jews are still allowed to mail letters," Elena said in a huff. "Last I checked."

Jews had lost so much; everything. They were being evacuated, isolated, deported, put into work camps. They had a curfew. Though Elena was right Jews were still allowed to mail letters. Josef or Elena wouldn't be arrested simply for that.

"It's no more dangerous for her than it is for me," Josef said. "And you are the engraver of this stamp, are you not? You might arouse the most suspicion."

"It's dangerous for all of us all of the time," Elena said, matter-of-factly.

I nodded, but the danger was so palpable, the worry, the fear. It left a particular metallic taste in my mouth.

We put our letters into the floor space for the night, and Elena left the workshop to go into the kitchen and prepare supper. Josef gathered his things to leave, too, but at the doorway he turned back, spoke to me: "You have your papers now. If anything happens to the rest of us you save yourself, all right, Kristoff?"

"I would never leave her," I told him.

"Don't be stupid," Josef said.

❀

Inside the kitchen, Elena had heated some broth and we ate it with stale bread, in silence. Josef's words haunted me, and I wanted to get Elena to leave with me, now. "I have almost enough reichsmarks saved to buy tickets to America for both of us," I said to her as we did the dishes in the kitchen. "We should talk about a plan to leave as soon as possible. It's what your mother wants for you. You read what she wrote."

"Okay," she said. "But let's talk about it more in the morning. I'm tired." She put the last dish down, turned toward me, and reached her hand out for mine.

I took her hand. "I know what you're doing," I said. She shook her head. "Don't lie to me. Don't tell me what I want to hear and then do something stupid on your own." *Stupid*, the same word Josef had used.

"I'm not going to do anything stupid." She held my gaze, unflinching, so for a second, I almost believed her. "I promise. Kristoff," her voice softened. "I love you."

"I love you, too," I said.

She tugged on my hand, and we went up the stairs together, to the attic.

The air was frigid, but that didn't stop Elena from taking off her clothes. Nothing frightened her. Not even the bitter almost-winter chill.

She slipped into bed with me, the way she had so many nights, and she kissed me, almost forcefully. I ran my hand against her back. Her bare skin felt icy, and she shivered a little as I touched her. "I'll get another blanket," I said.

"No." She reached for my shoulders and pulled me back toward her so I wouldn't get out of the bed. "Don't go." She kissed me again. She pulled herself on top of me, and our bodies moved in a way that had become so familiar, so easy. We were one person, together. Even our breathing seemed in harmony, our chests rising up and down and up and down, as one.

Afterwards, she laid her head against my chest, her ear against my heart. "If we get separated," she said quietly into the darkness, "I'll meet you in America. You'll go without me . . ." Her voice trailed off. She was half asleep. She didn't even know what she was saying.

"We're not going to get separated." Secretly I planned to take both her letter and my own to the post tomorrow morning, before she had a chance to. I couldn't risk her walking to town alone, no matter what she or Josef said.

"Promise me," she said.

"I promise." I stroked her hair absently between my fingers, and I drifted off to sleep.

When I awoke the next morning, she was already gone.

Los Angeles, 1989

S HE TOOK THE LETTERS," my father says, turning to look out the window. I'm still trying to absorb his story, put together what he told me, along with what I already know from Miriam and Gram. "They were both gone. I found one in the snow, at the edge of the woods. I don't think she made it to town before the Germans got her." He lets out a strangled cry, like he's reliving it all again, right in this moment.

"Oh, Dad." I put my hand on his shoulder, but he doesn't react, just stares out the window as if he can still see Elena, somewhere, just beyond the hills where I often think he can see my mother.

I try to make sense of everything he just told me. My father, my dad. Fifty years ago he engraved stamps for Austria, for the Nazis, and for the resistance. I always knew his first language was German, though I never heard him speak a word of it, ever. He loved telling me about history, the world's past, but he never talked about his own past, before he came to the United States. I'd always thought it was because he was so young when he came over, just a boy—that was the word he always used himself—that he couldn't remember another life in Europe the way Gram could. But maybe his silence was a choice. *I was a different person then*, he said. I always knew he'd converted to Judaism when he'd married my mom and that he was so steeped in religion, my mom used to tease he was more of a Jew than she was. But now knowing all this . . . this man he used to be, this woman he once loved, it almost all makes sense.

I look at him again. His face is contorted, and he has tears in his eyes. He reaches his hand up and puts it against the glass of the window. "I never saw her again," he's saying, not necessarily to me. "Never again," he repeats.

"But you came to America to meet her here, just like she asked?" He's still staring out the window, but I keep talking, more to myself than to him, trying to piece it all together. "You came to find Frederick Faber, but he was already dead. And then you met Gram and Grandpa Gid. And Mom." Benjamin was right. None of this was a coincidence. I wonder if my mother knew any or all of this. Maybe she did. But Gram doesn't. So maybe my mother never knew either.

And this letter that Benjamin and I have been clinging to these past few weeks, it was never sent. "You wrote a letter to Elena after she disappeared that morning, but then you never sent it? You kept it all these years. You collected all those stamps . . ." I suddenly understand it; I understand him. All the trips to thrift stores, yard sales, sifting through other people's trash, holding on to all those stamps. His collection. Not just paper and ink. The stamps were a connection to the past, his past, to this person he once was, this woman he once loved.

"I loved her," my father says. He turns and puts his hand on my cheek. "But I love you, too. I don't want you to go, Rissa. I don't want you to leave me, too."

"I won't," I say. And I sit with my father for a long time and look out his window with him. I sit with him until Sally interrupts, tells my father it's time for lunch. "Turkey sandwiches, Ted, your favorite," she says, smiling too wide.

"You'll tell her I'm here," he says to me as he listens to Sally, stands to go to lunch. I'm not sure who he thinks I am now, where he thinks we are, and who he's really asking after. "If you see her, you'll tell her where to find me."

"I will," I promise. But it feels just like the promises I always make to him when I leave here, when I promise to find his airline tickets, to look for his departure date, his checkout time from this hotel. It's an empty promise.

※

I head straight to Benjamin's office after I leave the Willows. In the story my father just told me, Kristoff is a different man. Not just my father with a changed name, but a stranger, a person I never knew. I keep reminding myself that it was him, that he lived through all of that. It's a wonder that he survived, that he got out of Austria, made it here. That I'm sitting here. The thought gives me chills, though it's hot inside the car.

I park haphazardly, taking up two different spots, and I run from my car through the parking lot, opening the front door of Benjamin's office hard enough that the bell hits the glass and makes a loud clanging sound.

"Katie?" Benjamin stands up; he's surprised to see me, and he smiles.

"I found Kristoff," I say. I'm out of breath. And Benjamin walks around to the front of his desk, takes some papers off a chair for me to sit on.

"Our Kristoff?" he asks as I sit.

"My Kristoff." Benjamin's face falls; he thinks I'm trying to exclude him. "No, no, I didn't mean it like that," I say. "My Kristoff because Kristoff is my father."

"Your father is Ted," Benjamin says, in that logical way he has of seeing everything.

"And Frederick was Charlie when he came here, remember?"

Benjamin frowns; he's still not sure, and I might almost doubt the truth of it, too, except my father's words were so real, so vivid, when he told me this morning. I tell Benjamin how his details overlapped with Miriam's and Gram's and Dr. Grimes's assumptions about the stamp. And how now it all makes sense to me: my father's lifelong obsession with stamps. Looking for them. Collecting them. Preserving them. Loving them. And I tell Benjamin about his paintings at the Willows, the edelweiss in the woman's hair, the same flower that was on our stamp. I've taken one with me, courtesy of Sally on the way out, and I show it to Benjamin, who examines it closely, then hands it back to me.

"He was a stamp engraver in Austria during the war." Benjamin's voice is filled with awe. He sits on the front edge of his desk and leans in toward me. He's close enough that our legs almost touch. "Your dad?"

"My dad," I repeat, and I tell Benjamin the rest of the story my father told me, about forging papers, about how the edelweiss was *proof of unusual daring*, proof that he loved Elena, about how they forged their own papers to become the characters Elena loved from

Little Women, and how he never saw Elena again after that morning when she went to mail the last letters.

"Wow," Benjamin says, and then he's quiet for a few minutes, speechless. "What do you think happened to the other letters?" he asks, when he recovers. "The ones that Josef and Schwann were supposed to mail? Do you think they actually sent them, that they got those people their papers even after Elena was taken?"

"I don't know." It seems so small in the face of the whole rest of Europe, Austria, all the Jews who died in the camps. My father and Elena and Josef and Schwann—does it really matter whether they saved ten people or fifteen or twenty? *Yes*, for some reason it feels like it does. The tiny town of Grotsburg where everything was eradicated by the Nazis, everything burned, is no longer just a missing dot on a modern map, but people who are connected to me, my family, my own history.

"I guess Elena was probably taken to Mauthausen herself and joined her mother. Or she was killed that day," Benjamin says. "Either way, she probably didn't make it through the war."

I ache for her, this woman I never met or knew, this woman my father loved when he was a different person. This woman who saved her own sister and her father and strangers, but did not save herself when she had the chance. My father said she forged his papers, she made him promise to leave, even without her. I'm pretty sure she saved him, too. "I promised my dad," I say, my voice breaking. "That if I found her, I'd tell her where to find him." I'm trying really hard not to cry, but I can't stop thinking about my dad as Kristoff, this other man, all the danger he and Elena faced, all the life he's lived since then and all the life that was stolen from her so many years ago. And I can't help myself. The tears well up.

Benjamin leans in closer and puts his hand on my shoulder. His face is close enough that I can see his eyes are blue-gray in this weird fluorescent office light.

"He really loved her," I say. "And she was taken from him."

His expression turns a little in understanding. And then he jumps off the desk and before either one of us can hesitate, separate, he pulls me up from the chair, wraps me in a hug. His arms are stronger than I would've expected, and he smells like Irish Spring and some sort of aftershave that reminds me of the beach, the cold salty sea spray in Coronado.

We hold on to each other for a few minutes, and I don't ever want to move, but the bell clangs over the door, and Benjamin lets go first.

I turn around, and a young blonde-haired woman stands in the doorway, looking a little confused. "I had an appointment." She glances at her watch, as if to double-check the time. "But if I'm interrupting, I can . . ."

Benjamin looks over me at her. "Miss Kemp?" She nods. "I'll be right with you." He looks back to me, puts his hands in his pockets, and shrugs. This stamp has consumed us for weeks. But he has other clients, ones who might actually make him some money.

"I should go," I say, but I don't for a minute. Because it feels like I should say something else, something more. *Our work here is done* pops into my head. But that sounds so stupid. I want to tell him I'll call him later or make plans to meet tomorrow for breakfast, but what reason does he have to spend time with me now? I found Kristoff, the answer to his question about the unusual stamp. We have nothing to talk about, no reason to meet up anytime soon. So I turn to walk out.

"Katie," he calls after me as I walk past Miss Kemp. I turn back to look at him. His hair is messy, unruly, and his glasses are a little crooked. Maybe I bumped them when we hugged? He notices, and pushes them back up his nose. "Take care," he finally says.

"Yeah," I echo back. "You too."

❀

I don't get a Christmas tree this year, for the first time since I started dating Daniel. Instead I go up to the attic and dig out the old menorah I'd taken from my father's house along with his stamp collection when I'd first moved him into the Willows.

Hanukkah begins just before Christmas, on the 22nd, and for the first time in years I find myself in my old neighborhood, at my old temple. They always have a menorah lighting, crafts and dreidel games for kids. I haven't been since my parents and I came when I was a kid, but this year I go alone, if only just to feel connected to the girl I once was and the place that I came from. I want to feel a part of something bigger and more important than me. This is my holiday. My father's and Gram's holiday. And Elena's and the Fabers' once, too.

On Christmas morning I give Benjamin a call. But he doesn't answer his phone, and I guess he got out of the office, maybe even out of the country. I leave him a message telling him I just wanted to see how he was doing, how he was holding up over the holidays. And then I drive down to Coronado, and spend an entire glorious week by the ocean with Gram.

When I get home, there are no messages on my machine. But I

find the rest of my father's stamp collection piled up on my porch with a note:

Thought you'd want this back. I looked through it all. Nothing else Faber/Austrian or of any significant value.—Benjamin Grossman

His note is so formal, all business. He's done with my father's stamps. And with me. Whatever we shared, briefly, is over.

Los Angeles, 1990

I ALWAYS LIKE NEW BEGINNINGS, fresh starts. It's a new year, a new decade. After I get back from Coronado in January I know it's time to find a new job. But first I find a realtor and put my house on the market. I don't want to live with so many old memories. I want to start over.

Then I call Jason and tell him everything I learned about the stamp and about my father. "Wow." He whistles on the other end of the line. "I knew there was a story there."

"Yeah," I say, biting at my thumbnail. I want Jason to offer me a job, offer to pay me to write this story. When he doesn't immediately, I come out and ask: "So are you hiring me to write this or not?"

"On one condition," he says. "I want to know what the letter says."

"The letter?" It takes me a second to realize what he's asking, because for a while now I've been fixated only on the stamp.

"The letter your father wrote Elena. We would print the text of it, with the article." His voice rises with excitement.

"I can't open the letter," I say. "It's not addressed to me."

Jason laughs a little. He thinks I'm kidding. But I'm not.

"No, really. It's not mine to open."

"But you said yourself, Elena is almost certainly dead," he says.

"Still . . . I don't feel right opening it. My father wrote her a love letter. We can't just print that in *Voice* magazine for the whole world to see. It was meant to be private."

"But your story isn't complete without knowing more about Kristoff and Elena's love affair," Jason points out. "Your story doesn't really have an ending yet. You don't even know what happened to Elena."

"You're right," I tell Jason. But I realize I'm not going to work for him. That's not really what this was about this whole time.

I'm going to hang on to this letter as a piece of my father, his past, his history. And I'm going to keep trying to figure out what happened to Elena, but not for Jason, not for *Voice* magazine. For my father, for myself.

※

In February I finally get a new job working for Gladys Weinstein, a hippie-ish woman who's about the age my mother would be, had she lived. She runs a small start-up magazine, *Jewish LA*, and she hires me to write the content. I reacquaint myself with the Los Angeles that I knew as a kid, and the Jewish pieces of life I'd all but left behind. I buy Shabbat candles, and sometimes I light them on Fridays, if I'm home and the mood strikes me. Mostly it does, these days. My father told me how he really first became a Jew the night he thought he'd lost Elena forever, how she'd caught him whispering the prayer wrong. There were so many Fridays Elena wasn't able to light the candles out of fear, and I can light them whenever I please. I feel I owe it to her, to my father, somehow, not to forget all this.

In the spring I sell my house to a young, newly married couple, who are still annoyingly bright-eyed about marriage and love and possibility, and I find a one-bedroom apartment in Santa Monica, where I'm close enough to walk to the Willows. It suits me better anyway.

I adopt a terrier from the pound, and I often walk her on the beach. I walk her over to the Willows a few times, and we sit out in the garden atrium with my dad. He enjoys the dog, even if every time he sees Lucky he believes he's meeting her again for the first time.

In April, I drive down to Gram's for Passover, and we have a Seder, the two of us and some of her friends from her bridge club. They all talk about setting me up with their grandsons, and I murmur polite excuses as to why I can't. *I'm not ready*, I say.

"What about that sweet Benjamin Grossman?" Gram whispers to me conspiratorially, across the table. She tells her friends how he drove down here with me once, and how she thought he was cute.

"I haven't even talked to him in months," I say, but what I don't say is all the times I've thought about him, wondering what he was up to, what he was doing, if he was awake in the middle of the night when I was. "And Benjamin was only interested in the stamp," I add. "Nothing else."

"If you say so," Gram says.

❀

June brings with it the hottest day ever recorded in LA, and when the city tops out at 112, I'm grateful to be closer to the water in my new apartment. It has a balcony and even today, there's a slight breeze coming off the Pacific Ocean. My proximity to the water feels like a new gift.

Gladys calls me in the morning and tells me not to come into work. Our small office isn't air-conditioned, and luckily, my apartment is. I offer her respite here, but she says she's heading to the mall, where she can stay cool and shop. I tell her I'll work at home, but she just laughs and says, "Oh, Katie, take the day off. No work required when it feels like Hell outside."

Lucky and I spend the day watching soap operas on the couch, and I'm surprised when around dinnertime I hear a knock at the door. No one is crazy enough to be out soliciting today, but the person knocks again and I get off the couch and glance through the peephole. Benjamin stands on the other side, looking sweaty and disheveled, his curly hair a mess, his glasses a little steamed up from the heat. And everything we shared together, those foggy days in Wales, all comes surging back to me.

"You moved," he says, without even a hello first when I open the door. And I remember that he's so direct, always to the point. It makes me smile to see him here, exactly the same. "I had trouble finding you." He peers past me, into my apartment, which is a mess, laundry piled on one end of the couch, library books piled on the floor. Dirty dishes in the sink, if he can see that far. "Smaller than your old place," he says.

"I didn't need all that space just for me. And this is closer to my dad. And the water." I open the door wider. "Come on in. It's too hot out to stand there."

Benjamin walks inside, and Lucky rushes him. He kneels down to pet her, and she licks his hand and he doesn't pull back. I hadn't pegged him as a dog person before now. "She's new, too?" he says.

"She is. Whole new decade, whole new apartment, whole new dog, whole new job, whole new life." I make room for him to sit on the couch by shoving a pile of laundry onto the coffee table. "You want a drink?" I ask.

He shakes his head. "No, I'm good. I can't stay. I just . . . I just wondered how you were doing, that's all."

"Today? It's like a hundred million degrees outside." I left that message back in December, and I've driven by his office or up to his neck of the woods a bunch of times since, hoping to run into him, wondering the same. I've just done it in nicer weather.

"You're doing well," he says, more to himself than to me.

I nod. I am, and I'm glad he can see it. "How about you?" I ask. "How have you been?"

Instead of answering he takes the seat I'd offered on the couch, and gives me a small smile, which I take to mean he's doing well, too. "I guess the real reason I came over here is to tell you that I'm still looking into your stamp," he says.

"Really?" I sit down next to him. "I mean I have been, too, I just thought you'd have other stamps to look into."

"I do," he says. "But your stamp was . . ."

"What?"

"Different," he finally says, looking down at his feet. He doesn't look back up right away, so I tell him that I've been trying to figure out what happened to Elena. Jackie from the Holocaust Society suggested that I look through the microfiche of Red Cross lists at the UCLA library but I couldn't find her name. I've also been corresponding with Dr. Grimes and he's let me know East Germany is releasing some records from the wartime soon, once the reunification is final. We're hoping Elena's name or details about her story will be among them.

"I got in touch with some stamp dealers in Germany and Austria," Benjamin says when I'm finished. "I kept thinking about the other letters. There were like fifteen or twenty of them, right? So what happened to them? Someone might have saved one somewhere. And now that Germany is reunifying . . . Well, I thought maybe one of our stamps would turn up over there. In the East even."

"Sounds like a long shot," I say, remembering what Jackie told me about sifting through the Holocaust information, looking for survivors.

He nods. "That's why I didn't tell you I was doing it." So he was still looking, doing this for me, and trying to protect my feelings, too? "But then it paid off," he says.

"You actually found one?" I forget to take a breath for a moment. There's another stamp like ours, my father's? Another connection to his past?

"Herr Jacobs, a dealer I contacted in Berlin—I received a letter from him this week. He said he has come across a similar stamp recently. That he has one in his possession. I want to go there in the fall," Benjamin is saying. "More airlines are starting commercial air service into Berlin, or will be once the reunification is final. Then I can see Herr Jacobs and his stamp in person. And maybe we could see if we can look into those records the East is releasing while we're there and see what we can find about Elena, too." He stops talking, as if he got carried away, then catches himself on the word *we*. "I mean what *I* can find, while I'm there, sorry."

"No," I say. "I want to go to Germany, too. I'll pay for my own ticket this time." He smiles, as if remembering our trip to Wales, and I wonder if he thinks of it fondly, the way I do. "Just one thing," I add. "Do you mind if Gram comes with us?"

Germany, 1990

EAST GERMANY, or I guess I should just say Germany, looks nothing like what I'd expected. The place that used to be Gram's tiny village, Hertzscheimer, is now rolling farmland surrounded by green hills and forests about sixty kilometers east of Berlin in Brandenburg. We rent a car and Gram, Benjamin, and I drive out there on our first day in Germany. I'm expecting wreckage, disaster, but all I see is beauty: open grassy land, sheep grazing. It's hard to imagine a village of Jews was here once, that it was destroyed, decimated, burned off the earth nearly fifty years ago. Or that the people who lived here since were contained behind a guarded brick wall, and kept isolated by the communism of the East for so many years.

We drive around for a little while, and Benjamin spots a *Naturpark*. I pull in and park the car. We all get out and walk on a wooded trail down to a small lake. Gram is wide-eyed, silent. She shivers from the chill in the fall air, colder than anything we're used to in California. "I never thought I'd be here again," she finally says.

"You've been here before?" I'm not sure if she means Germany, or the lake just in front of us. "This park?"

"Yes, sweetheart. *Wo wir als kinder spielten.*" Then she seems to remember herself, me, that I don't understand her German. "Where we used to play as children," she says. "I thought they would've destroyed it all, but it's still *schön* . . . beautiful," she says.

❀

When we're back in Berlin, at the Palasthotel, Gram goes up to our room to take a nap, and Benjamin and I decide to walk around the city for a few hours. We have an appointment to meet Herr Jacobs at four o'clock in what was once West Berlin, and Gram is going to come with us in case we need a translator. (Though Benjamin has spoken with Herr Jacobs on the phone once, and he says he speaks English, somewhat.) We're staying in what used to be the GDR, East Berlin, in a hotel that once was reserved for distinguished guests and has only recently opened to Germans and tourists like us. The decor is so brown that the inside reminds me of a cave, despite the fact that the building itself is opulent, and the surrounding block could even be described as oddly charming.

We check the map; we want to go see the wall. It's under three kilometers from the hotel, and the afternoon air is crisp. "It'll feel good to walk," I say when Benjamin asks if I think it's too far to go on foot. I feel cooped up after the long flights, the time in the car this morning. I want to experience Berlin, the way Gram did once as a girl. I want to see and feel the breath of the city. We figure out a route, and we walk in silence.

After Benjamin showed up at my apartment in the summer, we haven't talked much these past few months, other than to touch base about the details of the trip now and then. Gram needed to renew her passport, and we needed to figure out when it would be feasible and most affordable for us to fly. In the end we decided to wait for Lufthansa to begin commercial flights into Berlin again, once the official reunification had taken place. And so we'd discussed all that, intermittently, over the phone. But nothing else. I hadn't asked him how he was doing, or how he feels about his third upcoming Thanksgiving without Sara and Davis. I don't mention any of that on our walk either. At first, I'm not sure what to say, and then the silence between us begins to feel easy, comfortable. I don't need to say anything at all.

We turn onto Oranienburger Strasse, and I notice the domed building that stands out from the modest brick buildings surrounding it. There's a plaque next to the door, and a Star of David on it catches my eye. "A synagogue?" I say. I'm surprised, but maybe I shouldn't be. The war was so long ago, but I'd always thought of Berlin, especially the East, as a city without Jews. I stop and walk up to look at the plaque. The writing's in German, but I can understand enough to get the point. "This must've been destroyed in *Kristallnacht*," I say. "Then rebuilt in 1966." I trace the date at the bottom of the plaque with my fingers.

Benjamin wears a camera around his neck, and he lifts it up, snaps a picture of the plaque up close. He steps back and takes one of the building, the beautiful dome, me standing in front of it. "I'm going to print these for you when we get back," he says. "You could write about this synagogue, for your magazine."

"That's not a bad idea," I say, trying to hide my surprise that Benjamin knows about my new job. I haven't told him anything about it, other than the fact that I have one. Has he been checking up on me this past year, the way I've been checking up on him?

We keep walking, only stopping occasionally for Benjamin to photograph something. And when we get to the wall, we see it's still in the process of coming down. Men are working on deconstructing it right now. There's so much of the actual structure intact, which is surprising, given that it's already been a year since the wall "fell." It's ugly; a cement and brick monstrosity. I remember the wall "woodpecker" we saw on TV last fall in Wales. The woman in the raincoat who'd hated the wall because it had kept her from her family, who chipped it away in tiny pieces with her pickax. Benjamin and I fell asleep holding hands that night, the sounds of the woman chipping away at the wall on the BBC in the background.

Today the sun is shining brightly; the park near the wall appears festive, colored leaves on all the trees. The only sound the noise of bulldozers, taking the wall apart, piece by piece.

❀

Herr Jacobs's office is in a tiny brick storefront on the other side of the wall, on Luisenstrasse, near the University of Berlin. The unassuming sign on the front of the building reads *Philatelie*, and even with my limited German, I know we're in the right place.

We walk inside, and in an odd way it reminds me of Benjamin's office. A small crowded desk, a tiny television propped on a corner. It's funny that halfway around the world a stamp dealer is still a particular kind of person. Herr Jacobs walks out from the back when he hears us enter and he is much older than Benjamin, closer to Gram's age. *"Guten Tag,"* he says, eyeing the three of us. His eyes come to rest on Gram, as if he can't place who she is in this story, and I guess Benjamin didn't mention her beforehand. But she's the one who steps forward and begins to speak to him, without hesitation, in German.

"*Ja*, you are Americans?" he says back, in stilted English. "With flower picture?" I pull the plastic sleeve out of my bag to show him the letter. I point to the stamp and he pulls his spectacles from his head, and then examines the stamp through the plastic with the magnifier attached to one lens of his glasses. "Yes, it is same thing," he says, after a few moments. "Hold there, please."

He walks into the back and comes out a few minutes later with a newspaper. He looks through it, folds the page back, and hands it to me.

"What's this?" I ask.

"You ask if see flower picture," he says to Benjamin.

"Stamp." Benjamin's voice sounds measured, the way it always is. "I asked if you'd seen this stamp?"

Gram starts to speak in German, presumably to explain the confusion with his English.

"*Ja,*" he insists, shaking his finger at the newspaper. I look at it, and it's all in German, but I appear to be looking at the Help Wanted section, or some kind of advertisements. Not news stories. He moves his finger down the page, and then he stops. "Flower picture."

He's pointing to a small drawing of a building, what seems to be the synagogue Benjamin and I saw this morning. I recognize the dome. And inside the dome is a tiny edelweiss, looking almost exactly like the edelweiss on our stamp, in St. Stephen's Cathedral, Vienna. "What is this?" I ask.

Herr Jacobs shrugs, not understanding perhaps, and Gram tries to translate again. He says something back to her in German. She nods her head. *"Ja, ja, ja,"* she says excitedly.

"What?" I ask her.

"He says it is the Women's Movement for Peace, a group of women from both sides of the wall who have been fighting for freedom and peace in Germany for years. They're advertising their upcoming meeting. They always did it this way, in code, so the Stasi wouldn't know." He says something else in German and she says, "But now they still do it. That is their thing. The flower, that is their . . . symbol? Yes?"

"Ja," Herr Jacobs says. "Flower is symbol." He says a bit more in German.

"The flower is a code for where and when they will meet," Gram says. "His wife is a member, or was. She passed away last year. But Herr Jacobs still notices the ads in the paper. For her." She turns to look at him, seeming to recognize his sweetness in still remembering her that way.

But Herr Jacobs doesn't seem to notice. "Flower picture," Herr Jacobs says emphatically. "Flower stamp. Same artist, *ja?*"

"No, that's impossible," I say. "They can't be the same artist."

Herr Jacobs frowns and so does Benjamin. *"Ja,"* Herr Jacobs says, and he switches back into German once again, speaking rapidly.

"He says the lines . . . are the same," Gram says, her face contorting with concentration. She's struggling to keep up; he's speaking so fast. "In both of the flowers. They have the same lines."

"They're both edelweiss," I say. That's why we've come all this way—Herr Jacobs had simply seen another edelweiss in another building, in an advertisement in a newspaper. I hand the paper back to Herr Jacobs. *"Danke,"* I say.

"No." He pushes it back to me. "You keep. I have many others."

❁

We're quiet on the way back to the hotel. I fold the newspaper, put it in my bag, and look out my window at the storefronts of Berlin. We drive through the Brandenburg Gate without stopping, and then just like that we're back in the East.

"What do you make of it?" Gram says quietly from the backseat, as we drive by the synagogue. "I mean it is a little odd, isn't it? Another edelweiss in another building. All these years later?"

I glance at Benjamin, who doesn't react outwardly. He keeps his eyes trained on the road. I turn around and look at Gram. "I think it's a coincidence," I say, though as I say this I remember what Benjamin said that night in the car ride back from San Diego. *He doesn't believe in coincidences.* I almost expect him to say that now, too, but he doesn't. When I glance back at him, he's staring at the street ahead, frowning.

"But to imagine," Gram says. "If Gid and I had stayed and made it through the war. If I would've been stuck in the East. Would I have been brave enough to join this group, the Women's Movement for Peace, do you think?"

"Of course you would've been," I murmur.

"I don't know," she says. "I might have been too afraid of the Stasi. I don't know," she says again. She stops talking and watches out the window, as if picturing a whole other life.

❀

Gram and I are sharing a room at the hotel, and Benjamin is just down the hall. Gram falls asleep early, but I'm wide-awake. I walk to the window and take in the view: a cathedral, all lit up in the night sky. In spite of the drab brown decor of the hotel, it really is beautiful here. But Benjamin told me that East Germans were never allowed to stay at Palasthotel before the wall fell, that the hotel hadn't even accepted the local East German currency.

I think about the Women's Movement for Peace, this group that secretly announces their meetings in plain sight by printing a small drawing in the local newspapers. My father's story of hiding a flower in a stamp fifty years ago, trying to escape the Nazis, mirrors this group of women in my lifetime, advocating peace in the face of danger and threat from the Stasi. Women who are probably not that different from me, had my family gotten stuck in East Germany, behind the wall.

Proof of unusual daring, my father had said of the edelweiss, and maybe it is just the same here today.

There's a soft rap at the door, and I hurry over and look through the peephole. Benjamin stands in the hallway on the other side. I grab my key and open the door.

"I knew you'd be awake." He offers me a half smile. "I wanted to look at the paper again."

"Gram's sleeping. Hold on." I grab the paper from my bag, slip out into the hallway, and shut the door behind me.

We walk the few doors down to his room, and inside it's identical to mine and Gram's, all brown. He takes the paper from me, and I walk over to his window. He's on the other side of the hallway, so no view of the cathedral, only a view of the building behind us, and all I can see is darkness.

"I agree with him," Benjamin says.

"What?" I turn back around. Benjamin is sitting on the edge of the bed, and I sit next to him. Our shoulders touch, but neither one of us moves away.

"The lines *are* the same. It does look like the same artist."

"But it can't be," I say. "My father's thousands of miles away in the Willows."

"I know. But I don't think Herr Jacobs brought us here on a wild-goose chase. I mean what if . . ." His voice trails off.

"What if what?"

"What if someone involved with this organization knew about your father's stamp, maybe has one or received one once? Then copied it somehow?"

"I get it. You don't believe in coincidences," I say. "But maybe the edelweiss isn't a coincidence. It's an important flower in this part of the world. In Germany and Austria."

"Maybe," Benjamin says. He points to the bottom of the picture, at the numbers inscribed beneath it. "Herr Jacobs said it was a symbol for where and when. Look at the numbers here below the picture."

I look—10239015—and try to make a quick conversion to military time in my head. "Tomorrow at three?"

"We should go," Benjamin says. "Bring our stamp. Ask if any of the women have seen it before."

We'd planned on going to the records ministry tomorrow, trying to search the newly released public records for any mention of Elena, but Benjamin seems so eager to do this instead. And I have to admit I'm curious about these women, too, edelweiss or no, and so I agree with him.

❋

The next afternoon we get to the Neue Synagogue just before three. Gram says she wanted to see it again anyway, that she remembers being here as a little girl with her grandparents. "Someone had a bar mitzvah," she says. "A distant cousin." She says it like the details are just coming back to her.

But once we walk inside, we realize that the building is in the process of being restored. It doesn't appear to be a place of worship at the moment, only a construction site. "I'll ask for the rabbi," Gram says, and she approaches one of the construction workers, and speaks to him confidently in German. He laughs, shakes his head, says something back.

"What did he say?" I ask.

She frowns. "He says all the rabbis are in the West. The West has the rabbis. The East only has the cemeteries."

We walk back outside. Gram examines the plaque that Benjamin and I looked at yesterday. "They can't be meeting here," I say to Benjamin.

"No," Benjamin agrees.

"Maybe we misunderstood the picture?"

Benjamin turns and scans the street. A girl rides by on a bike, but she's young, a teenager, maybe on her way home from school. Too young to be involved in a subversive women's movement, and she rides past the synagogue anyway. She stops her bike across the street, and goes into what appears to be a café. "Over there," Benjamin says, at the same time the thought occurs to me. "I bet they're meeting in there."

✳

The inside of the café is crowded, and Gram offers to order for us in German while Benjamin scouts a table in the corner and goes to save it. I wait in the long line with Gram. "They didn't have coffee here in the East, for many years," Gram says to me. "They drank chicory instead."

"No coffee?" It is a small thing, but it seems a larger symbol for how bad it must have been for the people living here.

There's coffee now, thankfully, and I carry the cups to our table for me and Benjamin while Gram holds on to her mug of tea. We sit down, drink our drinks, look around.

"This is all very exciting," Gram says, blowing on her tea, then taking a sip. "I haven't had such an adventure since . . . Oh, I can't even remember when." She contemplates, takes another sip of her tea. "Maybe the sixties, when Gid and I went to Jerusalem." I vaguely remember when Gram and Grandpa Gid went to Israel. I was maybe ten or eleven and they brought me back a Star of David necklace, with a pretty blue stone in the middle. It was, for many years, the fanciest piece of jewelry I owned. "Thank you two for letting me come along," Gram says.

I squeeze her hand under the table, and Benjamin thanks her for coming with us, for translating with Herr Jacobs yesterday. Then he excuses himself to find a restroom.

"He's wonderful," Gram says, once he's left the table. "I really like him."

"Do you?" I smile a little and sip my coffee.

"He's very real, very honest." She keeps talking. "There's no pretension, like with . . . well, you know." I nod. She's not wrong about him. "He's such a nice man, too. And he likes you a lot, Katie." I laugh a little. But I wonder if there's any way she's right? Benjamin is walking back toward our table. Gram notices, too, and doesn't say any more.

"They're in the back," he says to me, a little breathless. "A whole table of them."

"What? How do you know it's them?"

Benjamin motions for me to come with him, and Gram offers to stay and hold our table. She winks at me as I stand up, but I pretend not to notice, and I follow Benjamin to the back of the café.

I see the table Benjamin is pointing toward, the group of women, their heads huddled together as they drink coffee. The sound of their laughter floats through the café. I'd been picturing this group of women as a severe bunch of communists, dressed in brown as drab as our hotel room, frowning as they got together to plan. But instead, they remind me oddly of Gram's bridge club, having a friendly get-together over coffee.

"I don't think——" I start to say, but Benjamin interrupts me by grabbing on to my hand. The feel of his fingers on mine, again, here, is jarring and I stop talking. He's trying to get my attention, that's all, but I think about what Gram just said. *He likes you.*

"It's her," Benjamin says. His voice comes out hoarse, raspy. He clears his throat. "The woman from your father's painting."

"That can't be." But I look at where he's looking: the woman at the head of the table, her hair in long gray waves that fall against her shoulders, the unmistakable upturn of her wrinkled cheeks, the arch of her forehead.

I walk up to the table, and Benjamin follows behind me, still holding on to my hand. "Elena?" I say. All the women stop talking, turn, look at me. My heart is pounding. I start to sweat; it suddenly seems excessively hot in here.

The young woman whom I saw riding her bike speaks up. "You have wrong table," she says in stilted English, and she frowns deeply.

"Elena Faber?" I say, a little louder this time.

"No one here with that name." The young girl (maybe she is older than I first thought? twenty?) makes a shooing motion with her hand. I am a fly, or at the very least a stupid American tourist who has no business approaching their group.

The woman Benjamin spotted, the one I called Elena, stands. She is clearly in charge, and she says something to the group in German. I wish Gram were standing here so she could translate, but I judge it to be something along the lines of *I will deal with the stupid American tourists* because I catch the words *amerikanischen Touristen*.

"*Ignorie sie, Amata!*" one of the other women says to her.

"Amata . . . Amy?" I whisper to Benjamin, remembering what my dad told me, that his and Elena's new names were Germanized versions of characters from *Little Women*. Benjamin laces his fingers tighter with mine and we hold on to each other. "Amy March?" I say, louder, and all the women stop talking, turn and look at me, with a new curiosity, a fascination. Then they look back at their leader. I am certain now that it is her. I am certain and yet I can't believe it. It can't be true. She's here? She's alive. *The same artist*, Herr Jacobs said. *The same lines*. Elena had known the stamp, the edelweiss drawing, as well as my father.

"Come on, we will talk outside," she says in nearly perfect English. She walks toward the front of the café, and Benjamin and I follow her.

❀

"If you are from the CIA, I already told them. I have nothing to say." She walks briskly down Oranienburger Strasse, in the direction Benjamin and I walked yesterday when we went to the wall. The air is cooler out here, and I stop walking for a second to catch my breath, but she keeps going and I have to jog to keep up.

"We're not from the CIA," I say. "We're not here to question you or hurt you. We've been looking for you." She keeps walking briskly, and Benjamin and I are practically running. "Miriam has been looking for you," I say.

She stops, spins on her heels, and looks at me, then Benjamin, then back at me. "Miriam?" Her face turns. Her toughness falls away for a moment, and she looks as though she might cry. "She's alive?"

"Yes, she lives in Cardiff. Wales." I leave out the part about the depressing Raintree, her broken hip. After all, she'd said it was only temporary and I'm hoping she's long home and healed and back with Herbie by now.

"Oh," Elena says. "Oh . . . all these years. My Miri . . ." There's a bench just down the street, and she walks toward it, holds on to it for a moment as if she might fall if she doesn't, and then she sits down. She pulls a pack of cigarettes out of her bag, and holds them toward Benjamin and me, a peace offering. We both decline, and she lights one for herself, slowly inhales, exhales. "Miri hired you to find me?" she asks.

"No," I say. "We've been looking for you and we found Miriam, first. Last year."

She takes a drag on her cigarette, then squashes it under her boot and stands. She doesn't trust us. She's going to start running again. "The letter," Benjamin says, tugging on my bag, and I pull it out.

"We have something that belongs to you," I say. "We've been wanting to give it back to you."

"I am an East German woman," she says dryly. "I don't have anything to pay you."

"But you used to be an Austrian girl," I say. "And we don't want your money." I hold out the letter, and she looks down at it. She gasps and turns white, as if I am holding a ghost.

"Where did you get this?" she says.

"My father," I say. "Kristoff."

Austria, 1939

I CLUTCHED THE LETTERS TIGHTLY in my hands, careful not to damage the stamps. It was snowing, and my toes were freezing, wet through the worn soles of my boots, but I kept walking through the woods toward town, shielding the letters under my coat to keep them dry. *Only a few steps more*, I kept telling myself. It was a lie, but I kept on walking.

Only a few steps more. Just a few more.

All I had to do was make it into town, drop the letters at the post on Wien Allee. All I had to do was mail these letters, and everything was going to be all right.

At the edge of the woods, I reached the clearing, and through the swirl of snowflakes, the pink-blue onset of dawn, I could see the remaining red-roofed buildings in the town up ahead.

Wien Allee. I was almost there.

The sudden cold butt of the gun against my temple surprised me. I didn't even cry out before the man grabbed my arm, and the letters fell from my hands, onto the unblemished snow.

I was going to be killed, and I knew all of a sudden that I didn't want to die. I did care about staying alive. I didn't want to leave this earth and Austria and my mother and Kristoff. Not like this.

I struggled and out of the corner of my eye I could see the man holding the gun to my head. "Josef?"

He lowered the gun, stepped back, and went to pick up the letters.

"Josef, you scared me half to death. What are you doing?"

"I had to get your attention. Stop you from going into town. German soldiers are everywhere. They're already at your house," he said.

"So? They've probably just come to pick up Kristoff's newest stamp plate."

I'd left Kristoff at the house, sleeping, so peacefully. I'd kissed him on the cheek, whispered to him how much I loved him. He'd stirred a little. He'd felt my love, even in his sleep, but he hadn't awoken.

Last night I'd promised him that we would leave for Bremen soon. I promised him that I wouldn't do anything stupid. But I had no intention of going to America with him now, not when we were doing so much good work and when we finally knew where my mother was. Josef had been trying to convince me to get Kristoff out of the country for months. I was good enough to engrave the papers on my own. And we both knew Kristoff wasn't cut out for the kind of work we were doing. Josef kept telling me the only way to save Kristoff was to let him go. He was right, I knew he was. But still. I hadn't been able to do it just yet. I'd thought I'd deliver the letters this morning, go back to the house, and then get Kristoff to Bremen. I wanted to take him there myself, be certain he made it to safety, the way I had with Miriam.

"No," Josef said sharply. "They're on to us." I shook my head. I didn't believe him. I couldn't. "I know what you did," he said. "They do, too."

"No one is going to notice a girl with a stack of mail, even a Jewish one. And Kristoff is a mess. He's much too nervous to go to the post."

"No," Josef said. "Not these letters. The stamp. You sent one to your mother, didn't you?"

Josef was right. I'd mailed a letter to my mother a few weeks ago with one of our stamps. Josef raised his gun, and for a second, I thought he might shoot me. "I . . . I didn't," I said, without conviction.

"Dammit, Elena, don't lie to me. One was missing. I counted them last night. And I thought to myself, where could it have gone? What could Kristoff have possibly done with it? But then I realized, it wasn't Kristoff. It was you."

He was right. There was no use lying about it. "It was just one letter, one stamp," I admitted. "And I didn't write anything in the letter that the Germans could make any sense of. I just quoted my father's favorite book about the edelweiss. That was all. But she'll know. She'll look at the stamp and read my words, and she'll know we're all safe."

"We're done. The second that letter hit the camp and the German censors looked at it they noticed that stamp. They've come for Kristoff already, and they'll be coming for us, too." Josef was trying hard not to raise his voice, but his face turned an alarming shade of red.

"No." I shook my head. "It was just one letter. Just one stamp," I repeated meekly.

"Come on," Josef said. "Schwann is at my house. He can drive us. The Germans might not know I'm involved yet. So we might be able to get out. But we have to go. Now." Josef grabbed on to my arm and pulled me toward him, not all that gently.

"I can't leave Kristoff." I yanked out of his grasp and began walking quickly back toward home. I couldn't leave him like this. I couldn't let the Germans take him, hurt him. I had to save him.

"Elena, stop or I'll shoot you," Josef said gruffly. I stopped walking, turned around, and he was pointing the gun straight at me again.

"You wouldn't dare." I crossed my arms in front of my chest, defiant. Josef had known me my whole life. We'd practically grown up together. But if anyone had it in him to shoot me, regardless, it would be him.

"If I have to shoot you in the arm to save your life, so help me God I will." He said it so sternly, so forcefully. I believed he would.

I tried to judge how fast I could run, toward the house. Toward Kristoff. If I could outrun Josef, Josef's gun . . .

"Elena," Josef said. "Don't be stupid. The Germans might not kill Kristoff, but they will definitely kill you if you go back there now."

I was certain Josef was wrong; they would kill Kristoff. I had the sudden image of Kristoff, *my beautiful Kristoff,* his tall lean body, torn apart by a bullet hole, blood pouring from his chest. He was all alone. He would die all alone. And it was my fault. I wanted to stop them, to save him, but if the Germans were already at the house, then it was too late. And going back would be suicide for me. I let out a cry that I muffled into the sleeve of my coat.

"Come on," Josef said more gently. He lowered the gun and put a hand on my shoulder. "What would Kristoff want you to do? He would want you to save yourself."

Josef was right. I knew he was. It sunk into my bones, a cold chill that would not leave me for a very long time.

Josef hooked the gun in his waistband and held on to my arm. I walked with him through the woods, to his house. I got into the car with him and Schwann and we drove away, abandoned our home.

Germany, 1990

THAT WAS THE LAST MORNING I ever saw Kristoff," Elena says. "A few weeks later Josef and I went back to Grotsburg at my insistence, and everything was gone. My family's house, his family's farm . . . It was all burned to the ground." She pulls another cigarette out of her bag and lights it with shaking hands.

"I don't understand," I say. "My father didn't say anything about the Germans coming for him that morning. He said he found a letter in the snow at the edge of the woods that he thought you'd dropped when you didn't come back. He thought *you* were taken by the Germans."

She takes a drag on her cigarette and looks off, toward the direction of the wall.

"Did Josef lie about seeing the Germans at your house that morning?" Benjamin asks.

"Yes," Elena says after a moment, and another drag on her cigarette. "If Kristoff is still alive, as you say . . . then I suppose he must have." I would expect more of a reaction from her, this woman my father described as so fearless, this woman still fighting for peace in Germany, all these years later. But she already seems resigned to this conclusion that Josef lied to her. Why isn't she angrier?

"What happened with the rest of your letters, your stamps?" Benjamin asks her.

"Josef and I mailed them in Vienna, all except the one we accidentally left behind in the snow in Grotsburg. But we got all the papers we'd made to the proper people with a little finagling. Not too long after that the British SOE came to us, and then Josef and I worked with them for a few years. We helped them with some of their stamps, distributed propaganda within Germany." I remember the stamps Dr. Grimes showed us in his textbook. Did she have a hand in those? "And then the war was over," she says. "And Josef and I settled in Berlin."

"Together?" I ask.

"Yes," she says. "At first we were just working together, as we always had. But then the years passed, and I believed Kristoff to be dead. And I began to see Josef differently."

That's why she hadn't reacted as I'd expected a few minutes ago. She fell in love with Josef. She moved on. The way my father did when he fell in love with my mother. I want to be angry that Josef lied to her, that they left my father behind, but he probably saved my father's life and maybe Elena's, too. If my father hadn't thought Elena was dead he never would've left Austria, come to America to look for Frederick, or married my mother. I wouldn't be sitting here now. The enormity of all of it hits me, of the way these tiniest movements and choices so very long ago have decided so much about my own life. I sit down on the bench, next to Elena.

"Things were good for a little while. We were happy," Elena says. "And then one day the wall went up in Berlin, just like that.

We were in the West for a party one day, and then the next day there was no going back." She grinds her second cigarette under her boot and then she doesn't know what to do with her empty hands. She twists her fingers together a little. "Josef and I were doing everything we could to get the wall down. But Josef was arrested in the seventies for 'spreading subversive propaganda.' The Stasi carted him off, and he died in Hohenschönhausen a few years later. It was a terrible East German prison, worse than Auschwitz, some said. The GDR denied it ever existed. You won't find it on any maps. But that's where they took him, where he died. I am certain."

We are all silent, perfectly still. "I'm so sorry," Benjamin finally says.

"So am I," Elena says matter-of-factly. After a few more moments of silence, Elena says, her tone softening, "Tell me more about Kristoff."

I tell her what I know, how he came to California in search of Frederick, and maybe her, how he found my grandparents and fell in love with my mother instead. "Gideon Leser was your grandfather?" Elena smiles for the first time. "He saved my father's life."

"My father's, too," I say. I wish Grandpa Gid were still here, that he could see this moment. He would take credit for nothing, none of it, though it is his to own. I wish Gram had walked out with us at least, so she could hear this.

"I tried to write to my father, after the war," Elena says. "But I never heard anything back." I tell her what Gram said about how Frederick, Charlie, only lived another year or so after he came to San Diego. "Well," she says. "At least he did not die like a dog watching his country be destroyed. I am forever grateful for that. My mother wasn't so lucky, she died in Mauthausen. I made a terrible mistake sending her that stamp, and I have never forgiven myself."

"It wasn't your fault," I say. There were thousands and thousands of names on the Red Cross lists I'd read on microfiche, so many innocent people murdered. "So many people died in camps."

But she just shakes her head, sadly, like she doesn't believe me. "I tried to look for Miriam after the war, too, before the wall went up, but we never had the money to go to the UK to search for her, and then after the GDR took over, I doubt any of my letters ever even made it out of the country." She turns to look at me. "You have actually talked to her? Seen her?" I nod, and she smiles again. She's beautiful when she smiles. Her entire face comes alive—all the years of war and hardship haven't stolen her beauty from her.

"I have her contact information in my purse." I pull it out and hand it to Elena. I've already added the information to my address book at home, so I don't need this copy that I've been dragging around with me since our trip to Wales.

She takes it, thanks me, stands. "I'd better get back. The women will start to worry." And she begins to walk back toward the café. Just like that.

"Wait," I call after her. "Your letter." I pick it up from the bench where she left it.

She shakes her head. "I haven't been Elena Faber in so many years. Perhaps your father might want to hold on to it still?"

"No." I shove it at her. "He wants you to have it. And he'd love to see you," I add. I really want to keep the promise I made to him that if I found her, I would bring her to see him. "He's living in a nursing home in California, LA. He wouldn't be able to make the trip out here. But maybe you'll come to him?"

"Oh." Her body deflates. "He's in a home? He's ill?"

"Physically he's fine. But his memory isn't . . . well, he was losing things, time. He has Alzheimer's and he couldn't live alone any longer. But the Willows, where he lives, is a beautiful place," I assure her.

Elena looks down, then takes the letter and puts it in her bag. "He lost me. We lost each other so long ago," she says. "Perhaps it is better just to leave it all in the past."

Now that we found her, I don't want to let her go. I want to drag her back to California with me, present her to my father at the Willows, like a prize I might have been overjoyed to win at the pier as a little girl. *Here's your gem*, I might tell him.

But she moves to walk back inside the café, and I realize there's nothing I can do to stop her. I grab one of my cards out of my purse and shove it at her. "Here, please. Stay in touch at least."

She smiles wanly but takes the card. "You seem like a sweet girl, Katie," she says. "He got very lucky to have you. Lucky to have such a wonderful and free life with you in America. He doesn't need me."

"But . . . he does," I stammer. I want to tell her how he's been drawing her lately, remembering the past, remembering how he loved her.

"No," she says before I can say anything else. "I am nothing but an old ghost. And he has you."

Los Angeles, 1990

I SPEND THANKSGIVING MORNING at the Willows with my dad. They serve a lunch in the atrium at noon for residents and their families: turkey and mashed potatoes and stuffing—all catered and surprisingly good. My dad and I eat at a table for two, and we talk about Thanksgivings past. We talk about my mom, and how she once set a turkey on fire when she tried to get creative and deep-fry it. It's one of those memories that I'm not even sure I really remember, but it's become a story I've told so many times that sometimes I feel like I've invented it. My mom used to laugh about it, years later, and remembering that is our favorite part.

I haven't told my father about the trip to Germany yet, and I'm not sure if I ever will. Part of me wants so badly to tell him that Elena is alive, but then I realize I'll have to tell him the rest, about how she got there and what Josef did. And that, even knowing he's alive, she didn't want to come to see him. She's a different person now. So is he, of course. But her memory is intact. She's living her life in the future, in a Germany that's finally free after so many years of her fighting. My father, on the other hand, is living his life in a muddled past.

"Where's your husband?" my father asks, forgetting both Daniel's name and the fact that we're divorced. He looks around the room, as if maybe Daniel is here somewhere, and he's gotten misplaced.

"Oh, he's not here," I say. "We're divorced, remember?"

"Ahh, yes, of course." He always smiles when I tell him that now, as if he still holds on to the memory, the feeling, that he always knew deep down it wasn't going to work out between Daniel and me.

"I'm going to Gram's for dinner tonight," I say.

I plan to drive down after I leave here. I called and invited Benjamin last night, on a whim, but I left him a message, and he hasn't called back. We've talked a few times since we got back from Germany. I called him once to thank him for all his help the past year and to ask if he had any ideas for what I might do with the rest of my father's collection. It's taking up an entire closet in my tiny apartment. He called me last week to tell me how another client of his had a genuine Faber in his collection, and asked if I wanted to see it before they auctioned it off. I said I would, but we had yet to arrange a time. And then last night, I offered up the invitation to Gram's. It felt weirdly personal in the face of our other interactions these past few weeks and months, but he was so sad this time last year, and I didn't want him to be alone.

"You'll give her my best," my father says. Then he adds, "I'm afraid I won't be able to make it back. I'm needed here."

"Of course," I murmur, not sure who's speaking to me now, Ted or Kristoff, what world he has lost himself to at the moment inside his failing mind. I lean over and kiss his balding head. "I'll see you next week," I tell him.

✾

When I get back to my apartment, Benjamin is sitting by the front door, reading a book. He jumps up when he sees me, and I smile. "You said you were leaving at one in your message, but then when I got here and you were gone, I thought maybe I'd already missed you."

"Nope." I unlock the door and let us both inside. Lucky glances at me, then jumps on him, and he pets her until she calms down. "Just visiting my father first. They had a lunch over there. So you're coming to Coronado with me?"

"I don't know. I thought I was. But then I got here and I thought I probably won't be the greatest company."

"When are you ever the greatest company?" I deadpan. He laughs a little. "You're coming," I say. Not a question, a command. "What are you going to do here by yourself except for wallow? And that's not what Sara would want you to do. She loved Thanksgiving, right? And besides, Gram adores you. She'll be upset if you're not there."

"Really?" His face softens. He likes Gram. I could tell by the sweet way he looked after her on the plane rides back from Berlin, carrying her suitcases, helping her into her seat, offering her his headphones.

"Yes," I say, though I haven't told Gram I've invited him. But I also know she will be thrilled to see him.

❋

Two hours later, Gram welcomes us both into her cottage with a hug, then ushers us into the dining room, which is already packed with her bridge friends. I put Lucky in the backyard, and when I get back Gram has already pulled out all the photos Benjamin took in Germany (which apparently he printed and sent to her, unbeknownst to me) to show all her friends during dinner. The ladies who, six months ago, were dying to set me up with their sons, offer me approving nods and basically leave me alone, so I don't bother explaining to them that Benjamin and I are just friends.

Everyone eats too much, drinks too much wine, including me and Benjamin, and Gram offers up her guest room so we don't have to drive back tonight. She has only one bed in there, so Benjamin offers to take the couch. Gram simply says, "Everyone sleep wherever you want. I don't judge." Then she kisses us both and heads off to bed.

"She's funny when she drinks," I say, though I don't know how much she really drank. Gram would wholeheartedly make that comment sober. But Benjamin laughs, and starts washing some of the dishes Gram left in the sink.

I go over and help him. He washes. I dry. Until everything is clean and out on Gram's counters. "You going to bed?" Benjamin asks me. He dries his hands on a dish towel and turns to look at me.

"Probably not." The kitchen clock tells me it's after ten, but I'm still a little buzzed from the wine, and I don't feel remotely tired.

"You want to take your dog for a walk? I'm still full from dinner, I could walk around a little."

"Sure, we can head across the street to the beach. Grab your jacket. It's cold down there this time of year."

I get Lucky and we head out front, and walk down the street by the Hotel del Coronado, which is lit up, this beautiful historic beacon by the sea. Benjamin hasn't seen it like this, and he stops for a minute to take it in. We walk down another block, toward the ocean, and I shiver a little as wind shifts off the water, and the temperature drops.

"You know what's weird?" Benjamin says as we walk along the beach. "I never expected any of this."

"What?" I take my shoes off and let my feet sink into the sand, and we walk down toward the water where the sand is harder, colder, but easier to walk on.

"Your grandmother. This dinner. You. I mean, when you walked into my office a year ago with your father's collection, I didn't even see you."

"Gee thanks." I laugh a little. "Guess I just blended in with his stamps."

"No, I don't mean that," he says. I can't see his face. It's too dark, but I guess he's blushing, embarrassed.

"I know what you mean," I admit. "I almost didn't get out of my car and go into your office that first morning."

"I'm glad you did," Benjamin says.

"Yeah, me too."

"I've been thinking these past few months about Kristoff and Elena's story, about what happened to them, what the stamp meant to them. But this morning when I got your message, I realized what their stamp meant to me." He's talking quickly, and he pauses to catch his breath. "If it hadn't been for that stamp, I never would've seen you. I never would've really looked at you."

He stops walking, and so do I. He turns to face me, to look at me now. The moon is full, glinting off the water. I can make out the shape of his face, the downturn of his lips, his serious expression.

"And what do I look like?" I ask.

He puts his hand to my cheek, slowly, as if he expects me to pull back. But when I don't, he strokes my cheek with his thumb. "You're really beautiful," he says. "And smart. And you're kind. And you love your family a lot. The way you look after your father and Gram . . ."

I don't know why but I feel like I'm about to cry. "You've had too much wine."

"I'm not drunk," he says. "Well, maybe a little."

I laugh. I'm a little drunk, too. "You know," I say, feeling bold from wine, from Benjamin's sweet words. "We could go to dinner sometime back in LA. Talk about something other than stamps, maybe."

"I'd like that," he says. He leans in a little closer, like he's going to kiss me, but instead he brushes his lips against my forehead briefly and then steps back.

But I pull him back close to me, and I stand up, lean in, and I kiss him on the lips. It's been a while since I kissed anyone, but I can't remember it ever feeling exactly like this, warm and perfect, and new, and like my entire body is sighing with relief, *finally*. I hadn't realized how long I've been wanting to do this until right this very moment.

"That's what I meant to do," he says when we pull back.

"I know," I say.

"And not because I'm drunk."

I laugh. "I know," I say again.

Maybe my father was right. There isn't just one ending, one answer, one person who can make us happy, or not. Maybe we can all begin again, become different people.

Benjamin takes my hand, and he and Lucky and I walk back to Gram's house.

Los Angeles, 1991

ONE MORNING AT THE END of January, I wake up to my phone ringing at seven. *Benjamin*. But I open my eyes, and he's sleeping here next to me. I smile for a second, before I worry that something is wrong with Gram or my father, and I jump out of bed to run into the kitchen to answer the phone.

"Miss Lawrence," the woman on the other end of the line says. "It's Gretchen from the Willows."

"Is my father okay?" I ask, alarmed. Sally got married, then moved away and left her job at the end of last month and I don't know Gretchen yet, or how fast she is to call me if my father is agitated.

"Yes, yes, your father is fine. Sorry, I didn't mean to scare you." I glance at the clock, wondering if I'd misread the one in my bedroom, but no, it is definitely seven a.m. "It's just . . . someone's here, demanding to see your father. She's not on the approved list, and as you know, visiting hours don't begin until eight. She got really annoyed with me and started yelling in another language. I wanted to call the police, but she said I should call you . . ." Her voice trails off, as if she's considering if that was a mistake, and maybe she should've just called the police.

My mouth is open, but for a moment I can't speak. *Elena?*

"I mean, should I call the police?" Gretchen asks.

"No, no, don't call the police. I'll be there as soon as I can," I say.

❋

Fifteen minutes later Benjamin and I are rushing into the lobby of the Willows. Benjamin came here with me once, last month, when the Willows decided to light a menorah on the first night of Hanukkah and I'd invited him to come and meet my father. They talked stamps, and my father's face had lit up, though I'm pretty sure he had no idea that Benjamin and I are dating, and I doubt he'll remember Benjamin today. But *I'm* glad he's here.

As we walk inside, I convince myself that maybe I read too much into what Gretchen said on the phone. "Maybe it's not her?" I say to Benjamin.

"What, some other woman yelling in German that she wants to see your father?"

"Gretchen didn't say *German*. She said *another language*. I assumed."

"It's her," Benjamin says, and of course, calm, rational guy that he is, he's right. As soon as we turn the corner into the main lobby I see her sitting in a chair. She's wearing a long floral dress, the colors too bright. Her hair falls in long gray waves, all around her face, and she clutches her giant black bag tightly in her lap, seeming afraid Gretchen or one of the other nurses might steal it.

I wave to her, and she stands, and frowns at Gretchen. "See, I am at the right place."

I realize I have met Gretchen before—last week when I was here. I just didn't know her by name yet. She's a petite woman who looks too young to already have her nursing degree. I would've pegged her as no more than sixteen, and she looks terrified of Elena now.

"It's okay," I say to her. "Ms. Faber—wait, March—does know my father. I didn't realize she was coming or I would've added her to the list."

"I told you," Elena practically spits in her face.

"There are rules, ma'am," Gretchen says. "I have to follow the rules."

"Rules," Elena grunts. Elena doesn't follow rules.

"And visiting hours still don't start for thirty minutes." Gretchen taps her watch and looks pointedly at me.

"Come on." I touch Elena's arm. "We can go across the street, get a cup of coffee, and then we'll come back at eight." She stares at me skeptically, and I still can't believe she's here. "I promise," I say.

❄

We sit in the smoking section at Pete's so Elena can have a cigarette. She lights one as soon as we slide into the booth, and then she exhales.

"I didn't think I'd ever see you here," I say to her. "You should've called. Told me you were coming."

"Yes. Well, I didn't want to make a thing of it." She takes another quick drag on her cigarette and then extinguishes it. "I am quitting these," she says. "Actually, I have already quit."

"I can see that," Benjamin says, and she frowns at him.

"You go everywhere with her?" Elena asks, looking from him to me, then back at him. It sounds like she's scolding him.

"No." Benjamin's face turns a little red. But recently, he has.

"You should," she says. "You two are a very cute couple." She rubs her fingers together. She clearly really wants another cigarette, but she doesn't reach for one. She quit. "I saw my sister last month," she says, turning back to me.

"You went to Cardiff?" I remember the foggy steps I took there, what have come to feel like the first steps I took toward digging my way out of my old life.

"Yes," Elena says. "I went to Cardiff. Miri says to tell you both hello."

"How is she?" I ask tentatively.

"Her hip is on the mend, and she is back at home with her husband."

"Oh good." I'm glad Miriam left the depressing Raintree.

"It was so wonderful to be reunited with her, to know she is good and happy and safe. After all this time. You did that." She looks at me, then Benjamin again. "You found her. You found me." She clears her throat. She's trying not to cry. She blinks her eyes and looks away for a moment. But she regains her composure quickly, turns back to me and continues talking. "Miri asked about you, about the letter you gave me. She wanted to know what it said. The truth was, I hadn't opened it. I thought I never would. But she wouldn't let it go. She said I was crazy not to read it. Not to come here. Now that I could."

"So you read it?" Benjamin asks.

She nods, and pulls it from her purse. She pulls out a pair of reading glasses, too, puts them on, opens the envelope, and unfolds the letter inside.

Austria, 1939

THE MORNING ELENA DISAPPEARED Kristoff couldn't warm up. He shivered for hours, his teeth chattering, even after he lit a fire, dressed in warmer clothes, huddled under blankets. He had found a letter in the snow, just at the end of the woods before the clearing, and he clutched it still in his fingers hours later—the last thing Elena had touched. He held on to it until the dampness soaked through the envelope, turning the paper into bits. It was unsendable now. He'd wasted a precious stamp. But he didn't care. He didn't care about Austria. The Nazis. Their stamps. The recipient of this letter, a woman they had made new papers for. He didn't care about anything but Elena. Eventually he threw the letter into the fire, burning it all, even the stamp.

He searched and searched for her. He walked through the woods in the snow for hours at a time, until his toes were too numb to walk anymore. Each time he'd walk back to the house, hoping he'd made a mistake, hoping he'd come back and simply find her there, kneading bread in the kitchen, laughing. He imagined her saying, *Silly Kristoff, I was here all along!* But every time he returned, the house was empty. She was gone.

He went to the Bauer farm and tried to enlist Josef's help, but he found the place seemingly abandoned. All the lights were on inside, the front door unlocked, but no one was home. Josef, too, was gone. And Kristoff feared that he'd also been taken by the Germans. Kristoff knew it was only a matter of time before the Germans realized what he had done, before they came for him, too. But he didn't care any longer. Without Elena it was hard to feel.

Two days and two empty nights passed, and Kristoff dreamed of Elena. He would awake and feel like she was so close. That she was still here, somewhere. He started to believe that Elena was still alive. *It is Elena*, he told himself. She was so tough. If they had only taken her to a work camp, she might escape, she might find her way back to him. He wouldn't leave the house. He would wait for her here. He would.

✾

But then, there was banging on the door in the middle of the night, and Kristoff heard Herr Bergmann shouting for him to open up, his voice rough and angry. Kristoff knew he had to leave right now, or he, too, was going to die. He remembered what Josef had told him, not to be stupid. And he didn't want to die.

He ran out the back door and into the workshop, opened the floor space, and hid inside. A few minutes later, he heard muffled sounds from above. Elena must've been so frightened all the times she'd done this, though she never admitted it to him. The thought of her, scared, alone . . . He wanted to howl. But he couldn't make a sound. Above him he heard Herr Bergmann's boots, Herr Bergmann calling Kristoff's name. Someone else saying, *"Er ist weg."* *He is gone.* Kristoff huddled into himself under the floor, daring himself not to move, not to breathe. It got quiet, and he thought they gave up, they left. But he didn't dare crack open the floor, until he began to smell smoke. When he stood, he saw flames shooting from the roof of the house.

Kristoff grabbed only the stamps, his forged papers, and his envelope of reichsmarks and he ran toward the woods. He didn't dare go back into the house for a change of clothes, a slice of bread, his sketch pad from the attic.

❀

He had promised Elena he'd go to America, find Frederick, even without her. They would meet there. They would. He told himself this over and over again, the words echoing in his head like a chorus as he walked.

He didn't have Schwann to drive him, so he walked and walked. He eventually hitched a ride with a farmer for part of the way and then took a train. He wasn't Jewish, and no one knew he'd plotted against the Nazis, and it still took him two weeks to get to Bremen. Once he made it there, he spent nearly all of his money on a ticket for the next boat to America in two weeks' time and then the rest on a room near the port.

He slept restlessly, still dreaming about Elena. Dreaming her here with him, and then he awoke, devastated to remember again and again that he was all alone.

He decided to write a letter to Elena that he would mail with their stamp before he left. Just in case she came back to the house to find it burned down, to find him gone, the letter should be waiting for her at the post.

My dearest love,

I am writing this from Bremen, where I will do as you wished for me and board a boat to America next week. When I get there, I will find Gideon Leser, and your father, and I hope that you will be able to do the same soon. That I will see you in America and we can be together as we talked about. Live in a little house by the water. I want to spend all the rest of my days with you—no, all my hours, my minutes. It has been torture not seeing you these past few weeks, and I make it through only by closing my eyes and imagining you are with me still. You will always be with me.

I hope you are safe, and that you read this letter soon. I hate that I am leaving without you, but I couldn't stay. They are onto us. They came looking for me and destroyed the house. It was too dangerous there. We should have left weeks ago. I feel like I'm betraying you by leaving without you, and yet, I don't know what else to do. I know this is what you wanted for me.

I wish you had woken me that last morning before you left. So I might've said goodbye. Kissed you one last time.

But then, I know you don't like goodbyes.

I will never say goodbye to you. Only see you again soon. I know I will.

With all my love,
Kristoff

Kristoff walked to the post to mail his letter before he boarded the ship to America, but when he got there, he couldn't bring himself to go inside.

He thought about his letter being read by the Germans, destroyed. If they had Elena, if she was still alive, would this letter only make things worse for her should they read it?

And so he tucked it in the pocket of his jacket and promised himself he would send it once he got to America, once the war was over.

Los Angeles, 1991

WHEN ELENA FINISHES reading the letter, translating into English for us, we are all in tears. I'm picturing my father, so in love with her. *I was a different person then.* He was Elena's person, and he had loved her so much.

"He could not say goodbye," she repeats. "Only see you again soon."

"And that's why you came here?" Benjamin asks.

She nods. "When you said his memory was failing, I didn't think I should come. But then Miriam called me a fool, and I read the letter. And he's right here. Alive, after all this time. The wall is down. I sold some furniture to get money, and I got a passport and plane ticket, just like that. And now I've finally made it to America." She pauses and takes a sip of the coffee the waitress has just plunked down in front of us. "He might not remember me. But I remember him," she says. "And Miriam was right. You were right. I have to see him again."

✻

At eight o'clock we walk across the street to the Willows and Gretchen lets us all go back. I walk ahead of Elena, and Benjamin walks behind her. From the hallway I can see my father has just gotten up. He's shaving in the small mirror in his bathroom with his electric razor and humming an old show tune to himself. I wait a moment before going in, uncertain if this will shatter his world, or if it won't even crack it. The latter seems worse to me.

I take a deep breath. "Dad," I call into the room, and I knock gently on the open door. "It's me. Katie."

He turns the razor off, puts it down on his sink, and peeks his head out of the bathroom. "Kate the Great," he says. "To what do I owe this surprise? And so early in the morning."

I walk into his room, nervously. "Dad," I say. "I don't know if you remember, but you've been drawing someone in art class." He frowns, looks at his feet. He's not wearing shoes yet. Only white socks. "Someone from your past, from back when you were a different person. You told me about her. We talked about this, do you remember?"

He doesn't answer, but he opens up his nightstand drawer. He had apparently stowed a drawing in there and he unrolls it now. He stares at the picture, traces the face with his finger. Elena is watching all of this from the hallway behind me, and I hear her sigh. Then I hear her footsteps approach closer, into the room.

He looks up, sees her, and takes a quick step back, dropping the picture, as if he's seeing a ghost.

I take the picture from the floor, roll it back up. "I found her,"

I say. "Actually, Benjamin and I both did." Benjamin walks into the room, too, when I say his name, and he takes my hand.

Elena steps forward. She and my father are staring at each other as if they have stared at each other already for a thousand years and also as if they are only seeing each other for the first time. "Hallo, Kristoff," Elena says.

I hold my breath, waiting to see if he'll recognize her, if he'll know her. He doesn't say anything at first, but he reaches his hand up, brings it to her chin, her cheek, like he's feeling the lines, the way he drew them, activating some sort of muscle memory that's lain dormant for fifty years and has survived in spite of his insidious disease. "Perfect lines," he says.

"You know who I am?" She's asking a question, but she says it with certainty. She already knows the answer.

He considers it for a moment. "The stamp engraver's daughter," he says. True to his disease, he probably can't remember Frederick's name right now, or maybe even Elena's, but I can see it in his face, he can remember the joy of loving this woman, the pain of losing her. "I loved you for a long time," he says. His voice has a dreamlike quality. He's remembering her in another time, another place. He seems to understand the wonder at finding her here.

"Yes," Elena says. "We lost each other long ago. But then your daughter found me again."

He lets out a small sob and pulls her toward him; he wraps her in a hug. He rests his cheek on her hair, and he whispers something that sounds like, "Apricots."

"Maybe we should go," Benjamin says to me. "Give them a little time."

"We're going to go wait out in the lobby," I say, but neither one of them seems to notice us anymore.

"You won't leave me again," I hear my father saying as Benjamin and I begin to walk away.

Elena answers him: "I will never say goodbye to you. Only see you again soon."

Author's Note

I keep a letter in the top drawer of my writing desk that I wrote to my grandparents as a child. The envelope has a twenty-cent U.S. flag stamp, postmarked 1983, and the letter is written in my five-year-old handwriting, telling my grandparents how much I missed them after they returned home after a recent visit. My grandmother must have saved it, because twenty-five years later, when she moved into a memory care home (much like the one Katie's father lives in), my mom found the letter in a drawer in her house and mailed it back to me. I have kept it in my own drawer ever since. And every time I catch a glance of it, I remember how letters used to mean something and how we're missing some of that now in the digital age.

My grandmother passed away a few years ago, but before she did, most of her memory left her first, and like Katie and her father, every time I spoke to her, I felt I was speaking to her in the past. She would often tell me she could picture my face when she heard my voice on the phone, and I imagined her picturing five-year-old me, the one writing that letter. And though she could never tell me what she had for breakfast or what she'd done that morning, she could often recount episodes that had happened when she was younger, in spectacular detail. She'd also tell me about the hotel she was staying in and wonder when she'd be going home from vacation, or ask me where her plane tickets were. The idea for Ted and the fictional memory care facility, the Willows, came first from my relationship with her.

All of the characters in this novel, Ted included, are fictional, but many ideas in the book are rooted not just in my own personal experience with watching my grandmother's memory decline, but also in real historical events.

Though all the stamps and the engravers in this book are fictional, there were real engravers who took part in the resistance. Czesław Słania was one real such engraver who forged documents for the Polish resistance. And stamps and stamp plots also played a real role in the resistance. The ones my fictional Dr. Grimes recounts in the book are all real. I read that after the *Anschluss*, the Germans really did create stamps depicting Austrian scenes, though the stamp Kristoff creates in this novel came from my imagination.

Though Elena also is fictional, I was inspired by the real women who risked their lives and worked with the resistance, notably Sophie Scholl, whom I first discovered while visiting the powerful resistance exhibit at the U.S. Holocaust Memorial Museum in Washington, D.C. Also true was the fact that concentration camp prisoners were allowed to send (and receive) mail, on preprinted camp letter cards, with specific rules and limitations. This seemed remarkable to me. Though I also read that incoming mail was censored, and often had the stamps removed to look for any messages underneath.

The *Kindertransport* that saves Miriam was a real rescue effort that came about just after *Kristallnacht*, taking thousands of refugee children on trains and then boats to Great Britain between 1938 and 1940. Many of the children, like Miriam, lived out the rest of their lives in Great Britain and never saw their families again.

The events surrounding the fall of the Berlin Wall in 1989 are also based on fact. The details of Elena's life in East Germany and the reunified Germany that Katie visits in 1990 are based on my research, down to the Palasthotel, which was not open to East German guests before the wall fell because the hotel didn't accept the local currency, and which was reportedly filled with all brown decor. The group that Elena is a part of in Germany is loosely based on what I read about the real group, Women for Peace, where women in both the East and the West organized and tried to stage protests against the GDR and nuclear armament.

Before I started writing this book, I knew almost nothing about stamps or philately. I never thought about the people who made stamps, designed them, or even collected them. I showed up one day at the Postal History Foundation library in Tucson with only a very rough outline of this book, and I told the librarians there that I was writing a novel about stamps. They very kindly gave me books, articles, pictures, and guides (organized by year, country, and engraver, like the ones Katie takes out of the library), and started me on the journey toward understanding the importance of stamps. Like Katie, I used to see stamps as only paper and ink, as a way to get my mail from one place to another. But by the time I finished writing this book, I came to see them also as gems.

Acknowledgments

Thank you to the wonderful team at Riverhead Books, my publishing family: Geoff Kloske, Kate Stark, Jynne Dilling Martin, and especially my amazing editor, Laura Perciasepe, whose careful eye and remarkable dedication make her a continual joy to work with. Thank you also to the fabulous Penguin Random House and Riverhead sales, marketing, and publicity teams, with special thanks to Lydia Hirt, Mary Stone, Michelle Giuseffi, and Alexandra Guillen.

I am deeply indebted to my agent, Jessica Regel, whose support, brilliance, and kindness always keep me going. It was a conversation with her that first sparked the idea for Kristoff and Elena's story, and another conversation that made me believe I could actually pull this off. Thank you, Jess, for everything! Thank you also to the wonderful team at Foundry Literary and Media.

Thank you to all my writer friends, who offer ideas, read drafts, and lend support on a daily basis. I'm so grateful for your friendships: Maureen Leurck, Tammy Greenwood, and Laura Fitzgerald.

And thank you to my family and extended family, my biggest cheerleaders and best publicists, especially Gregg, who also understands and takes over when I'm absorbed in a fictional world.

Thank you to all my readers for sending me e-mails, inviting me to your book clubs, libraries, homes, and cities. Thank you most of all for reading and allowing me to keep doing what I love— write and talk about books!